"I never expected to see a Rochelle dare appear in my chambers again,"

Winewski's legendary sonorous voice boomed.

No doubt the family scandal was about to be rerun.

I straightened my shoulders and managed a cool smile. "Nice to meet you, Judge."

"We'll see about that, Ms. Rochelle. Unlike your grandfather, I run a tight courtroom and tolerate no improprieties."

His implication was clear. My grandfather had become a crooked judge. I had paid enough for my family's sins. No one was going to make me turn tail.

"I don't intend to make any." Keeping my gaze locked on the judge's I experienced a small victory. He looked away first.

Dear Reader,

This month marks the first anniversary of Silhouette Bombshell. And just when you thought the bookshelves couldn't get any hotter, we're kicking off our second year with a killer lineup of innovative, compelling stories featuring heroines that will thrill you, inspire you and keep you turning pages! Sit back, relax and enjoy the read....

Once a thief, always a thief? The heroine of author Michele Hauf's *Once a Thief* says no way! But when her archenemy frames her for theft, she's got to beat him at his own game to keep her new life, a new love and the freedom she won at such great cost....

When hijackers steal her billion-dollar satellite and threaten to use it as a weapon, a NASA scientist must work with a know-it-all counterterrorist expert to save the day. The heat is on in Kathryn Jensen's exhilarating *Hot Pursuit!*

A Palm Beach socialite-turned-attorney gets into a killer's sights when she's called on to defend a friend for murder, in *Courting Danger* by Carol Stephenson. It'll take some fancy legal moves—and a major society shake-up—to see that justice is served.

And how far might someone go to win a million dollars? The heroine of *The Contestant,* by Stephanie Doyle, begins to suspect that one of her fellow reality TV show competitors might have resorted to murder—could it be the sexy ex-cop with the killer smile?

Enjoy all four, and when you're done, tell us what you think! Send your comments to me c/o Silhouette Books, 233 Broadway, Suite 1001, New York, NY 10279.

Sincerely,

Natashya Wilson
Associate Senior Editor, Silhouette Bombshell

Please address questions and book requests to:
Silhouette Reader Service
U.S.: 3010 Walden Ave., P.O. Box 1325, Buffalo, NY 14269
Canadian: P.O. Box 609, Fort Erie, Ont. L2A 5X3

COURTING DANGER

CAROL STEPHENSON

Published by Silhouette Books

America's Publisher of Contemporary Romance

SILHOUETTE BOOKS

ISBN 0-373-51365-8

COURTING DANGER

www.SilhouetteBombshell.com

Printed in U.S.A.

Books by Carol Stephenson

Silhouette Bombshell

Courting Danger #51

Silhouette Special Edition

Nora's Pride #1470

*Legal Weapons

CAROL STEPHENSON

credits her mother for her love of books and her father for her love of travel, but when she gripped a camera and pen for the first time, she found her two greatest loves—photography and writing.

An attorney in South Florida, she constantly juggles the demands of law with those of writing. I-95 traffic jams are the perfect time oases for dictating tales of hard-fought love. You can drop Carol a note at P.O. Box 1176, Boynton Beach, FL 33425-1176.

To my agent, Roberta Brown, for your unwavering belief and support; you are a writer's dream guiding light.

My deepest gratitude goes to Judith Arco for patiently answering my questions about the criminal law process. Any errors are mine or artistic license.

Chapter 1

I'm a hired gun.

Not the blazing bullets kind…the legal kind.

After all, attorneys are the only publicly sanctioned form of revenge and payback our society allows. If someone damages your car or hikes your rent, instead of stringing him or her from the nearest tree, you go to court and duke it out.

However, if you do decide to take matters into your own hands or otherwise flaunt the laws of our country, you'll still need someone like me: Katherine Rochelle, criminal defense attorney, the ultimate in legal weapons.

We can be found in the yellow pages; you can't miss the ads with the pictures and bold assurances of our qualifications to defend you. If we appear to be larger than life, we have to be, for you are placing *your* life in our hands.

What you don't realize is that behind our serious demeanors, diplomas and certifications are individuals as flawed as you are. My brethren drink, gamble, lie, cheat and steal. They fight with their spouses and raise kids who land in trouble.

For some that's a dollar sign above their heads, not a halo, having sold out their ethics for the almighty buck or other glory.

For others, like me, the struggle to keep our principles and honor intact as we fight for justice leaves our armor dented and tarnished. Sometimes we needed crutches, like the kind I had now.

I paused before the double wood doors and fumbled in the pocket of my ivory silk jacket for the ever-present roll of antacid tablets. A little stomach insurance wouldn't hurt before I entered the chambers. Even this early in the morning, a cacophony of sound filled the Palm Beach courthouse hallway: heels clicking on the marble floor, briefcase locks snapping, voices echoing—questioning voices, irritated voices, hurried voices. I tuned it all out to focus on the challenge before me.

A familiar burn began in the pit of my stomach so I took a few deep breaths. Here in the alcove, ammonia and orange furniture polish from last night's cleaning warred with attorneys' colognes. Inside a new scent would be added: fear. Fear of the accused, fear of the judge, fear of failure.

Anticipation stirred to life, kick-starting my pulse. It had been six long months since I'd had been in a courtroom. What did it matter that this was only a county court misdemeanor hearing where the main thing heard was criminal traffic offenses?

It was action. Soon enough I would work my way into circuit court where weightier crimes, such as battery, armed robbery and murder, were tried.

Granted, the hiatus I'd taken to work with my two girl-friends, Carling Dent and Nicole Sterling, in setting up our own criminal defense firm certainly had been fulfilling. Our law school dream—the Law Offices of Dent, Rochelle and Sterling—was now a reality.

However, it still bit that I had been a casualty in a scandal at the U.S. Attorney's office. Losing my job hadn't sat well. Neither had waiting for our offices to be finished.

Practicing law was like falling off the horse; if you waited too long to get back on, you wouldn't.

I was more than ready to get back in the legal saddle. I reached for the door handle, but the overweight bailiff standing to the side shook his head. "You can't go in yet, miss. The judge don't let anyone inside until ten minutes to court time."

The docket was scheduled to start at 9:30. I glanced at the slender Chopard watch on my wrist: nine-sixteen. I cocked an eyebrow at the bailiff, but he merely folded his arms across his stomach in an "I won't be budged on this" manner. The way he kept looking around indicated tension.

In a low tone I asked, "Is there a problem?" X-ray machines and guards at every entrance were a way of life at the courthouse, but you never knew.

"No, but we had an incident last week."

A male attorney, checking the docket sheet, glanced up. "The judge pissed someone else off?"

The bailiff's lips quirked but he managed to keep a straight face. "The judge was just doing his job."

The attorney grimaced. "Great. Can't wait for today's performance." He moved away and I crossed the hallway to wait.

"Well, look who's here." A man's loud nasal voice scraped my eardrum. "If it isn't Katherine Rochelle."

After I could get past the vision of six wiry hairs combed across the gleaming pale skin of the man's head, I locked gazes with Leo Feinstein. Age wasn't being kind to my former law school classmate. In fact, it was gouging his face with a steel brush.

"How nice that the state attorney let you out of your cubicle, Leo."

His flush did nothing for his massive bald spot. "You were a nice woman, Katherine, until you hooked up with those two pals of yours."

He meant that I had been an amenable debutante, in danger of fading into nonexistence as a human being, until Carling and Nicole had rescued me. A man like Leo didn't care for strong women attorneys like Carling or Nicole who ran circles around him every day in court.

"Hey, someone left today's paper." Always the cheapskate, Leo bent over, his faded navy-blue polyester tie dangling forward.

The bold headline of an article on the front page caught my attention: Is The Courthouse Restoration Jinxed?

The answer? Absolutely.

Unable to stop myself, I gazed through the wide bank of tinted windows that lined the main corridor. Across the street shimmering under the bright Florida sunlight was the old courthouse. Black skeletal fingers of scaffolding encased it much like the frustration that gripped me whenever I looked at the 1916 structure.

Would it never release its secrets?

When the 1970s brick wraparound was first stripped away, revealing the building's facade as it had existed thirty-five years ago, I had haunted the construction perimeter. Had I half expected to see my grandparents walk down those steps as they had when they had disappeared all those years ago? Had I hoped their unknown killer would experience contrition at the déjà vu of seeing the original courthouse and confess?

How much death had those halls witnessed?

So lost was I in my contemplation of the past that I jolted when Leo spoke. "Isn't it something that a woman was killed there the other night?"

The woman had a name and a life she hadn't deserved to lose in that tomb of horrors.

"Her name was Grace Roberts," I stated.

"Hey, that's right. Your family's a big supporter of the restoration. Did you know her?" Leo's greed for gossip hadn't lessened in the years since graduation.

I shifted my briefcase from one hand to the other. "Love to chat, but I'm due in court."

Leo jerked his head, dislodging one precious hair so that it spiraled straight up. "Are you here for Winewski?"

My stomach did a perfect flip. "Yes."

"God, how the mighty have fallen." His smile reminded me of a vampire all set for the final love bite. "Katherine Rochelle attending a lowly misdemeanor hearing rather than gracing the lofty halls of federal court. Not to worry. I'm the prosecutor today, and I'll keep in mind that you won't know your ass from your head in there. I'll try to go easy on your poor sucker of a client."

Terrific. It appeared the rumor mill that was the West Palm Beach legal community had generated a nasty spin on my leaving the U.S. Attorney's office. Either Harold Lowell, my former lover, or the female U.S. attorney who had replaced him, had been bad-mouthing me.

"Don't do me any favors, Leo. I can handle myself."

He sneered. "Yeah, I heard plenty about how you handle yourself outside the job." His attention zeroed in on my chest. That ruled out the U.S. attorney even though she had fired me for "incompetence."

To my chagrin, I had learned a hard lesson about being a whistle-blower: your co-workers avoid you like the plague. After all, you've brought disruption in their jobs and gotten a popular man into hot water. When they had looked at me, I had seen their speculation—had I turned him in merely because of a lover's quarrel?

Yet underneath the speculation I knew their real fear was they would lose their jobs because they had illegally contributed to Harold's campaign fund for attorney general.

However, I knew the current chief attorney was smart enough not to risk a lawsuit by maligning my reputation.

Since Harold was already on the slow road to disbarment and conviction for all sorts of federal crimes and had nothing to lose, my money was on him. The bastard.

In times of trouble, though, adages are wonderful crutches, especially ones drummed into the very pores of your being. If my great-aunt Hilary had said it once, she had said it a thousand times, "Rochelles never sweat in public."

I arched a brow, giving my aristocratic freeze-in-hell look. "Gee, Leo, I'm quaking in my shoes. Don't tell me that you actually manage to stay awake for a whole hearing nowadays?"

Law school classmates have long memories and one of mine was that of Leo snoozing through nine a.m. Criminal Law.

Leo's mouth opened and closed like a fish gasping for breath. He stormed across the hall into the courtroom, sending the doors swinging so wildly that the bailiff rushed to steady them.

Was my petty moment of besting Leo worth a guaranteed payback from hell? My lips twitched.

Definitely.

I strolled across to the chamber and nodded to the still-huffing bailiff as I entered. I made a beeline to the opposite side, away from where Leo stood, and sat at the end of the bench seat. Letting him cool down wouldn't be a bad idea.

Studiously ignoring Leo's glare, I read the graffiti etched on the back of the wood bench before me. Although cameras and microphones had been installed in the rooms when the current courthouse had been built ten years ago, technology hadn't defeated the artistic endeavors of the accused and defiant.

The newest artist had definite opinions on Judge Kurt Winewski's anatomy. I chuckled, but the laugh died in my throat as I glanced up. A group of attorneys had gathered around Leo, who was talking a mile a minute. A few gawked at me, their expressions ranging from curious to baleful. The latter belonged to those lawyers whose clients I'd prosecuted during my days as an assistant U.S. attorney. I hadn't won any popularity contests then, either, due to my prosecutorial zeal, and it appeared I wasn't going to now.

Let them look and gossip.

But it wasn't fair that my own integrity was getting maligned. A crook was a crook, right? So what if the criminal happened to be a fellow attorney? I was the one who had been wronged, not Harold. My only fault was once more having no—that's nada, zilch, zero—judgment in men.

Absently I watched people fill the room. Why hadn't I immediately seen through the charisma of my boss and lover to his rotten inner core? It wasn't as if sex with him should have blinded me; that had been uninspiring and blessedly infrequent.

For whatever reason, I hadn't suspected anything until I had found Harold's little black book in between my sofa cushions and, after decoding it, realized it didn't contain women's phone numbers but illegal contributions for his campaign fund. I had been faced with only one option: I had gone straight to the federal authorities.

"All rise." The bailiff adjusted his utility belt around his girth as he struggled to stand.

Tucking away the past, I stood with everyone else and watched the judge march to his bench. For one moment the seal of Florida hanging on the wall framed Judge Winewski's head like a gold halo…or a crown of thorns some would mutter, given the judge's use of his power.

Beneath white bushy brows his piercing regard swept the courtroom, a maneuver designed to keep the audience standing a moment longer. At once he honed in on me with a look of condescension and distaste, as if a disgusting bug had crawled into his domain. Even though we had never met in person, I knew he recognized me.

Sometimes bearing the Rochelle trademark looks of honey-blond hair, vivid blue eyes and tall, lithe build was a definite negative. I didn't need to open the gold filigree locket I wore to realize that I was the spitting feminine version of my grandfather. The family had harped on that unfortunate fact my entire life as if they expected my soul to have been stamped with all his faults, as well, like a generational doppelgänger.

"I never expected to see a Rochelle dare to appear in my chambers again." Winewski's legendary sonorous voice boomed to the courtroom's farthest corners.

What was this? Sweep-out-Katherine-Rochelle's-dirty-linen-closet day? No doubt the family scandal was about to be rerun.

I straightened my shoulders and managed a cool smile. "Nice to meet you, Judge."

"We'll see about that, Ms. Rochelle." The man who once had bounced my mother on his knee wagged his finger as if I was a recalcitrant child.

"Unlike your grandfather, I run a tight courtroom and tolerate no improprieties."

His implication was clear. My grandfather had been a crooked judge. The cold flame of injustice replaced the nerves churning in my stomach. I had paid enough for my family's sins and my own stupid mistakes. No one was going to make me turn tail.

"I don't intend to commit any." Keeping my eyes locked on the judge's as he plopped into his seat, I experienced a small victory. The judge looked away first.

"Call the first case," he ordered.

Everyone sat and the court fell into a rhythm of defendants and their lawyers presenting their cases.

I flipped opened the client's folder and studied the charging affidavit. Simone Jean-Charles. A thirty-year-old Haitian immigrant with four children to support on her housekeeping earnings. The divorce settlement obligated her ex-husband to pay the car-insurance premiums for one year. Of course, he hadn't and when Simone had been stopped for a busted taillight six months ago, she'd been ticketed for expired insurance. Then the ex had promised to take care of the ticket. Of course, he hadn't and her license had been suspended.

Simone's bad luck continued when she had been stopped by an Officer Pitt because her car resembled one involved in a jewelry store robbery. He had checked her license and charged her for driving with a suspended license. A misdemeanor but my client needed to drive to keep her job. Although I was working on straightening out the insurance mess, a conviction on the latest charge could be economically devastating.

I glanced at the police report and compared the entry to the arresting affidavit. I smiled. Glancing up, I spotted Simone entering the room. I gathered my briefcase, rose and crossed to the center aisle, preparing to take my place by her side when her name was called.

The current on-deck attorney was pleading his case. Judge Winewski rapped his gavel. "Denied. This man's driving license is suspended." The attorney shrugged and turned to his client.

"You can't do this!" his client yelled. "I'll lose my job."

His counsel tried to calm him, but the man cursed a blue streak, drew back his arm and landed a direct blow to the attorney's nose. Blood spurted as the lawyer fell backward.

"Bailiff," the judge called out, but the guard, sitting in a chair too tight for his girth, could barely lumber to his feet.

As if on cue, everyone raced for the exits, including the judge.

Self-preservation warred with the ingrained Rochelle family code of conduct, but since the wounded lawyer kept yelling at the top of his lungs, I knelt beside the attorney trying to silence him.

Mistake. Berserko's fingers gouged my shoulder. He locked his arm tight around my neck, dragging me to my feet. Not an easy task as I'm five-eight and had four-inch heels on.

"We're going out that door, girlie." Berserko's breath stank of booze, garlic and desperation.

No, we weren't. He had picked the wrong woman on the wrong day. I faked a stumble, twisted and whacked him over the head with my briefcase.

Berserko shrieked in pain but he wasn't down.

Yet.

I spun and jammed my Jimmy Choo stiletto heel into the man's groin. White-faced, the man dropped like a stone to the floor, writhing in agony.

"Would someone like to arrest this man?" I called out. "I'd like to get on with my hearing."

The judge's door cracked open. The bailiff scrambled up and rushed over to cuff the prisoner. Winewski ventured out, his incredulous gaze darting from the prisoner to me.

I tugged the corners of my fitted jacket. "Judge, I believe next on your docket is the case of the *State versus Simone Jean-Charles*. If the Assistant State Attorney can be located…" I lifted a brow.

"Feinstein, get in here!" the judge bellowed.

The hall door creaked and moments later Leo stood behind the opposite table, but he kept casting a nervous glance at Berserko being escorted outside.

"Mr. Feinstein, if you can quit worrying about your hide and focus on the matter of Simone Jean-Charles, we might finish before lunch."

"Judge, I have an *ore tenus* motion to suppress," I said.

"The excitement going to your head, Ms. Rochelle?"

"No, Your Honor. If you would look at State's Exhibits One and Two, the arresting officer's affidavit and police report."

Leo, his face flushed as he struggled with his file, snapped, "Which exhibits?"

"One and Two. Get with the program, Counselor." The judge shuffled a few papers. "I have the exhibits. Proceed, Ms. Rochelle."

"The probable cause basis for the traffic stop of my client was information Officer Pitt received when he called in her tag number that her car was connected to a robbery."

"So? That's a textbook stop."

"Compare the number the officer called in and the number on his report. He transposed the last numbers."

"Eh?" The judge's brows drew together.

"The officer stopped the wrong car for the wrong cause, Judge. Anything he found is the result of an illegal search. The charges should be dismissed."

"Any response, Mr. Feinstein?"

Leo's mouth opened and closed.

"Thought so. Defendant's motion is granted. The charges are dismissed. Next case."

Oh yeah, I felt like doing a happy dance, but instead I whispered to Simone that everything was going to be okay. I sauntered across the courtroom out into the hall. The moment the door swung closed behind me, I pumped my fist in the air. "Yes!"

I was back.

An hour later I squealed my gold-colored Jaguar to a stop behind the shell-pink stucco one-story building that housed the Law Offices of Dent, Rochelle and Sterling. I entered through the back door into the warren of offices and cubicles that was the heart of our operations. I paused, absorbing the dull clatter of keyboard keys and low voices on phones.

Not for the first time, pride burned in me. This was ours. This law firm represented the hopes, dreams and wills of three women who had formed a bond in the early days of law school. I would do my part to hold up my end. I wouldn't let my friends down.

After walking down the abbreviated hall, I entered the

second office on the right, dropping both my purse and briefcase on my desk. As I sat with relief, I noticed a telephone message propped against the phone and grimaced. Big, bold letters, words underlined.

"Great. Perfect morning so far."

"Talking to yourself?" Carling Dent, her sharp elfin features split by a wide grin, asked as she entered. Because she was dipping a tea bag in her mug, her normal bounce was more like a flounce.

I motioned for her to close the door. Halfway across the room she stopped and stared.

"What happened to you? Since when did morning hearings turn into a demolition derby?"

"Just my luck." Shucking off my jacket, I examined the gaping side seam, mentally adding a trip to the cleaners on my to-do list.

"All right, Kate. Give." Carling plopped herself into a plush client chair. "Did Winewski and you go a round?"

I wiggled out of my ruined panty hose, balled them up and tossed them into the wastebasket. "Hardly."

Anyone who saw this dark-haired babe and what they imagined to be a vapid gaze with her soft green eyes was in for a rude awakening. Carling was sharp as a tack and had the instincts for nailing a person to the wall.

"Wasn't he a friend of your grandfather's?" she asked.

"Former," I corrected as I pulled out a package of panty hose from my bottom drawer.

"Gave you a hard time?"

"Started to." I slid the nylons over my pedicured feet and stood to pull on the hose. "Then the defendant on the docket before me took exception to Winewski's suspending his driver's license. After decking his lawyer, he made the mistake of grabbing me. He figured because I was a 'girlie' he could use me as a shield."

"Next time he'll be sure to ask about your sports trophies. Naturally, you were the victor."

I smoothed out my skirt but smothered an oath when I spotted the blood on my favorite royal-blue blouse. It would never come out. "You should have seen Leo Feinstein run for the high hills the moment trouble broke out."

"Leo had traffic detail?"

Rummaging in the drawer, I found a patterned silk scarf that wasn't too bad a match for the remnants of my outfit. "He's down to six hairs."

My friend snickered. "Get this. I heard that he's planning to do hair implants."

I suppressed a shudder. "I don't even want to think about where the hair will come from. He's too cheap to spring for anything on the high end."

As I wound the scarf around my neck, Carling sprang up and rushed around the desk. "My God, Kate. Your throat!"

Granted, it hurt to swallow, but her look of horror sent me scrambling for a mirror. Gingerly I peeled away the collar. The vivid bruise ran from red to purple in a solid band across the base of my throat. Carling's fingers were gentle as she touched the skin, but I still winced at the stab of pain.

"That bastard had you by the throat, didn't he!" she demanded.

"Yes." I buttoned the top of my blouse. The material was silk and wouldn't scratch the abused skin too much. I then looped the scarf one more time around my neck for extra coverage.

"You should see a doctor. What's your schedule for the rest of the day? I'll cover. You leave now and seek medical attention." She snapped out the series of orders like a general going to battle.

"You'll even cover the summons from Aunt Hilary?"

The look of abject horror on her face tickled me. I gave her a quick hug. "I didn't think so."

She swallowed, hard. "I can call and tell her you're indisposed."

I opened the door to the small closet, took out a black blazer and put it on, remembering to transfer the antacid roll into the pocket. Although it covered only part of the damage, this jacket would have to do. No time to go home and change. Aunt Hilary needed to make her club luncheon.

I pivoted. "Well, how do I look?"

Carling folded her arms and took her sweet time surveying me from head to toe. "Like someone who has been through the ringer and is trying to cover up."

My arms dropped. "Thanks a lot."

My friend's lips curved in a big smile. "You'll do, *Katherine.*" Her emphasis on my name didn't go unnoticed. In the world I had once inhabited, my formal name was always used. Carling had been the first daring enough to shorten it. And it was into that former environment I was now heading.

Carling gave me a thumbs-up. "Good luck."

"I'm going to need it," I said under my breath as I crossed the room.

"If you don't return in an hour, we'll send out a search party to the cemetery of dead debutantes."

"Ha-ha." I opened the door and reached into my pocket.

"Kate." I looked back. Carling would make a great mother. "You're stronger than you think."

I slid my hand clear and displayed my empty palm. "This advice from a woman who would rather cut a vein than confront my great-aunt." I winked and left before she could recover. Getting the last dig in was always a challenge with her.

Outside I blinked against the glare of the sunshine and crossed the postage-stamp parking lot in a few strides. As I drove out of the lot I thumbed another antacid tablet from the roll.

For once traffic wasn't snarled along Flagler Drive. While oil tycoon Henry Flagler may have started West Palm Beach as a bedroom community for the servants and workers of Palm Beach, to keep them out of sight from his rich cronies he brought in on his railroad, today West Palm Beach was its own city. Technology, banking, tourism, and even the entertainment industry had prospered here. True, it had a tawdry underbelly, but it had a personality of its own.

I loved it.

I drove across the bridge over the Intracoastal Waterway and on the other side entered the preening world that was Palm Beach. Regal royal palm trees lining the pristine road swayed in the breeze. Chic shops and restaurants thrived with customers. Valets in jaunty white jackets or crisp white shirts ran back and forth, parking a succession of Mercedes, Rolls-Royces and Jaguars.

I turned onto Ocean Boulevard and drove past one stunning mansion after another. Only light waves ruffled the Atlantic Ocean while the late March sky was crystal blue, not a cloud in sight. A picture-perfect tourist day in paradise. So why couldn't I relax and enjoy it?

Because I no longer belonged here.

Turning onto a driveway of hexagonal pavestones, I punched in a security code and waited for the massive wrought-iron gates to open. I passed immaculately cultivated gardens, lush with fronds of palmetto, areca and foxtail palms and vivid blossoms of verbena, hibiscus and bougainvillea. I parked in the semicircle at the front of the palatial house, took a deep breath, and with the practiced grace of the debutante, swept from my car.

I needed to be at the top of my game. This morning had been a cakewalk when compared to the judge, jury and executioner waiting inside.

Chapter 2

"Good morning, Edwin."

"Good morning, Miss Katherine." Edwin greeted me from the Palladium-styled doorway. Although he had been my great-aunt and uncle's butler for only a few months, he was cut from the same mode as the long line of Rochelle butlers before him. Always there before you knew you needed him.

Of course the household staff was so large that there were many unseen eyes and ears to note the arrival of a car. Still, it was decidedly spooky how Edwin would appear at the door before the bell sounded.

"Madam requests your presence on the rear loggia." In keeping with his training, Edwin's only reaction to my less than stellar appearance was a micro-fractional disdainful lift of his brow. Otherwise, his face remained expressionless as he stepped back to let me inside. "She's finishing her laps."

But of course she was. If there was one constant in Hilary Rochelle Wilkes's life, other than duty, it was her swimming.

"Thank you, Edwin."

I moved across the spacious foyer, skirting the center dominated by the overhead Baccarat chandelier. Suspended from the thirty-two-foot domed ceiling, the dazzling gilt bronze fixture dripped with opulent crystals. Once as a kid, I had watched as a hurricane-force gust of wind caught the chandelier and tossed it up in the air like a tennis ball before letting it drop. A falling shard of glass had speared my upper arm. Even the top plastic surgeon called to the emergency room by my aunt and uncle hadn't prevented the half-moon scar that was a permanent reminder.

As I reached the hallway leading to the ocean side, I cast one regretful glance toward the twin stairways that curved and twisted to the upper levels. A cautious person would've kept a change of clothes in her former bedroom. Only a rash person would burn all bridges by removing all her possessions in a desperate bid for identity.

I straightened the edge of my jacket and walked down the sweep of marbled corridor. For a moment I paused in the double French doors framed by amber silk brocade curtains to collect myself.

The view was primo Palm Beach: bands of green, gold and blue. Every rainy season the beach, like a worn wedding ring, would be tarnished, narrowing to a slip under the onslaught of storm-driven waves. Every year the inhabitants would lobby to have the beach restored. Mustn't mess with property value. The rich and famous had seasonal homes on the beach, so that the beach must be perfect.

I used to believe the city council sent workers onto the beach every day before dawn to arrange shells so that the temporary residents would have the thrill of finding one. Once I crept down in a quest to catch the shell scatterers at work, but I only managed to step on a Portuguese man-of-war left by the tide. That ill-advised outing had catapulted me to a finishing school in Switzerland.

I crossed the patio and then went down the steps to the pool deck. With a smooth flip that barely rippled the water, my aunt made her turn at the deep end of the pool. In her youth Hilary's prowess as a swimmer had earned her a spot on the Olympic team. Her bronze medallion held a place of honor over the fireplace in her sitting room. Although her years of competition were long behind her, she maintained a rigorous swimming regimen. I would match her stamina against today's generation of women anytime.

"Are you going to stand there all day dreaming?" Wearing a peach tank swimming suit that showed off both her athletic form and golden tan to their best advantage, she stood in the shallow end. Ignoring the steps, she placed her hands on the side and pushed clear of the pool.

"No, Aunt Hilary." I walked to the stack of towels and handed one to her. Although her actual date of birth was a secret as safeguarded as the gold in Fort Knox, Hilary had to be in her late sixties, early seventies, but she radiated the health of a forty-year-old. Her strict swimming regimen kept her thighs firm, her body lithe. Although her wet hair was sleeked back, I knew a superb hairstylist kept the trademark Rochelle hair a gleaming blond and arranged in a style contemporary in fashion but not inappropriately youthful.

After she dried off, I handed her a terry-cloth robe. Only then did she present her cheek for my air-kiss. She crossed to the wrought-iron-and-glass-top table and sat down. I followed, taking a chair that faced the sun and the inquisition I knew was coming.

"You look like something that dreadful cat of yours dragged in."

"Gee, thanks, Aunt Hilary. You look fabulous as always."

"Don't get cheeky with me, young lady. Not after all I've done for you." Hilary could look down her regal nose and make a person squirm at twenty paces. I resisted the fidget but issued the expected apology.

"Sorry."

Without a word a maid appeared with a tray of frosted Waterford glasses of iced teas, and after serving us, just as silently disappeared. While Hilary sipped the sweetened brew with a twist of key lime, I studied her over the rim of my glass.

I had to hand it to her. No matter what the situation, my great-aunt always radiated strength, power and composure. Too bad Hilary was as cold as the Hubbard Glacier inside.

Whoa, watch the poor-little-rich-girl routine. After all, where would you have been without Hilary when Mom so lovingly dumped you on the doorstep?

Presented with a wailing baby, Hilary with her code of family duty had more than risen to the occasion. She had given me a home, such as it was. She had given all that she could.

It was not her fault that the burden of being a Rochelle had long ago burned out any softer emotions in her. And not my fault that I could never measure up to her level of perfection.

I placed the glass on the table without the slightest clink, as I had been taught. I folded my napkin, and along with it a child's desperate need for love, and tucked it beside the glass.

"Aunt Hilary, you know I'll always be grateful for what you did for me."

The faint lines of displeasure framing her mouth eased. She nodded and leaned back in her chair.

"Your new office is doing well?"

I couldn't resist a quick grin. "The Law Firm of Debt, Default and Miscarriage is doing great."

Her fine brows knitted. "I beg your pardon?"

"An insider's joke. When Carling, Nicole and I were in law school, we used to joke about opening a practice with that name."

Remembering those days in the local bar frequented by the law students, and my friends' discussions late into the night, satisfaction once more surged in me. By God, we had done it. After all the pain, setbacks and disappointments the three of us had experienced in our careers, we had joined forces to open our own firm. We would make it on our own, defying the all-old-boys' network that still prevailed in this neck of the legal world.

"Oh, I see." My aunt cleared her throat. "I would imagine you'll be handling only civil matters given what happened to you at the U.S. Attorney's office."

Ah, here we go. She finally was getting to the reason she had summoned me. She was going to make a last-ditch effort to convince me to take a "title only" position with one of the family's businesses. Hilary always manipulated a person until she had you trapped in a corner with no escape.

I kept my voice cool and level; she must not hear any uncertainty or vulnerability in my tone.

"No, we're a criminal defense firm, which means I'll be helping people charged with anything from misdemeanors to felonies." That is, as soon as I could get my own clients rather than taking files over from Carling and Nicole. Their former positions with the Public Defender and State Attorney offices had given them a decided advantage in referrals. My past wasn't so kind. It was not every day a CEO caught with his hand in the employee pension cookie jar— the kind I used to prosecute—walked off the street into a small law firm.

Maybe, just maybe, my victory this morning would help to rebuild my damaged reputation. Using my trust-fund monies for the start-up costs of the firm only made me a financial partner. For my self-respect I had to pull my own weight with client referrals.

"I have a…favor to ask of you."

Although I maintained a relaxed pose, my Hilary antenna quivered. What was she up to? She demanded, ordered and, in short, expected people to snap to do her bidding. The word "ask" was not in her vocabulary. Certainly, her imperious summons this morning hadn't suggested this new approach.

"A favor? From me?"

"On a professional basis."

I couldn't help myself, I gaped. "You want legal advice?"

Anger sparked in her crystalline blue eyes. "You still call yourself a lawyer, don't you?"

Ah, her infamous disdain. With one efficient slash she could cut you off at the knees.

My own temper flickered. "Not call. Am."

"Have you heard the latest about Grace Roberts's death?"

Disbelief once more swelled inside me. Grace, the vivacious and efficient young woman who had maneuvered her way into becoming my aunt's assistant, was dead. Violent death to people I knew was becoming a constant in my life, and that nasty realization had caused more than one sleepless night this past week.

"Nothing more than the brief coverage in the morning paper."

"You're aware she was killed in the old courthouse." Hilary kept her eyes on my face. If she was waiting for a reaction she was going to be sorely disappointed.

"Yes." Then, damned if my hand, on its own volition, didn't stray toward the tube of tablets concealed in my pocket. My aunt's eagle-sharp gaze tracked my movement. I brought my hand forward, empty.

"They've arrested Lloyd Silber for her murder."

"What?" My mouth dropped open. Lloyd, director of the courthouse restoration project, was about as debonair and dedicated as they come.

"Close your mouth, Katherine. You could catch every mosquito along the beach the way you're gaping."

"Yes, ma'am." I swallowed. "Why do the police think Lloyd killed Grace?"

Hilary shrugged. "The usual. A young, pretty volunteer. A straying man who wasn't about to divorce his wife."

"Lloyd and Grace were an item?"

"That's the rumor."

No way. Grace was engaged to a drop-dead gorgeous executive of a high-tech company. More than once she had rubbed my nose in the fact after my relationship with my former boss had crashed and burned. Grace had had visions of a many-carat diamond ring and a waterfront mansion dancing in her head. She wouldn't have wasted one flutter of her eyelashes on an older man like Lloyd who had lost everything when the limited-partnership tax laws had changed.

"I can see your mind is already at work, springing to Lloyd's defense."

"It's just not possible—"

Hilary held up her hand. "This is exactly why I wanted to see you. For once in your life, I want you to leave well enough alone and say no."

"You've lost me."

"Meredith Silber, poor fool, believes her husband is innocent. She called me this morning to ask if I thought you would represent him."

My breath hitched and excitement skittered along my nerves. The Silbers wanted me?

"I want you to refuse."

My brief spike of adrenaline flattened. "Why? I know you've never wanted me to become an attorney but—"

"But would you listen to reason? Of course not. You talked grand plans about the pursuit of justice. Where has this insane need gotten you? Once more in disgrace. Do you enjoy dragging the Rochelle name in the mud?"

Indignation frosted my voice. "I had nothing to do with that mess at the U.S. Attorney's office and you know it. Harold Lowell was accepting campaign contributions under the table from his staff and other influential people. What was I supposed to do? Just sit there and let him get away with it?"

"No, for once your moral fanaticism exonerated you. But your taste in men remains abominable."

She had me there. I attracted every loser in the universe.

My face must have reflected some of my chagrin, for Hilary nodded with satisfaction. "Exactly. If you had done what I had advised and gone into the family business, you would've met some nice executive and be married by now. But no, you never would listen to me."

I pinched my nose. "This is getting us nowhere."

"So typical of you, Katherine. Changing the topic when I'm trying to talk reason."

"I've lost track of what you're trying to get me to do."

"Not represent Lloyd, dear."

"Why not? He needs a good attorney who'll believe in his innocence."

"What he needs is a *great* criminal attorney, and quite frankly, that's not you, Katherine. What did you do at the U.S. Attorney's? Prosecute a few executives who stole from their companies? Give them a slap on the wrist with a fine and send them to one of those white-collar prisons for a few years?"

Hilary leaned forward. "The government plans to seek the death penalty against Lloyd. This is his life at stake."

She was right. I had dealt with only high-brow criminals in a world where the sole stake was money. First-degree murder was a different matter.

"Dear, Lloyd is going to need an attorney who can get him a good deal and you're not up to it. How many of your so-called court victories can be attributed to the fact that you were dating the boss? That he might have given you easy cases? Even your uncle and godfather noticed that Harold sat as second chair on your trials more than was normal."

Resentment burned in my stomach. It looked like the rumors had literally hit home. Only Carling and Nicole believed in me and my capabilities. Granted, I might not be experienced enough to try a murder case, but I certainly could plea-bargain with the best of them.

"Glad to know you think so highly of my abilities. Just for the record, I never rode on Harold's coattails."

"Be reasonable. You can help best by steering Lloyd's wife toward the names of several good attorneys. A few of us on the restoration board are quietly raising money to help out. Of course, we can't do so openly because of Grace."

"Of course." Mustn't take a stand that the press could pounce on. I rose. "I have to be going."

Unease clouded her eyes. "Katherine, you won't do anything foolish?"

I crossed the terrace to the doors. "Now why would I start being anything but a disappointment to you?"

"Katherine!"

I paused.

"Why do you always fight me? I only want what's best for you."

"If that's the case—" I turned halfway "—then why don't you ever listen to what I want?"

"Oh, I've listened." My aunt's lips thinned. "But you never seem to know what's best for you. At times you are utterly unreasonable just like…" Her voice trailed off.

I stilled. "Like my mother?"

"No, like my brother. Always so righteous. Always so wrapped up in such an abstract concept of what justice is that you never can recognize the realities of life. Life isn't black-and-white, Katherine, it's filled with gray."

"That's a lesson you've taught me well."

All too well. The defining moment had been when I was fifteen and home for summer-school break. My aunt had accused a servant of breaking a Dresden figurine, even though Uncle Colin had been the culprit because he'd had one too many. All my arguments and pleas had fallen on my aunt's deaf ears. When it came to her husband, Colin could do no wrong. He denied the incident and that was enough for her. Not only had the servant Carmelina been fired, she had been deported back to Colombia.

Six months later Carmelina and her family had been at the wrong place when a gunfight had broken out between a drug cartel and the police. Carmelina had died instantly, the earnest eighteen-year-old girl who had only craved and worked for a better life for her family. When I had come across another Colombian servant, distraught and crying in the kitchen over a letter from home with the news, I had gone to Hilary. Her only comment had been, "Death happens," and that I should get use to it.

As if I wasn't already all too familiar with death and the everlasting grip of its consequences. Exhibit One, my grandparents. Exhibit Two, my mother.

It had been at the moment I stared at her in disbelief over her callousness that my desire to be a lawyer who fought for others had been born.

Hilary rolled up a cuff of her robe. "I've tried my best to steer you from going down the same reckless path Jonathan traveled."

To the point of suffocation. "If you had only answered my questions about my grandparents—"

Hilary's chair scraped as she rose. "And tell you what? That Jonathan and Marguerite vanished one night? That the ensuing investigation uncovered his dirty secret—that he took bribes as a judge? That the police closed the case after concluding my brother and his wife had probably been murdered and their bodies dumped in the ocean? I see no need to display the family's soiled linen."

Only the barest flush across Hilary's cheeks betrayed her anger. "As much as you love putting them on a pedestal, Jonathan and his treasured Marguerite weren't perfect. She wanted too much and he was too weak. If you don't learn to control your rash ways, you'll share the same miserable fate as my brother."

Even as I stared at her, the abyss between us widened, a lifetime of missed opportunities. As I stood on that knife-thin edge of no turning back, in a protective reaction I wrapped my fingers around the locket at my neck. Luckily it hadn't been damaged in the courtroom scuffle.

Oddly, the piece of jewelry containing my grandparents' pictures had been my guiding light since I had found it in my mother's jewelry case in her former room.

No matter what Hilary and the rest of the world said about my grandparents, I had never believed it. True, as a lonely child surrounded by self-absorbed adults, I had fantasized that they were the parents I never had. As a young girl I could only see the warmth of their smiles the camera had captured. As an adult I recognized the core-deep integrity in their expressions that the camera had captured. Maybe I didn't know who I was, but I knew in this moment the person I didn't want to be.

"I'm sorry that you don't understand me, Aunt Hilary, but I have to lead my own life and make my own mistakes."

"I give up trying to reason with you." She gave a slight dismissive movement with her right hand and turned away to walk toward the entrance to her suite of rooms. "Try not to drag the family name through another escapade." She disappeared into the house.

I tucked the locket under my blouse. Hilary was right on one point. While I couldn't do anything about the old family scandal, I could undo the damage I had done to the Rochelle name by getting my own act together. Time to get started.

As I hurried down the hallway, a door opened and a man emerged. "Katherine, hold on a minute."

So much for making a clean escape. I halted and plastered on a smile. "Hi, Uncle Colin." I kissed his ruddy cheek and then spotted another man inside my uncle's den.

"Paul, what a surprise! I thought you were in D.C. before the Judicial Committee."

The tall man stepped forward to the doorway and pressed a cool kiss to my forehead. "The approval process is on hold while the senators go home to make sure their constituents know they exist."

I chuckled. My godfather, Paul Schofield, an U.S. appellate judge, had received the nod from the President to be the next U.S. Supreme Court Justice, but the approval process was taking forever.

"How much longer, do you think?"

His shrug was casual but I could see the tension in his lean, tanned face.

"Who knows? Perhaps when they've determined I was bottle-fed and wore cloth diapers."

"I can't believe how invasive this inquiry must be for you."

However, if ever a man had a clean slate for prying eyes, it would be my godfather: a state prosecutor who became an extremely successful personal-injury attorney, married well like my uncle, a U.S. District judge and now on the appellate bench. As cogent and articulate as his written opinions were, he would be a tremendous Supreme Court Justice, perhaps going down in history as famous as Justice Learned Hand.

"Katherine, there's something we would like to discuss with you. Could you step inside for a moment?

This sounded like trouble and I had already had my fair share in the span of two hours. I dragged in a deep breath before moving into the den. I had always hated this room and the heads of dead animals staring at me from the walls. I understood Colin's need to escape from his rarefied world married to a Rochelle, but couldn't he hunt with a camera rather than a gun?

"What's up?" I folded my arms and studied the two men as they glanced at each other.

What a contrasting pair. My great-uncle's stocky build had served him well as a college football player on a scholarship, but age had thickened his middle and transformed his lantern jaw into being jowly. Still, my uncle remained a good-looking man. His thick tawny-gold hair had silvered without thinning, lending him a genteel look. Blessed with a generous mouth, an easy disposition and twinkling hazel eyes, he had cut quite a charming swath in social and political circles until he had landed my great-aunt as his wife. Only his splotchy complexion betrayed his recurrent escape from being henpecked via one too many bourbons.

On the other hand, time had weathered Paul's craggy features into handsomeness. Underneath heavy brows, his deep-set gray eyes glinted with intelligence. White frosted his ebony hair at the temples. Italian-tailored wool suits transformed his rawboned frame into old-world elegance.

Still, the men had forged a bond. One a public defender, the other a prosecutor, they had met at opposite sides of the bench and litigated their way up to fame and fortune. Only Colin's legal career had stalled after a stint as Florida's Attorney General.

Colin cleared his throat. "Katherine, what Paul hasn't mentioned is that the appellate investigation is now focusing on his family and immediate acquaintances."

"That's because Paul is too good to be true."

"Exactly." Colin nodded, his expression grave. "We need a man like Paul on the highest court bench."

"Absolutely."

"That's why I have to add a special plea to Hilary's request that you not represent Lloyd Silber."

Betrayal sliced deep, the hurt curdling in my heart. Of all the people in my life I thought would understand the need to find justice for the wrongly accused, it should have been Uncle Colin.

He had been my father figure, the man I had emulated. His tales about cases he had heard on the bench had been my inspiration to go to law school.

"Don't look so stricken, dear." Colin awkwardly patted me on my shoulder. "I know it's been unfair what you have gone through, that you're a good girl."

I cleared my throat. "Woman, Uncle Colin. I'm a woman now."

He turned even a deeper shade of red. "Of course you are, dear. But you're just getting back on your feet, building a practice. Taking on what will be a news-headliner case would do more harm than good right now."

My lips were stiff. "And be an embarrassment for Paul."

Paul shook his head. "Don't ascribe sentiments to me. I'm very proud of how you've pulled yourself together. But you need to work up to handling the big stuff. Even Colin and I paid our dues before trying murder cases. In the hands of an inexperienced attorney, more harm than good may be done. A man's life is at stake."

"Thanks for the vote of confidence."

"Katherine! Don't take that tone with Paul. If you want to blame anyone, blame me. I was the one who thought we should discuss the matter with you."

But behind Colin I felt the presence of my aunt, manipulating the strings, to give me a double whammy. I turned and walked to the door.

"Where are you going?" Concern edged Colin's voice. I knew he loved me, but when it came to choosing between me or Hilary and Paul, I knew the answer wouldn't be me.

"Oh, I thought I'd hang out at the county jail and maybe

watch some *real* attorneys at work during arraignment hearings since, according to you, I don't qualify as one."

I shrugged. "And while I'm there, I just might arrange to meet with Lloyd Silber." Without waiting for Colin's reply, I went down the hallway.

I couldn't leave fast enough. The house had never been my home.

The afternoon passed in a blur. I first contacted and met with Meredith Silber at the couple's town house in North Palm Beach. A petite, elegant woman, Meredith could speak with me in private for only a brief period of time. Family and friends filled the rooms and kept interrupting any attempt at conversation. Thank God, I was able to sit with my knees together during the crucial interview. Otherwise, Meredith would've noticed that they were quaking from nerves.

However, I held myself together and came away with her quiet plea to at least meet with her husband. After checking in with my office and telling my partners about the possible case, I drove to the jail and took a seat in one of the facility's conference rooms. As I waited at the utilitarian table for the guards to bring Lloyd in, I wrinkled my nose.

The meeting room smelled the same as ever. No matter how strong the cleanser used, it could never erase the pungent smell of sweat, anger and fear.

Then a guard opened the door and let Lloyd in. I sat back, startled by the change in his appearance. In the course of two weeks, when I last saw him at a social function, the director had aged considerably. His brown eyes were tired with deep grainy circles of black under them. A heavy five-o'clock shadow stood out against the pallor of his skin. However, his background as a naval officer left its stamp in the way he sat ramrod straight in his chair.

Life had dealt him a number of hard knocks, but Lloyd always brimmed with energy. Now he sat almost lifeless, as if the very vitality had been sapped from his veins. His face was devoid of any expression. Only if a person looked carefully would they spot the resentment burning bright in his eyes.

"Thanks for seeing me, Katherine." His voice was rough. "Not many of my friends want that pleasure at the moment."

"They'll call once we get you out of here."

"Am I getting out?"

"You'll have a first appearance hearing tomorrow morning. With your clean record, family and community ties, I anticipate the judge will allow bail. It may be high because of the murder charge."

Embarrassment flickered across Lloyd's face before the shuttered expression resumed. "At the moment I don't happen to have any spare change lying around."

Oh yes. His wife, Meredith, had been quite clear about their financial situation. In the past I had wondered why a man like Lloyd would take on a low-paying job such as the restoration project, but now I knew. At his age without money, he had been hoping to make prestigious contacts.

"You do have friends, Lloyd. A few are raising the collateral for the bail."

He looked down at his hands clasped on top of the table. "Another debt to repay."

"It's either that or stay in jail."

His lips twitched. "Always the pragmatist, Katherine."

I cleared my throat. "Speaking of being pragmatic, I have to advise you that I've never represented a client charged with murder. However, I'm quite an experienced negotiator. I reviewed the charges before meeting with you, and I'm confident that I can get you a good deal."

Without warning, he leaned across the table and snagged my wrist.

My mouth dried. We were in a conference room without windows. If the on-duty officer wasn't paying attention to the security cameras, Lloyd could break my right wrist and worse before help could arrive.

With my left hand I carefully palmed my pen, prepared to jab him if need be.

"I didn't kill Grace." His blunt nails cut into my tender flesh. "I wasn't having an affair with her. I love Meredith too much to betray her like that. You must believe me."

I sensed the anger through his grip, I heard the conviction in his voice, and when I gazed into his haunted eyes, I recognized the truth. Hadn't I looked into a mirror countless times during the U.S. Attorney corruption investigation and seen that same lost expression in my own eyes?

Lloyd hadn't killed Grace Roberts.

I released the pen and laid my hand on top of his. "I believe you."

"Thank you." He swallowed, blinking back tears. He released me and slowly leaned back into his chair.

"Now what?"

Under the cover of the table, I massaged sensation back into my right hand before I picked up my pen. "Now tell me everything you know about Grace, about the restoration project and any enemies you may have made."

Lloyd groaned and scrubbed his face. "How many hours do you have?"

I flipped to a fresh page on my paper pad. "As many as it takes."

Chapter 3

The stadium-size parking lot had emptied considerably during the time I had been meeting with my client. Only a scattering of patrol and civilian cars remained. The late-afternoon sun cast deep shadows in the corners. Of course, my car was parked on the far side so I cut a diagonal toward it.

Halfway across the lot I heard the slight sound of rubber scuffing against the pavement. I glanced around but saw no one. The fine hairs on the nape of my neck lifted as if stirred by a nonexistent breeze.

I picked up the pace and at the same time shifted the car key into my right hand. Although I heard nothing else, I still breathed a mental sigh of relief when I reached the Jag. Being a city girl, I flicked on the miniflashlight clipped to my key chain and panned the narrow beam into the back seat. No one.

Who could blame me for having jumpy nerves? I'd had one miserable day. I inserted and twisted the key.

Someone jerked my briefcase from my left hand, almost dislocating my shoulder.

I spun only to see a hooded person running toward the street.

"Hey!" I took off after the thief. "Give that back!"

After a few steps I kicked off my shoes, wishing I could throw them like a knife and impale him right between the shoulder blades.

In my stocking feet, I continued the chase, zigzagging among the cars. If I could maneuver him toward the south edge, then maybe I would be in luck and the security for The Donald's golf course might be on patrol. The Trump course was more closely guarded than the jail any time of the day.

I winced as a stone sliced my foot. There went another pair of hose! The kid was fast, I had to grant him that. In my tight skirt I wasn't gaining any ground. Time for a different strategy.

At the top of my considerable lungs, I yelled, "Take the bag but dump the contents!"

The thief ignored me and cut around one of the county buses used to transport prisoners. I pumped my arms and put on a burst of speed, but by the time I reached the bus, he had disappeared. I paused, catching my breath, while I tried to gauge where he had gone.

No movement, no sound, no clue.

Now, like an idiot, I could stumble about in the gathering dusk, giving him an opportunity to jump me again, or retreat to my car.

"Damn!" Turning, I gimped back to the jail parking lot, picking up my discarded shoes along the way. I rather liked that briefcase, but thank God, the jerk had gone for the blatant designer initials on the case and not for my more discreet Hermès tote. Although it was a pain in the ass, I could've easily recopied the court files contained in the case. Not so for the contents of my tote. Unzipping the top, I pulled out the slim leather portfolio.

My notes from the Silber interview were irreplaceable. I'd dictate them up as soon as I reached the office. I opened my car door and slid inside.

But first, I had a bone to pick with the sheriff's office about the security of its parking lot.

Nearly an hour later the Jag and I, mutually running on empty, crawled into the firm's parking lot. Given the time, the staff was gone for the day although I could hear voices from Nicole's office located diagonally across from mine. Without making a sound, I limped down the hall.

Once I was inside the seclusion of my office, my aching feet demanded that I kick off my shoes. The next article of clothing to go was my jacket. With a mingled sigh of relief and groan of pain, I shucked off my ruined hose.

"Hey, sweetheart. Don't you think we should get business out of the way before we get down to hot and sweaty?" A man's voice, as rich and smoky as aged whiskey, emanated from the depths of the Queen Anne chair I had placed beside a table in the corner for working at nights.

I froze, my skirt still hitched around my waist and my heart doing a perfect backflip. I didn't have any appointments. My sole client was in county lockup.

As I yanked my skirt down, I squinted but couldn't make out my unwanted visitor's features. As I hadn't bothered to turn on the overhead light, the room remained dark. Good, he couldn't have seen much.

"Of course, I'm for skipping business altogether. Stripping off that blue silk thong over your endless legs would be a lot more interesting. It's been a hell of a day."

My face burned. Of all the obnoxious men, this one took the cake. Carling's office was next to mine so he had to be her client. Let her take his gigantic ego down a peg or two. In the meantime I wrapped the shreds of my dignity around me.

"Excuse me, but you're in the wrong office." Each word dripped with the iciest disdain I could muster. "If you're here for Carling—"

"Hey, you're here! For once I didn't hear your car squealing to a stop."

I looked around. Carling stood with her shoulder propped against the doorjamb. "I see you two have met."

I was supposed to meet this oaf? With a tinge of desperation, I said, "I was just going to escort your client to your office."

She let out a hoot of laughter. "In my dreams. After you told me about your new case, I knew you would need an investigator so I called the best. Kate, meet Gabriel Chavez, P.I." She flicked the switch on so the room flooded with light.

Oh no, not *him,* although I probably should be grateful for the opportunity to meet the infamous police detective whose dismissal had actually bumped me and the federal corruption investigation of the U.S. Attorney's office from headlines.

I blinked against the glare as the man rose and sauntered toward me. He had chosen that chair deliberately, I realized, both to protect his back and to see who entered before he was spotted. Here was a man accustomed to danger and wanting the upper hand.

Then I saw his face and was blindsided. God, talk about gorgeous.

Gabriel Chavez personified Latin virility: jet-black hair that curled, golden skin stretched taut over knife-edged cheekbones, eyes the shade of dark Godiva chocolate, a sculpted poet's mouth designed for long, soft kisses. Dressed in black jeans and black T-shirt, he had a tough, compact build with broad shoulders.

Then he smiled, a flash of strong white teeth. Oh yeah, here was a man who could charm the pants off any woman within a hundred feet with one glimpse of that dimple.

He extended his hand and manners dictated that I hold out my own. I intended only the briefest of grips, but nothing prepared me for the jolt of his skin against mine. A wave of heat singed every nerve ending from the tips of my fingers to the soles of my feet.

I stepped back and nearly fell when my heel banged against a chair. With a smooth move, Gabriel caught and righted me. His arms slipped around me, bringing me into perfect alignment against the hard, muscular angles of his body.

With an effort, I found my voice. "Um, I'm fine. You can let go now, Gabriel."

His bedroom eyes couldn't have been hotter and more amused as he slowly shook his head. "Call me Gabe. And I'm quite happy with the way things are."

I inhaled, to blister him, and gasped. Even the smallest movement on my part caused us to rub together.

He grinned. His warm masculine scent filled my nostrils, making me feel even woozier.

Setting my teeth, I wiggled my hand trapped between our bodies. I caught a pinch of his rib flesh and gave a sharp twist. He yelped and released me. I shook my fist at him.

"Listen macho man. I have been mauled and mugged two times already today and I've had it up to here!"

My outburst finally got a rise out of Carling, who had contented herself to watch our play-by-play with great interest. She rushed to me.

"What do you mean, you were mugged?"

"A guy…at least I think the thief was male…grabbed my briefcase as I was leaving the jail."

Now that my hormonal surcharge was subsiding, my feet were back to screaming for attention. I limped over to my chair and sat, dropping the tote bag on the floor.

"I gave chase but lost him when he ducked behind a bus."

"Let me see those." Gabe knelt before me and lifted a foot. His dark brow arched. "You chased him without your shoes on?"

I winced as he prodded a cut. "I thought it was wiser than breaking my neck from running in four-inch heels."

"You actually think? Did you think about the consequences of chasing some punk by yourself?"

I tried to tug my foot free, but his strong fingers were like a vise.

"I can take care of myself."

"Right, that's why you look like you've been run over by a truck." He glanced over his shoulder. "Carling, can you bring me a washcloth and a first-aid kit? These cuts need to be cleaned and bandaged."

No way did I want to be left alone with this man. We could call Nicole for help. I shot a pleading glance at Carling, but my traitorous friend was already out the door.

With as dignified tone as I could muster, I said, "You don't need to stay, Mr. Chavez. Carling and I can manage."

He winked. "We have business to discuss, remember?" His touch was gentle but impersonal as he examined the cuts on my sole. Wow, were my feet throbbing! I tried to see around Gabe's head to see how deep the cuts were.

Then I caught sight of the fire-engine-red toenail polish the manicurist had talked me into yesterday instead of my usual pink.

What messages did a woman send with that color? I almost surrendered to the urge to wiggle my toes to see if any polish was chipped.

I heard Gabe's low voice rumbling. With an effort, I focused.

"What did you say?"

"Carling says you need an investigator for the old courthouse murder case."

"Mr. Chavez, I don't think you're suitable for the position."

Uh-oh. He released my one foot only to wrap his fingers around the other ankle. Good thing I'd had my legs waxed as well yesterday. As he pressed his fingers, the action took on the semblance of a massage.

"It's Gabe, remember."

"What?"

"My name."

"I know who you are." My embarrassment made for loose lips. "Your exploits as a detective were headline news up right through the time you punched out your captain and you were fired."

My God, was that Aunt Hilary's biting primness I heard coming from my mouth?

Gabe lowered my foot; I could have whimpered.

"Was that a rebuke I heard? You of all people should understand about being on the receiving end of a scandal."

He had me there. Leaning forward, I looked into his dark fathomless eyes. "I'm…I'm sorry. It's been a long hellish day. No." I pinched the bridge of my nose. "That's a cop-out. You ever have a frightening moment when you become exactly like the people who raised you…even when you swore a million times you wouldn't?"

He nodded. "Both the good and the bad of our folks are stamped upon our makeup."

"Exactly. I just had an 'Aunt Hilary' moment and I apologize."

Gabe stayed in a crouch, his arm resting on his knee. "This Aunt Hilary raise you?"

I never spoke about my family with strangers, but in the quiet of my office, with this man who appeared willing to listen, the temptation was strong. Too strong. I needed to steer the conversation back to business.

"Gabe."

"Yes?"

"Carling and Nicole both speak highly of your investigation skills." If fact, they had waxed poetic about his results. When their regular investigator had suffered a heart attack and retired two months ago, he had recommended Gabe. At that time I had no clients of my own, so I hadn't bothered to meet Gabe and hadn't bothered to check his references.

"They're dynamite women."

The obvious admiration in his tone gave me a pause. Was his relationship with one of my friends personal? Jealousy's claws needled me.

"Look," I said in desperation. "I'm sure you'd be fine to use on a case with not as high a profile…." My voice trailed off. My family had said the same about me.

Gabe winked at me. "We're quite a pair with our history, aren't we?"

I nodded.

His expression intensified as he studied me. "Your partners said you got a bum deal at the U.S. Attorney's office."

My cheeks warmed.

"But you made a mistake and paid for it."

Even months later, chagrin was a hot ball in my throat that I had to swallow.

"Slept with the top guy—"

Oh no, not again. I wasn't about to listen to the career-favors-for-sex intimation. "Don't go there." My voice was tight with anger.

"Don't go where?"

"I did not get any special breaks for dating Harold. Period."

Gabe's eyebrow arched in skepticism. "I know Harold Lowell and you're a looker."

Just like a man to assume the worst. This time I welcomed Hilary's reproving tone in my voice. "What you don't know is that I eloped when I was eighteen, only to learn the boy had visions of trust funds and not love." I snapped my fingers. "My family secured the divorce within a few weeks."

He whistled. "Talk about a quickie."

Perhaps. But not quick in terms of emotional toll, although I wasn't about to admit that. I settled for a frosty glare. "Call my mistakes with men lessons learned the hard way."

Moreover, I wasn't about to follow my mother's path and blaze a sexual trail through the opposite sex.

"You must be talking about that rat Prince Harold." Nicole Sterling, carrying a white terry washcloth and first-aid kit, walked toward us. Tall and slender in her navy pin-stripe suit, she was model-perfect. Her concerned gaze absorbed my condition in one glance.

"You look like hell."

"Gee, thanks."

"Carling needed to take a call so she asked me to bring in the first-aid kit."

Gabe leaned back on his heels and flashed that killer smile. "Hello, Red. Looking gorgeous as usual."

"Looking to die young, Gabe?"

"No, ma'am."

"Then don't call me Red." She handed him the cloth.

"Sure thing, Red…I mean Nicole." He winked before he looked down as he probed and cleaned my wounds. I bit back a whimper.

"Did Katherine also mention that she was the one who figured out Harold's scam and turned him in to the federal authorities?"

"No, she forgot that fact." He squeezed a drop of salve onto his palm and carefully applied it to the cuts.

"Fine." I leaned back into the chair. "Let's talk about me as if I wasn't present."

Nicole propped her hip against the edge of my desk. "Lucky gal. Nothing like having a tall, dark and handsome man attend to you."

And dangerous, I thought. Very dangerous to a woman who lacked any intuition about the opposite sex. I said coolly, "If you see a man like that, let me know. Ouch!"

Gabe's expression was pure innocence. "Sorry. Did that hurt?"

"You know it did."

Nicole laughed. "Sounds like you two are going to have a great time working together."

I cast her a withering glance.

"Kate here hasn't made up her mind whether I can stand up to public scrutiny on this case."

I squirmed. I hadn't decided, but the truth said out loud sounded shallow.

"Nonsense. Your credentials are impeccable." Nicole paused a beat and fluttered her eyelashes. "And you owe me a beer for landing you another case."

Gabe grunted as he wrapped gauze around my foot.

"Thanks a lot. Your partner is already skittish as a perp under questioning."

Nicole picked up the Saint Louis paperweight on my desk and tossed it from hand to hand. Its facets flashed a rainbow of colors in the light. When my friend was working on a problem, she liked to keep her hands busy.

"We all appreciate the best."

He patted my bandaged feet and rose, spreading his hands. "Working for three beautiful women. How can life get any better?"

I rolled my eyes, and Nicole laughed. She put down the paperweight and walked over to the corner of the room where I kept a huge dry-erase board. "Since you're the walking wounded, Katherine, I'll man the marker. What do we know so far?"

Gabe proceeded to wander around the office, pausing here and there to check out a photograph or a knickknack.

I squelched a Hilary urge to instruct him not to touch anything, but instead removed the portfolio from the tote, and flipped through my notes.

"Grace's body was discovered at ten-twenty p.m. when the guard was making his rounds. Approximate time of death speculated to be after eight. Our client was home alone."

"So no alibi." Nicole's marker squeaked on the board as she wrote down all the facts.

"Police theory of motivation was lover's quarrel."

"Were they having an affair?"

I shrugged. "He denies it."

"Good-looking older man, pretty young girl. Jury may disbelieve him."

"True." I frowned at one page. "He mentioned the restoration has run into major snags. Additional subcontractors had to be hired in the hopes of bringing the project in on time."

Gabe paused in his prowling. "What kind of snags?"

"Delayed shipments, busted or stolen equipment, accidents." I lowered the pad. "The workers are complaining the site is jinxed. A few have even quit, saying the fourth floor was haunted."

Gabe examined the array of my skeet-shooting and swimming trophies on a shelf. "That's the floor where the woman was murdered."

Nicole chose a different colored marker. "So for suspects we have our client, his wife…." She wrote rapidly.

"Why Meredith?"

"Jealousy." Nicole and Gabe spoke in unison and grinned at each other.

"Textbook suspect," Nicole added.

"All right." Personally I doubted that Lloyd's small, reserved wife could muster the energy to kill anyone. She was more into complaining about her lowered financial situation. If she killed anyone, it would be her husband, to collect insurance payments.

"Others on the restoration committee, as they would have access and motive." My partner continued down the suspect column. "Any mutual friends and acquaintances of Grace and Lloyd. Of course, Grace's fiancé. Construction people. Who else?"

"No one—" I broke off as a horrible idea took hold. Oh brother, opening that can of worms would make my life miserable.

"What is it, Katherine?"

"Nothing." I shook my head. "Bad idea."

Gabe turned around and folded his arms. "Can't be that bad, *Katherine,* if it caused that panicky expression."

What, did he have eyeballs in the back of his head? I sulked.

"Grace's job was to collect memorabilia from the days the courthouse was in use. Art, books, furniture, photographs."

"We'll call this pool of suspects 'donors.'" Nicole added another line on the board.

Oh goody. My aunt and all her friends would be simply thrilled to be questioned in connection with a murder case. It would be the talk of the town for weeks.

I rubbed my temples where the telltale throbbing of a tension headache was starting. "So where do we start?"

"The murder scene." Gabe jerked his head toward the door. "Come on, beautiful. Let's get going."

"Where?"

"The courthouse. I'll make a call on the way to clear our admittance."

"Now?" All I wanted to do was crawl home, straight into a hot shower.

"Our client's first appearance is in the morning, isn't it?"

"Yes."

"The murder occurred at night, didn't it?"

"Yes." I frowned. "Who's the attorney here?"

With studied nonchalance he shrugged. "I'm attending law school at night."

Uh-oh.

"Look, there's no time like the present. I need to see how the scene looks like at night. Besides, with all the construction people, the integrity of the crime scene is going to be shot to hell if it isn't already."

He extended his hand. "Go home, change, and I'll pick you up in thirty."

I forced my aching body to leave the chair's comfort without his assistance. "Make it an hour and you have a deal."

"Thirty."

"Forty-five."

"Thirty."

I sighed. "Okay, thirty, but don't be on time."

"Seven sharp and I'll pick up burgers along the way."

True to his word, Gabe arrived promptly at seven, charmed my cat Willy, handed me a hamburger and pulled me toward his battered black Dodge truck before I could catch a breath. I had raced home, jumped into the shower and pulled on the first available outfit.

I wore jeans, whose crisp crease had earned a withering glance from Gabe, a black cashmere V-neck sweater, and no makeup. I was tired, my feet hurt like hell, and my temper simmered due to the irritating man beside me, but I was having the time of my life.

What I was doing was so totally removed from the glittering balls of Palm Beach society that I could've hugged myself for joy. Oh heck, why not? I wrapped my arms around myself.

"Are you cold?" Gabe asked as he pulled his rattling monster of a truck into a spot in the parking garage.

"No."

He leaned across me, and I got another tantalizing whiff of him as he reached into the glove compartment and pulled out a large flashlight. Oh dear. Gabe was one of those MacGyver types—prepared for any emergency.

Within a few minutes we stood before the old courthouse. My breath caught. At night with the glow of lights, it shimmered. The first stage of the restoration had consisted of removing the 1970s brick facade that had wrapped around the original 1916 structure. Now the neoclassic building with its graceful pillars stood out among all the other governmental buildings.

Such pretty trappings for so much heartache. It's just a

building, I reminded myself. It simply served as the site of tragedy.

At the entrance Gabe exchanged a few words with the security guard and then we were inside, crossing the hall to the stairway.

My shoes echoed on the marble steps in the old courthouse. Had my grandfather placed his foot in this slight depression? Had he held this banister? Had he and Grandmother walked through those doors and simply slipped away into the night? Had they been dragged out kicking and screaming?

We reached the top floor and took the passage to our left. Gabe switched on the flashlight and its high-powered beam sliced down the long dim corridor.

I smiled. "I was right."

"About?"

"You're like MacGyver."

"Loved that show as a kid." He patted his back pocket.

"Don't tell me. Let me guess. Your pocketknife?"

"You bet. As a top-notch investigator, I like to be prepared."

Ahead of us, the shadows stirred as if a darker one moved in their midst. For a moment I wondered if we had disturbed one of the building's alleged ghosts. Then I narrowed my eyes.

"I thought the guard said we were the only ones up here."

"Yes—" Gabe broke off as he swung the flashlight. The shadow moved as the person took off in the opposite direction.

"Hey, come back here!" I yelled and broke into a run. Someone was up to no good.

"What the hell? Kate!"

The beam of light bounced as Gabe started after me. I

called over my shoulder. "He must have been after the artifacts housed up here."

The light steadied and I saw the dark shadow turn and lift its arm. Metal glinted.

A Mack truck in the form of Gabe rammed into my ribs as a loud crack reverberated.

"Umph!" The force threw me forward yet twisted me at the same time. I landed not on the floor but on something only a bit softer.

Before I could draw in a breath, Gabe rolled me underneath his hard body, drew his gun, braced his arms and fired off one shot.

The ringing spread from my ears to my temples as if I was in the London Tower at noon. I could see that Gabe had pulled out his phone and was talking, but all I could hear was a buzz interfacing with the ringing.

He rose, tugging me up along with him. "Come on. Hurry. The police are on their way, and I want to get a look at what he was doing before they get here."

He reached into his jacket pocket and brought out latex gloves. "Here, put these on."

I snapped on the icky plastic. As we approached the vicinity where the intruder had been, I saw the strips of yellow tape strewn on the ground in front of one room.

"Ah, so someone else was interested in the murder scene."

"Gabe." I halted and gripped his arm.

"What is it?"

I swallowed, knowing that indeed the courthouse ghosts were alive and well tonight, for they had materialized to haunt me.

But I had to circle around to the truth. I couldn't immediately confront it.

"That can't be the room where Grace Roberts was killed."

"Duh." Gabe pointed the flashlight at the door. "Tape with the words *crime scene* on it. Surely you left the ivory tower at the federal level on occasion to know what the tape looks like."

So much for circling. I took a deep breath.

"That's my grandfather's old chambers."

"What?" He turned and gripped my upper arms.

I nodded. "That's the office where he and my grandmother were last seen before they disappeared thirty-five years ago."

Chapter 4

Gabe let out a long, low whistle as he ran his hands up and down my arms in a comforting gesture.

"The murder occurred in your grandfather's former chambers?"

Damn this place. How could the past reach through generations to hold another so entangled in the consequences?

I needed to go home and drag my aching body into bed, not to emerge for at least a week. But I had a client who needed me to find the truth.

Breaking away from Gabe, I stepped toward the door. "You're the former detective. What do your instincts tell you about this situation?"

"It was where Grace spent the majority of her time. Then again, there's no such thing as coincidence, not when murder is involved."

"This just gets more and more complicated."

After picking up his flashlight, Gabe followed and swept the beam around the room's interior. I stared in disbelief.

Before me was the re-creation of Jonathan Rochelle's inner chambers in the aftermath of a hurricane. Many of the strewn and overturned objects I recognized from the small storage room tucked at the back of my aunt's house. Although under Hilary's orders, the room had been kept locked at all times. Still on occasion a servant had left it open. Since my room was also on the same level, I had used those opportunities to sneak in and explore. What child could resist the secrets underneath drop cloths behind a locked door?

I stepped inside the chambers. Here on the floor was the bronze statue of justice that my grandmother had given her husband the day he had been sworn in. I knew by heart the words engraved on the figurine's base: To Jonathan, My Darling And My Hero. Love, Marguerite.

All that remained of a family heirloom vase were scattered blue fragments. Grandfather's worn book of landmark court decisions was pitched into the corner.

Tears burned my eyes.

"The bastard. He could've torn the pages." I started toward the book, but Gabe gripped my arm.

"You can't move anything."

Of course. Nodding, I wrapped my arms around my middle because the urge to grab the book I had read so often remained strong.

"That guy tossed this room looking for something. Anything you notice as being unusual?"

"I wouldn't know. I've never been inside the actual room before." All visitors had been kept to the temporary restoration offices on the first floor while the upper floors had been under construction.

"But you know the contents."

"Some. My family kept a few of Granddad's belongings in storage. I didn't even know that they had been transferred here." Circling, I surveyed the room. Taking center stage was a magnificent mahogany desk that had been imported from the Far East. Elaborate carvings covered all the sides.

"Look," I pointed, "the desk drawers are open."

Gabe avoided the debris and stepped behind the desk. "Nice work," he murmured as he ran his gloved hand over a carving.

"Granddad's pride and joy. My aunt used to say it matched the size of his ego."

I joined Gabe, prepared to search the drawers but an overturned frame drew my attention. The glass was broken and the faded photograph of the couple ripped to shreds.

"Your grandparents?"

I swallowed. "Yes."

Crouching, Gabe used a pen to slightly lift the frame and examine the back before carefully lowering the frame. "Doesn't look like it's been opened so chances are nothing was hidden behind the photo."

I started to protest but then closed my mouth. His conclusion that the intruder had been looking for something was an obvious one. Yet the photo's destruction seemed more personal.

The hair on my neck stirred. I felt disoriented, to be surrounded with so many of my grandfather's things after all these years. If I blinked, I swore I would see him sitting… No, don't be ridiculous.

Glancing away to stare at the far wall, I froze. Hung in an ornate gilt frame was a painting of Jonathan Rochelle in his robes. The artist had captured him sitting behind the bench, with one hand resting on top of a Bible. Even at rest, my grandfather exuded energy. From all accounts, he had been a dynamic man and strength radiated from him. His blue eyes sparkled with amusement as if he was laughing at me.

Then I saw the diagonal tear across the portrait. "Gabe!" I rushed across the room. "The painting's been slashed."

"We must have interrupted the thief before he could totally destroy it."

"Thank God," I murmured as I touched the raw edges. I would call my friend at the Metropolitan Museum of Art. He would know the best restoration expert.

Voices from the hallway warned we weren't alone anymore.

"Come on." Gabe gripped my arm. "We'd better get out of the crime scene before the cops get here."

The next hour passed in a blur as the police once more swarmed over the room and interviewed us. Numbly I answered those questions I could and deftly avoided those I wouldn't or couldn't answer.

Then Gabe was guiding me out of the building into the night. "Let's grab something cold to drink."

We walked in silence until we reached the first trendy bar along Clematis Street. Because it was off hours, the place wasn't crowded and Gabe found a table in the rear where we couldn't be overheard. After we placed our orders, Gabe leaned back in his chair, stretching out his long legs.

"Okay, shoot."

"Shoot what?"

"Tell me about your grandparents. You've been paler than a ghost since you made the connection that the room had been your grandfather's chambers."

I laced my fingers together. "I don't know where to start."

"How about their disappearance? I know some about the scandal. Judge Rochelle in with the Mob, taking bribes—"

I slammed the palm of my hand on the tabletop, causing the bowl of nuts to rattle. "He did not! That's a lie."

Gabe held up his hands. "Okay. What do you believe happened?"

The brief spurt of anger drained away, leaving me tired beyond belief. Still, any immediate prospect of crawling into bed remained a mirage.

I rubbed my now-throbbing temples. "I don't know what happened, only the official accounts. All I know is that the scandal left a scar on my life from the moment I was born."

"How so?"

To say I was normally closemouthed about my family would be an understatement. The only people who knew were Carling and Nicole. However, I saw quiet understanding in Gabe's eyes, not the morbid curiosity I usually confronted. I rolled my shoulders to loosen the tension before I continued.

"My mother was twelve when her parents vanished without a trace. She never got over it. She went from a rebellious teenager to a woman bent on self-destruction. She never settled down, only jet-setting around the world as much as her trust fund would permit. My mother slept with any man who wanted her and even those who didn't."

I shrugged. "At some point she got too careless and I was the result. She was 'in love' at the time and thought a child would bind the man to her. It didn't. The relationship went bust by the time I was born, and dear old Mom dumped me off on Aunt Hilary and Uncle Colin's doorsteps."

The waitress served us our drinks, and I sipped the tepid Pinot Grigio to moisten my throat.

"Your mother's sister raised you?"

"No." I lowered my glass. "Aunt Hilary is actually my grandfather's sister. Calling her 'great-aunt' reminded her too much of her age."

"Does she think her brother was wrongly accused?"

"I have no idea. She's banned any discussion."

My fingers tightened on the glass stem. "Once when I was six I made the mistake of asking a question during dinner. I had sneaked into the room where Granddad's things were kept after a maid had left it unlocked. His desk fascinated me so I wanted to know where he was."

I took another sip of wine and then stared at my empty glass in astonishment. I never drank an entire glass. Aunt Hilary had always said that alcohol dulled the intellect. My mother was a shining example. Except for the one binge that had led to my disastrous marriage, I avoided drinking.

Gabe signaled to the waitress. "Oh no, I can't." I placed my hand over the glass.

"Worried I might take advantage of you?"

"No, but I need to be able to think."

"It seems to me that you do too much thinking at times, Kate. You need to loosen up and let go."

"Therein lies the way to ruination for a Rochelle."

"Your mother?"

"Yes."

"What happened to her? Have you ever met her?"

That would be difficult to do since she broke her neck skiing au natural, drunk as a skunk, down the slopes in the Italian Alps.

When the waitress arrived with another wine and a club soda, I seized on the interruption. At times the line between talking about my family's history and baring my soul was razor thin. "We need to discuss the case."

"Fascinating." Gabe took a swig of his drink. Not as fascinating as watching his strong neck muscles flex as he swallowed.

"What is?"

"The way the No Trespassing sign reared up in your voice."

I shrugged. "I've already said too much. Family matters shouldn't be discussed in public."

"I assume I'm in the presence of Aunt Hilary?"

Horrified, I stared at him. I had done it again. Fallen back on her when I was feeling vulnerable. Did I not have any protective mantels of my own? When would I be my own person?

"Yes," I sighed, "but my mother's dead and gone and I'd rather not discuss her."

He reached across the table and took my hand, rubbing his thumb over my knuckles. "For now. But at some point you'll have to talk about her if only to let go of all that hurt inside you."

I tugged my hand, trying to get up, but his grip tightened. Frustrated, I glared at him. "I want to go home."

"We still have business to finish tonight."

"We saw the crime scene. It told us nothing about Grace Roberts's murder."

He continued to massage my hand, sending tingles of warmth shooting up my arm.

"No? It told us that somehow your grandfather is involved. What happened tonight was no coincidence. His chambers were not a random toss."

"It could've been a kid bent on trouble or someone trying to destroy any evidence from Grace's murder." Talk about grasping at straws, but I needed to make the effort in front of Gabe.

"The destruction of the photograph and painting were personal and you know it."

"Yes." The fact that Gabe's observation matched mine relieved some of my inner tension. I hadn't been imagining things in the chambers after all. "I sensed the anger."

"Whether revenge or something more is involved, we need to explore that avenue."

"True, but Grace was murdered in that room because of her involvement with the restoration. We need to keep with the game plan of the most logical suspects, namely the restoration committee and its volunteers. I have the list. Can you run backgrounds on them?"

"Sure." He raised my hand and flipped it over, pressing a soft kiss to my palm. "Babe, why do you think your grandfather was innocent?" His dark gaze unsettled me.

The wine cracked open the door to that part of my heart I kept secret from the world. I wrapped my fingers around the locket and tried desperately to fence around the truth.

"His decisions, his work, his community service."

"What else?"

I blinked back the tears that burned in my eyes.

"Because of the honesty I see in his face." I whispered, "I have his looks and his character, from what my aunt has told me a million times."

"So you have to believe that he was honest."

"Yes."

"Sounds reasonable to me." Gabe rose. "We have a long day tomorrow. Let me take you home."

Darkness shrouded the endless twisting hallway. As I walked along, I kept trying to open doors but all were locked. Panic's fingers gripped my throat but I managed to swallow my fear.

I would find a way out. I had to.

Ahead of me the shadows stirred, and I saw a figure.

"Wait!" I cried out as I began to run. But the person raced away from me.

No matter how hard I tried, I couldn't catch up with him. The hall was like a maze. Every time I thought I had reached the end, there was another stretch. Every time I turned, the figure disappeared down another hallway.

Sweat beaded on my forehead and my lungs burned. If I didn't know I was in the old courthouse, I could've sworn I was running uphill.

Finally, I saw the form pause before a door. The darkness shifted and lightened. Stunned, I saw my grandfather smile at me before he opened the door and slipped from view.

"Granddad, wait! It's Kate!" I hurried after him. Why didn't he stop? Didn't he know who I was?

I reached the door and slipped through the gap. The bright light blinded me and I froze. It took a moment before I could see clearly. Then I wished I was blind again.

The only furniture in the room with white walls was a raised table. Strapped to it was Lloyd Silber.

"You failed me!" he screamed, his accusation slicing through me like a sword.

"No! I've only begun the investigation. I'll get you out."

My grandfather, holding a book, appeared beside the table. "No, you're too late. You've failed to save him like you've failed at everything else in your life."

Then the book changed into a syringe, and my grandfather raised his hand.

Tears streamed down my face. "Granddad, you can't do this. You're not a murderer."

His mouth twisted into a macabre smile. "Why not, Kate? I'm already doomed." He brought his hand down.

"No!"

I shot up in bed, my chest heaving. Shoving back the tangled mass of hair, I took a few steadying breaths.

I was in my bedroom, not the courthouse. The early-morning light crept through the lace curtains. I glanced at the clock on the bedside table. Six o'clock.

Then I heard a sound. The soft tread on the hardwood floor coming from the front of the house.

Flinging back the damp twisted sheets, I swung my feet to the floor and dropped into a crouch. I scanned my bedroom and what part of the hallway I could see. Nothing.

Keeping low, I scampered around the corner of the bed. Since I kept my gun locked up, I didn't have many weapon options. Perfume spray would burn anyone's eyes like the devil, but I didn't want to get that up close and personal.

Wait a minute. Running my hand carefully under the bed, I curved my fingers over the baseball bat stowed there along with my other sporting equipment. Bed skirts hid a multitude of clutter.

Now armed, I padded to the door and held my breath. I saw a muted glow of light in the room I used as my office. I stole toward the entrance but Willy, with his innate sense of timing, appeared at my feet and yowled for his breakfast.

I rushed down the hall but I was too late. The office window was open, the sheer curtains fluttering in the breeze.

Holding the bat up, I went to the window and slammed it shut before locking it. I could've sworn every window had been secured before I'd gone to bed last night. The glass wasn't broken and there were no signs that it had been jimmied.

Puzzled, I turned on the desk lamp and looked around. No trace of an intruder. Not a tossed book or an open drawer. I must've interrupted him before he could search.

Or had there really been someone inside the house? In my weariness had I simply forgotten to lock up last night? I placed the bat in my chair. Maybe I was losing it.

Then I scrutinized my desk.

One thing that could be said about anal-compulsives. We know where and how we left our things. I always kept my appointment book in the center of the desk pad—and closed.

It lay open at an angle about two inches from the edge of my desk. I didn't have to read it to know it was opened to the page marking my meeting in the jail with Lloyd. Since I like to keep records, my appointment book doubled as a diary of events.

I glanced over to where Willy waited expectantly. "You know, I don't think the theft of my briefcase yesterday was an accident. I think someone wants information about the case."

Willy rose, flipped his tail with disdain and huffed off. So much for using a cat as a sounding board when his mind is set on breakfast. The idea sounded pretty incredulous to me as well.

I checked the wall clock. No point in going back to bed. Not with court at 9:30 and adrenaline pumping in my systems. Peeling off my damp silk nightshirt, I walked to the bathroom. I slipped into my swimsuit, fed Willy and, after grabbing my portable phone, I headed outside to the patio.

Moments later, I set the phone on the deck and dove into the pool. The initial shock of the cool water drove the breath from my lungs, but as I fell into a rhythm of swimming laps, my body became acclimated and the water felt like silk against my skin.

Stretch, pull, kick. With every stroke, the nightmare's grip on my nerves eased.

During my youth, I had taken up competitive swimming in the vain hope of winning Hilary's approval. Only after my divorce did I realize that swimming was as vital to me as breathing. The psychiatrist I had seen briefly had likened the pool to a mother's womb, saying that was why I turned to swimming so much.

Personally, I thought her conclusion had been pricey metaphysical baloney. If she had even been half listening to me, she would have realized my mother's womb probably had been a toxic cesspool of booze and drugs. How I had been born physically unscathed was truly a wonder of the world.

Turn, kick, stretch and pull.

After two embarrassing sessions, I'd called it quits with the mental health profession. I loved to swim and that was all that mattered. Those moments when my muscles would burn and my worries would go on mute functioned like deep sleep, enabling a release of my subconscious to explore options. Some of my best decisions came while I swam, such as going into practice with Carling and Nicole.

My muscles were warm and limber now; the sensation of peace stole over me. I was almost there at that special spot in my mind—

The phone's harsh musical notes ripped through the quiet morning. I sighed. While I could ignore the phone, the mood was shattered and I needed to get ready for court. Since I was at the far end, I quickened my freestyle.

"Good morning, beautiful."

Startled, I swallowed pool water and gagged. The chlorinated stuff went straight up my nasal passage, burning my nose and throat. The resulting tears lessened the effect of the glare I shot Gabe as I fumbled for the phone. Still off balance from Gabe's appearance in my backyard—my backyard barricaded from the outside world by a five-foot wood picket fence—I misjudged the distance and cracked my left elbow on the side of the pool.

"Ouch!" I almost dropped the phone into the water.

"Hello? Katherine?"

I dragged my attention to the phone as I rubbed my throbbing arm. At the rate I was going, I would need a body cast before the end of the week.

"Good morning, Aunt Hilary."

"You sound very strange, Katherine. Did I wake you?" My aunt's disapproval simmered over the line.

"No, I was up." Although I wished that I could go back to bed and start the day over again.

Gabe sauntered toward me, and I pressed my finger over my lips for him to remain silent. Of course he ignored me.

"Let me give you a hand up." With a grin he extended his hand.

Stunned silence emanated in waves on the other end of the phone. Then my aunt spoke in a frigid, condemning tone. "Is there a man with you?"

Technically, I was an unattached adult woman, who owned her house and ran her own business. Hopefully sooner and not later, I would have a man in this house, but this wasn't the time for that particular battle with Hilary.

Stumped as to how best to answer her, I lifted my hand to push back my dripping hair. Mistake.

Gabe gripped me under my arms and hauled me gasping out of the pool. Shivering from the sudden exposure to the cool morning air, I realized I hadn't bothered to bring out a towel. Great. When wet, my white workout tank suit turned transparent, leaving nothing to the imagination.

A situation that didn't escape Gabe's attention. As he surveyed me leisurely, I could feel my skin heat from the fire in his gaze.

"You think too much," he murmured.

"Someone has to think around here! You operate on pure testosterone." I stalked to the door.

"What did you say to me, young lady?" Hilary sputtered.

Damn, I'd forgotten to cover the receiver during my little exchange with Gabe.

"Hang on a minute, Aunt Hilary." On my way through the bathroom, I grabbed a robe. I entered the kitchen where a meowing Willy greeted me.

"Katherine?"

"I'm here, Aunt Hilary."

I scrunched my shoulder to hold the phone to my ear as I shrugged into my robe.

"And yes, that was a man you heard. He's the investigator who's helping me with Lloyd's case." I glared at Gabe as he ambled into the kitchen.

"You hired a private investigator?"

"Yes—"

"Why on earth would you do such a foolish thing?"

I sank onto a stool and rested my forehead against the palm of my head. Gabe made himself at home by opening cupboard doors until he found the coffee.

"I don't know, Aunt Hilary. Maybe because it's standard when there are a lot of witnesses—"

"It's a waste of money."

"I'll be the judge of that."

"And what about Lloyd's finances? Are you trying to bankrupt him? I called this morning to tell you that his friends haven't been able to raise much toward his bail."

Great. Just great.

"Then I guess I'd better argue for as low a bail as possible this morning at first appearance."

Gabe finished measuring the grains and turned on the coffee maker. He lounged against the counter.

"You're raising false hope. Colin said you should be busy bargaining for the best plea that you can."

"What if Lloyd's innocent?"

"I knew it. You're going to ruin that man's life."

"If the prosecutor goes for the death penalty, I may just save his life."

Hilary's voice became distant. "Colin, speak to her."

I lowered my head and thumped it against the countertop.

"Good morning, honey."

"Good morning, Uncle Colin."

Gabe placed a mug of steaming coffee in front of me. I grabbed it and gulped down a sip, nearly hissing when it burned my mouth.

"What's wrong?"

"Coffee's still too hot to drink."

"Then don't drink it."

"Of course, why didn't I think of that? What other sage advice does Hilary want you to impart at this hour?"

Colin cleared his throat. "I know how you want to do the right thing. But I'm speaking from experience. Defending someone accused of murder is tricky. No matter how well-meaning an attorney wants to be, how much she wants to crusade a cause, your client's life is at stake."

"But Uncle Colin, something strange is going on. There have been problems with the courthouse construction."

"What does that have to do with Grace's death?"

"Maybe nothing. But I'm going to check it out. And last night when my investigator and I were inspecting the crime scene, we caught someone destroying the room. It was Granddad's chambers."

Silence on the other end. Colin harrumphed. "I'll have to find a way to tell *her*." From his slight emphasis, I knew Hilary was still standing close by the phone. "Your godfather Paul won't like this either. The whole situation sounds dangerous, Katherine."

"I have Gabriel Chavez working with me. He's a top-notch investigator. Not to worry, Uncle Colin, I'll be careful. After court, I'm going to interview the restoration volunteers."

Hilary's voice sounded in the background. Colin cleared his throat again. "Oh, your aunt wants to remind you of the charity ball meeting this weekend."

"I don't think—"

Hilary came on the line. "Katherine, this is the final financial drive for the courthouse before it opens. We're on the board of directors. You must make it."

"I'll try. Look, I have to go. I'm due in court."

"Katherine—"

"Bye, Aunt Hilary." With a wince I disconnected the line. Boy, would I hear about this later. One simply did not hang up on Hilary. She decided when a conversation was over.

"Sounds like heartwarming support from your family," Gabe commented as he lounged against the counter next to me.

My head snapped up. "Why are you here at this hour of the morning?"

"You didn't give me the list of people last night. I thought I'd run the backgrounds while you're in court."

"Great." I took one bracing sip of coffee before rising and going into the living room where I had dumped my bag last night.

"You're going to speak with the restoration staff?"

"Yes." I pulled out my notepad and ripped off a page.

"Want me there?"

I considered that for a moment and then shook my head. "I've worked with them. They might talk to me more freely without a stranger present."

"Okay. Then when I get finished I'll head over to the police station and check out the case file."

"They'll give you access?"

"If I don't run into the captain." He grinned.

"Here's the list. I have to get ready for court."

"Need help?"

"Somehow I expect you're more expert at helping a woman out of her clothes than into them."

His eyes widened before he burst out laughing.

"Damn, Kate. I like you. You have quite a mouth on you."

"Out." I opened the door and waited expectantly.

He paused beside me and before I could react, pressed a hard, hot and all-too-brief kiss. "Yep. I like your mouth."

Then he was gone.

I closed the door and ran my tongue over my lips. I could still taste him like a fine brandy—warm, spicy and all-too tantalizingly male. I couldn't remember the last time that I had felt such a sexual tug, and I didn't like it one bit.

But since I couldn't slap a restraining order against my hormones, I would do the next best thing and take a cold shower.

Chapter 5

People packed the first-appearance hearing room at the Criminal Justice Center. The criminal world of West Palm Beach must have been jamming last night.

I made my way to one of the front benches and squeezed in beside a woman sobbing into a tissue. Despite the No Smoking order, the acrid odor hung in the air along with the miasma of colognes, deodorants and hairsprays. Any person sensitive to fragrances would be knocked dead entering the room.

Judge Theresita Rodriguez entered and quickly began her docket. The sheriffs led in the accused as each case was called. When I saw Lloyd in his orange prison jumpsuit being escorted in, I rose and went forward to the podium where the young woman State Attorney already stood.

We exchanged curious glances, weighing each other, while the bailiff read the charges. Dressed in a tan, inexpensive suit and her dark brown hair pulled back in a clip, the state attorney looked like she had just hung up her law school diploma. Not surprising. For these cattle-call first appearances, the State Attorney's office would deploy only its inexperienced junior attorneys. Hopefully today, I would learn the name of the assigned prosecutor so I could make contact and begin the discovery phase.

Judge Rodriguez peered over her reading glasses at Lloyd. "Do you have counsel?"

"Yes, Judge," I answered. "Katherine Rochelle for the defense."

"Good morning, Counselor. Mr. Silber, you've been charged with aggravated murder. Do you understand the charge?"

I nodded to Lloyd. He cleared his throat and leaned toward the mike. "Yes, Your Honor."

"What's your plea?"

"Not guilty, Your Honor," Lloyd said.

"We request a reasonable bail as this is my client's first charged offense," I added.

The state attorney intervened. "Rachel Sachs for the prosecution. The State opposes any bail."

The judge leaned back in her high-back black leather chair. "Why's that?"

"A young woman was brutally murdered—"

"Save the argument for trial, Counselor."

Rachel blushed, but I had to hand it to her, she plowed forward. "Given the heinous nature of the crime, Your Honor, the State considers him a danger to the community plus a flight risk."

"What's the evidence?"

"State Exhibit One is the arresting officer's report. It details the preliminary findings that this was premeditated murder."

"Response?" the judge asked, turning toward me.

"Your Honor, that report just draws conclusions. The officer sets forth no facts to warrant my client committed the murder let alone with premeditation." I took a breath. "Moreover, my client is married and has been a long-time outstanding citizen. He's received numerous citations for his service as outlined in Defense Exhibit One."

The judge's brow furrowed in concentration as she reviewed the documents.

The sheriff deputy whispered in the state attorney's ear. She nodded and took the mike again. "Your Honor, if I may advise the court of new information?"

"Go ahead."

"The deputy tells me that the defendant attempted suicide last night."

Stunned, I turned to my client. A dull flush spread across his cheeks, and he looked down at his handcuffed wrists, plainly unable to look me in the eye. I leaned close to him, whispering so the mike wouldn't pick up our conversation. "Lloyd, did you?"

He raised his face and I saw how bloodshot his eyes were. If ever a man had gone to hell and back, he stood before me. "I thought it would be best for Meredith."

"What's best for Meredith is to have her husband home again, with his name cleared."

His brow arched in disbelief, but he nodded. "I'm sorry. I've caused a problem, haven't I?"

"For now. But we'll work it out."

"Ms. Rochelle?"

I realized the judge was speaking. "Yes, Your Honor?"

"In light of your client's instability, I'm going to deny bail for now and place him on suicide watch."

"I would like to request a psychiatric evaluation." While

I didn't believe Lloyd was mentally disturbed, I needed to be sure that he understood what was happening.

"Granted."

"I would also like to request that the defense be permitted to raise the issue of bail again at the preliminary."

"Not a problem. I order that Mr. Silber remain in custody and a psychiatric evaluation be arranged as soon as possible."

The state attorney scribbled a note. "We'll make the arrangements."

"Who's the lead prosecutor on this one, Ms. Sachs?"

"Jared Manning."

The burning in my stomach increased. After only six years as a state attorney, Jared Manning was the department's best prosecutor. Rumor was that he was preparing for a run for the top spot in the next elections.

Figures. A headline case with all the trappings of murder, high society, sex. How could a glory seeker like Jared pass it up?

I was in big trouble.

Chaos reigned in the restoration committee's office on the first floor of the old courthouse. Taking one look at a young woman weeping into a handkerchief behind the front desk, I kept going. I needed someone rational. In Lloyd's office I found Derek Jones manning the phone. He motioned for me to take a seat. As I waited, I studied Lloyd's lead assistant. Derek reminded me of a watered-down version of Johnny Depp: all intensity with no concern for his appearance. His ratty hair stood on end, his eyes were bleary behind his glasses, and his wrinkled, untucked T-shirt contained mysterious stains.

Someone needed to give Derek a makeover and fast.

The front man had to juggle dealing with the government red tape, the wealthy donors and the construction crew. Derek, in present mode, didn't exactly inspire confidence. What he needed was an Aunt Hilary.

I grinned, wondering if I could sic her on him to get her off my back for a while. Except that would increase her presence around here. My smile faded. Not such a good idea.

Derek hung up. "Ms. Rochelle, what a pleasant surprise. Did your aunt need something?"

Money carried a long stick and those with the restoration project knew my family had dumped a substantial sum to the extent that one exhibition hall would be called The Rochelle Wing.

"No, Derek. I'm representing Lloyd."

His mouth tightened. "Why would you want to do that? We all loved Grace."

Hmm. Obviously, things weren't as solid between the two men as Lloyd had indicated.

"Including yourself?"

He folded his hands on top of the desk. "Grace was a beautiful young woman, full of life and energy. She didn't deserve to die."

"On that we can agree. Did Grace know you had a crush on her?"

He flushed and jerked a shoulder. "I never said a word to her. She was engaged."

"How was her relationship with Lloyd? Did you ever notice anything unusual?"

"No, but they often worked late in the museum rooms on the upper floors. There were rumors…" His voice trailed off.

"What type of rumors? That they were having an affair?"

"Yes, but I didn't believe them until her death. Why would she go for an old man when she could have—"

"You or the younger man she was dating?"

He shrugged.

"How long have the rumors been going on?"

"For the past few weeks. Grace had been spending more and more time volunteering."

So the rumors were recent. But what had Grace found so fascinating here? Spending time in a museum-to-be was no way to keep the flames blazing on a hot romance with the fiancé. Had she found a better opportunity? But with whom?

"How did Grace get along with the rest of the volunteers?"

"Fine. Everyone—"

"Loved her. Yes, you already said that. But if people were gossiping about her, that means there was friction going on. People usually relish the negative if they're jealous or don't like someone. Nothing people like more to do than bring a person down from a pedestal."

Derek leaned back in the chair. "I've never thought of that."

"Anyone in particular who was into the rumors?"

"I don't even know who first mentioned the possible affair, but Cindy Overbeck took offense every time the topic cropped up."

Cindy was the weeping woman out front. I jotted her name down. "Anyone else?"

"Peter Robbins. He's one of our newer volunteers. An attorney."

Was he the greener fields? I added his name. "Did Peter hit on Grace?"

"No, yes." Derek ran his fingers through his hair. "I don't know."

Yes, Derek did, and the answer to my question was yes. I noted "possible romantic competitor?" after Peter's name.

"Can you tell me who else is on the committee?"

Derek listed ten other people and gave me their usual schedules. I flipped to a fresh page on my notepad. "Lloyd mentioned there have been recent problems with the restoration work."

Derek groaned. "Problems? More like catastrophes."

"How so?"

After getting a rundown of basically the same incidents Lloyd had mentioned, I thanked Derek and left. Next up, a visit to the construction company. As I cleared the cubicle's corner, I collided with a man. Reaching out to steady him, I gasped with surprise. "Paul! What are you doing here?"

Smiling, I gave my godfather a hug. When I saw the man standing behind him, I stiffened. "Good afternoon, Judge Winewski."

"Ms. Rochelle." Avid curiosity burned in his gaze.

Paul kept his arm around my shoulders. "Kurt, you know my goddaughter?"

"She appeared before me in court yesterday."

"Good." Paul gave me a squeeze before releasing me. "I'm very proud of Katherine." His message that I had his blessing hit its mark.

Winewski's brows lowered so I couldn't see his eyes, but he muttered, "She did okay."

Although I was grateful for Paul's gesture, Winewski's grudging comment gave me a pain.

"Thanks, Paul. What are you doing here?"

"I was meeting Kurt for lunch and thought I would stop by and check on the progress. The restoration board is naming one of the courtrooms after me, you know."

"No, I didn't. I think that's fabulous."

Paul studied me. "I heard that you took Lloyd's case after all."

"Yes." Straightening my shoulders, I braced for the expected criticism.

"I'm sure you'll do your best. If you need to bounce any ideas off of me, I'll be happy to help you."

"Thank you, Paul." I rose and brushed my lips across his cheek. "That means a lot to me."

"Why don't you have lunch with us?"

Over my dead body. Sitting that close to Winewski was enough to make me lose my appetite. "Thanks, but I can't. Gotta go. I have several people to interview."

"Do you need a ride?"

"Nope, I'm parked in the garage."

"All right, honey. Call me no matter what."

"Will do." Nodding to Winewski, I made good my escape. Minutes later I reached the garage.

Too impatient to wait for the elevator, I took the stairs. Although the subcontractor had a trailer on site, the main office was on Blue Heron Boulevard, and I needed to start my questioning there. According to Derek, the owner rarely came to the courthouse project, letting his field supervisor handle everything. I also needed to track down Peter Robbins, the new volunteer.

Strains of Perry Mason's theme song emanated from my tote. Pulling out my cell phone, I answered. "Katherine Rochelle." I pushed on the door bar to the third floor.

"Hey beautiful, where are you?"

While I could blame the spike in my blood pressure to climbing the stairs, unfortunately I was in top physical form. What was it about Gabe's sultry voice that brought to mind afternoon delights on a workday?

"Gabriel." Even I was impressed by how repressive I sounded. "If we're going to work together, we need ground rules."

"Sure." I could see Gabe shrugging those yummy shoulders. "But I'll just break them."

Had to give the guy points for being honest. Since there wasn't a wall against which I could bang my head, I started toward my car.

"Did anything come up on the background searches?"

"I got one hit so far. A Cindy Overbeck."

The lovesick volunteer. "What do you have?"

"A misdemeanor conviction for shoplifting."

I blinked and then narrowed my eyes. "What on earth?"

"What's wrong, Kate?"

"My car windows are smashed." My poor Jag. The front windshield was now a spiderweb with one gaping hole in the center.

"Where are you?"

"Third floor of the courthouse parking garage—"

I heard a sound, the rasp of someone inhaling. I spun but saw no one. The sun cast shadows across the floor. Was someone hiding behind the second car to my right? The shadow shifted and there wasn't a breeze to be bought today.

"Gotta go," I murmured, and switched off the phone. Since I didn't know how damaged the Jag was, my only option was back toward the stair exit. I slipped out of my shoes and prayed for smooth concrete.

A man wearing a ski mask and carrying a baseball bat stepped into view. "I've got a message for you, girlie."

The guy had a paunch. Hopefully he was as out of shape as he appeared. Then I saw the gun handle sticking out from his waistband. Now a bullet I couldn't outrun, that is, if he decided the bat wasn't a sufficient communication tool.

"Great. Send me a letter." I turned and made a beeline up the slope to the exit on the next level.

The man yelled and I heard his grunt as he took after

me. The sound of wood clattering and then rolling on concrete reverberated. So much for any faint hope that he intended to use only the bat. I ran harder.

Almost too late I saw the orange cones and sign Closed For Repairs as I approached the exit. Great. I would have to loop back the way I came. But that meant a nice easy shot. I didn't fancy being a sitting duck.

Putting on a burst of speed, I snatched a cone as I sped up around the corner. Interspersed among the sedans and compact cars was a healthy smattering of SUVs and vans. Not the first one, I warned myself. Not the second.

But the third.

I flung one shoe as far as I could toward the next exit door. The years of javelin throwing during gym class in Switzerland served me well. The pump fell with a soft thud close to the opposite line of cars near the end of the incline.

I dropped behind a dirty white utility van and squeezed against the side by the wheel cage. If the guy dropped to look for feet, his view would be blocked. Or so my theory went. Although my adrenaline pounded, my breathing remained light.

On the other hand, my attacker's was labored as he rounded the corner. That didn't keep him from being quite the chatterbox.

"You bitch. I know you're hiding behind a car. I was supposed to only rough you up, but now I'm going to have some fun with you."

Wheezing and a pause in his talking marked his progress.

"You're going to lose a lot more than that shoe. Maybe if you come out now, I won't scar that pretty face of yours."

Fat chance. I lifted the cone.

"The message is to get off the Robins…um…that dead broad in the courthouse case."

Moron. He couldn't even remember his instructions.

His labored breathing came closer. I pressed against the van.

"You can't outrun a gun so you might as well come out."

The man appeared in the gap. He was on my side of the garage, peering between the cars opposite us.

As he stepped past me, I swung the cone in an arc, smacking its base right across the man's knees.

He howled and stumbled, dropping the gun. I brought the cone over my shoulder and then down at the back of his head. He slumped forward to the floor.

I released a long, slow breath. Moving forward, I kicked the gun across the garage floor. With a loud metallic noise, it skittered under a car. I gave the man's body a wide berth as I had seen enough heart-stopping moments in horror films where the dead guy wakes up and seizes his unsuspecting victim. Leaning against the van's front grill because my legs suddenly were wobbly, I pulled my phone from my pocket.

The roar of an engine, the squeal of tires of a car careening up the level sent a red light off in my head. I scrambled and threw myself into the protective cover behind the van again.

Praying my white silk suit would blend in with the van, I slid back into the shadows.

A dark, nondescript car—was it a Chevy or Oldsmobile or a Buick?—roared up the slope. It barely slowed when the dark-tinted driver's window lowered and white flashes blossomed. A split second later the cracks of gunfire ripped through the garage. The window of the car next to me shattered in a spray of glass. I threw my arms up to protect my face.

The unseen driver gunned the motor and sped off. Only when I heard it circle around and head down toward the exit did I step shaking from my hiding spot.

I almost lost my breakfast.

I had never seen a dead person before. No question my attacker was dead from the head shot he had taken.

Help! I needed to call the police. I fumbled in my pocket for my phone when I realized I had lost it in my scramble for safety. Without looking at the body, I glanced around.

There, by the van's front tire. Kneeling to pick it up, I heard the approach of another car. Oh God, the shooter was returning.

I braced myself for another spray of bullets, but the car engine stopped.

"Kate, where are you?"

The tension eased from my body. "Gabe. Over here." I tried to rise, but my traitorous legs suddenly had no strength.

Then Gabe was beside me, sliding his arm around my shoulders, helping me up.

"Are you all right?" His hands were gentle as he ran them over me, checking for injuries.

"No, yes…I think so." I bit the side of my mouth to keep myself from blathering like an idiot. "Police. Need to call them." I waved my hand in the general direction of what was left of the thug.

"I'll call them, but first let's get you to my truck." Gabe kept his body between me and the gruesome scene as he led me to the passenger side of his truck.

"Where are your shoes?"

"Don't know. Threw one. Dropped another." Oh God, why couldn't I speak in complete sentences?

"You're about to hyperventilate. Here," Gabe pushed my head down, "breathe deeply and don't talk."

I obeyed him while he called the police. Closing my eyes, I tried to will the image of the dead man's body from my memory. Although the pressure in my chest gradually eased, the queasiness in my stomach remained. Slowly, I straightened and braced my hands on the seat.

Gabe crouched beside me and stroked the hair from my face. "Baby, can you tell me what happened?"

My lips twitched. With my height and the demeanor I presented to the world, I wasn't exactly the type of woman any man had ever called *baby*.

"He trashed my car."

"So I saw." His fingers circled to the back of my neck and began to massage the knotted muscles. "What else happened?"

"He had a message to deliver, but I didn't give him a chance. I ran."

"Good girl."

"I hid and took him out with a parking cone."

His hand stilled. "You what?"

"Then the car came, bullets flew. The thug died and I didn't." My attempt to be nonchalant failed as I couldn't suppress the wave of shivers that racked my body.

Gabe gripped my shoulders and lightly shook me. "You have to get a hold of yourself, Kate. The police will be here any minute. You don't want them to see you like this."

I choked back the sob that was rising in my throat. He was right. I had to be calm, in control. I let out one long shuddering breath and then nodded.

"I'll be fine."

"That's my girl. I hear the sirens." When he held out his hand, I took it and he assisted me up. When the black-and-white unit came around the bend, I was standing, barefoot but in control.

The next hour passed in a blur of questions. I had to demonstrate where I first encountered my attacker and my ensuing flight during which Gabe's expression had hardened into stone. The only thing the lead detective hadn't made me do was go near the body. That part I was allowed to describe. Finally the questioning was over and I stood by Gabe's truck. I had already called AAA to tow my Jag.

Gabe appeared with my shoes in hand. I gasped and flashed him my first real smile. "You found them!"

I sat on the edge of the seat and held my hand out, but instead, Gabe knelt and slipped the shoes on my feet.

"You really shouldn't be wearing heels like this with those beat-up feet of yours."

"They're Ferragamos. The leather's like butter. Besides, I had court this morning."

"So you felt the need to torture yourself?"

"It's a woman thing."

"It's a stupid thing."

He rose and went around to the driver's side. He started the engine but, because of the narrow lane, he had to drive forward past where the police were loading the black body bag into the coroner's van.

It was stupid, I know, but I looked and once more saw the gore and blood that remained glistening on the concrete. My stomach lurched.

Gabe drove in silence, but the truck jolted over each section break between the concrete slabs. Ba-bump, ba-bump. I could visualize the tires spinning and spinning like a broken movie reel in my mind. Again and again the film flapped, with the same grainy images of blood and death repeating. I swallowed—hard—but my throat burned. As far as I was concerned, we couldn't exit that garage fast enough.

However, the light was dazzling after the garage's dimness. Too bright, in fact. My head began to swim.

"Gabe, stop the truck!"

He shot me a startled look but swung off the street into an alley. Before the truck had come to a complete stop, I stumbled out the door. Then I was bent over, throwing up.

Gabe's arm slid around my shoulders and his other hand held my hair back from my damp face. "There, baby, you'll be all right. Every good cop loses it on their first gunshot case."

I was too busy retching my guts out to throw him an elbow. I'd get even later.

Chapter 6

I couldn't look at Gabe as he bundled me into his truck. You would've thought I was made of fragile Venetian glass the way he was treating me.

How embarrassing.

I couldn't see my way past my mortification so I stared blindly out the window as he slid behind the steering wheel.

A Rochelle never displayed weakness in public, yet here I was, a Rochelle who had thrown up in an alley, right off Olive Avenue.

If that wasn't bad enough, my mouth tasted like I had drunk a cocktail made of rotten eggs and lemons. Naturally, because I was dwelling on the rancid condition of my mouth, my traitorous saliva glands began to water. I cringed at the thought of having to swallow. Proper conduct be hanged, I was ready to roll down the window.

Gabe reached behind his seat and brought up a bottle of water. "Here. Drink and spit."

Tears of shame burned my eyes but I grabbed the bottle. After uncapping it, I took a swig of the warm water and swished it around. Silently, the glass rolled down and I stuck out my head and spit. I repeated the process several times until the sour taste in my mouth became bearable. While I longed to brush my teeth, at least now I could manage until I was home. I fumbled in my bag for the tin of breath mints I always carried.

Gabe started the truck and pulled away from the alley. For the duration of the drive, we rode in silence. Five mints later he pulled in front of my house. Before he could switch off the engine, I had my door open, more than ready to retreat and regroup.

"Thanks. Gabe. I'll call you later."

Gabe opened his door. "I'm coming in."

The last thing in the world I wanted at the moment was to have another person around.

"To be perfectly rude, I'm not in the mood…" I was talking to an empty cab. I let out a hiss, clamped my mouth shut and slid out, almost taking a header to the sidewalk. I grabbed hold of the door handle.

Oh boy, my legs had the consistency of a rag doll's. Obviously, during the drive, the surcharge of adrenaline that had been powering me had drained away, leaving extreme exhaustion in its place.

Out of my peripheral vision I saw Gabe reaching for me. No way, I wasn't a baby who needed to be coddled. So what if I had seen a man with half his head blown off? I could handle it.

Steeling myself, I pushed off from the truck and, using the momentum, stalked up my impatiens-lined path. Normally the brilliant bands of red and white flowers cheered me because I had planted them myself, but not today.

Fifteen feet, ten. Come on, Kate, you can do it. Five feet. There, I made it without falling flat on my face.

I unlocked the door and didn't stop to check if Gabe was safely through before letting it swing shut.

After dropping my purse on the table, I headed down the hall. Maybe I couldn't prevent him from invading my space, but I could ignore him. Willy yowled from the kitchen and Gabe greeted him.

Good. They could keep each other company for an eternity or two.

I went into the bathroom and swung the door shut. After turning on the shower full blast, I grabbed my toothbrush. I squeezed out half a tube of toothpaste and scrubbed like there was no tomorrow. As the spearmint washed away any remaining sour taste in my mouth, I almost moaned with relief.

Then I glanced up, saw my image in the mirror and froze. Who was that woman?

Staring back was someone with toothpaste foam around her mouth and haunted, mascara-ringed eyes. Hair escaping from her once neat French braid hung in her face. Dirt and oil smeared her former immaculate white suit. Blood stained the front.

Blood. Not mine. That man's.

My stomach lurched but it could find nothing to throw up. That particular cupboard was bare. I had another person's blood on me and God knows what else.

My knees liquefied. I dropped the brush to grip the sides of the sink. Control, I must have control. I needed to feel clean again.

Spinning, I staggered into the shower fully clothed. I shuddered with relief under the blast of hot water. Bracing my hands on the wall, I let the spray sluice over me. Through half-closed eyes, I watched brown-colored water swirl around the drain. I willed the shower to wash away everything I had seen.

A sob ripped free, painful in its intensity as if it tore apart my soul. I pressed my hand against my lips to stop others, but I couldn't. Freed at last, one sob after another flowed through me. I crumpled to the tiled floor and curled my legs against my chest. Raising my face to the spray, I let my tears mingle with the water.

I didn't hear the shower door slide open. "Kate?"

"Go away." Since I couldn't run, couldn't hide in a six-by-four shower stall, I turned toward the wall.

"Come on, baby. Let's get you into dry clothes." Heedless of the shower spray, Gabe knelt beside me and placed his hand on my shoulder.

I stiffened at his touch. The last thing I needed when my defenses were down was kindness.

While a part of me wanted to succumb and let Gabe take care of me, my darker side, scarred from too many hurts and disappointments, warned me not to fall for the same old trap of a man professing concern for my welfare. Two times burned by former lovers were lessons learned that didn't bear repeating.

"Go away."

His eyes narrowed but he didn't remove his hand. "Don't be ridiculous. You've been through hell."

"So? I'm handling it."

"By sitting in your clothes in the shower? Don't be an idiot. What do you think I'm going to do, Kate?" He bit off an oath. "Throw you down and have wild sex?"

Gabe's naked body covering mine. Mindless sex without a care in the world... Suddenly, the confines of the stall narrowed. Steam misted the glass doors, shutting off the rest of the world.

I swallowed. "Don't be absurd."

As the water continued to drench us, I stared into his dark eyes. I believe that the eyes mirror a person's soul, and depended on this when making observations as an attorney. But Gabe's continued to mystify me. I could see anger in their depths, but the man himself remained veiled.

Other than my uncle Colin and godfather Paul, kindness from men came with too high a risk. To the power-hungry opposite sex I represented the whole enchilada: wealth and family connections. All theirs for the taking if they could only seduce me into being a mindless bimbo, blind to their machinations.

Exhibit One, my short-lived marriage. On the second night of our Caribbean honeymoon cruise I had learned that my husband planned to wheel and deal with my trust fund for the rest of his life. I still could feel the humiliation burning inside me as I'd had to secure another cabin for myself until I could catch a flight home at the first port, and then had to endure the divorce bought at too high a price: my innocence.

No, when a man was kind to me, a red warning light went off in my head. That signal was ringing loud and clear right now. I concentrated my focus on extricating myself from danger.

"Look, I said I'm fine." Somehow I braced my hands on the slick tile floor and scrambled to my feet. Every inch of my body groaned with pain, but at least my legs held. With his usual grace Gabe also rose.

"Why won't you let me help you?" Then his gaze lowered to my chest. I followed his glance and saw that my white clothing was now see-through. I might as well be naked.

Men. I squashed my flicker of disappointment at Gabe's too typical reaction. What did I expect? A man to want me for my brains? Fat chance.

"Please leave," I said quietly as I moved to turn off the shower.

"You're still in shock. Let me check you out." Gabe's arm embraced me, but I jerked away.

He arched a brow but let his hand drop. He leaned against the shower wall. "Want to tell me what this is about?"

"Nothing. I'm fine."

"If you say you're fine one more time I'm hauling you off to a doctor."

That did it. I whirled toward him, my hands fixed to my hips. "Listen, Gabe. I'm grateful for what you did for me in the garage, but I'm not some damn piece of crystal with a 'fragile' label slapped on it. I'm strong."

Gabe merely folded his arms. "I never said you weren't."

"Then stop treating me as if I were broken."

"There's a difference between caring for someone and caring about someone."

"Not in my world. And we haven't known each other long enough for you to—" I raised my hands and mimicked quote marks "—care about me."

Before I could react, Gabe straightened and wrapped his arms around me. In the future I would never underestimate his ability to move. For the next argument, I needed to be a football field away to insure enough distance. By the time my brain registered that I should be pushing him away, his head lowered and his mouth crushed against mine.

Ohmigod.

The heat blasted through me. The kiss wasn't merely a seizing, it was a taking. Forget my ex's tepid kisses. Forget all the calculated kisses I had ever received from other men. I was experiencing passion.

Had I really argued that I wasn't fragile? I felt like blown glass. Every bone in my body melted. I clutched his shoulders just to keep my balance.

Gabe groaned and slid one hand to the back of my neck and angled my head. His tongue traced the outline of my lips. Perversely I wanted to touch the fire, but some part of my conscience remained alert, making me hesitate. However, Gabe's thumb pressed against the side of my mouth, a silent demand for admittance. I opened and his tongue surged in.

Conflagration.

Seething, hot, toe-curling passion. The type I never thought I could experience let alone respond to.

Holding on to him wasn't good enough. I needed to feel the strong, hard lines of his body against mine. I slid my arms around his neck. He stroked his hand along the curve of my spine; I could have purred like my cat Willy. Then he was gripping my bottom, pressing me tighter against him, fitting his erection into a place I thought was dead.

Over the years I had learned to think of myself as asexual, allowing no man close enough to bring me to life. Even my former lover Harold Lowell hadn't been able to breach the barrier. Sex had been pleasant, even mundane, like scratching an itch. But never all-consuming.

Had I fooled myself into thinking I had killed all desire?

I wanted to forget for the moment and throw myself into the devastating flames. I raised first one leg and then the other so that I was wrapped around Gabe. However, I still craved more than being plastered against him like a second skin. I needed to be fused to him as if we were one. I tugged at his T-shirt.

His hand covered mine, halting my desperate attempt to strip him. Before I could protest, he was prying us apart.

My feet along with my pride hit the slippery tile. I pressed against the wall and hugged myself.

"Wha—at's going on?" Damn, my voice quavered.

Gabe reached out. I flinched. Absently, he tucked a wet strand of hair behind my ear. "I may be a lot of things, Kate, but I haven't sunk so low as to take advantage of a woman in shock."

I lifted my chin. "I thought I was the one taking advantage."

A smile tugged at the corner of his mouth. "Let's call it a mutual taking." He traced the path of a water droplet along the curve of my face. "Look, I told Carling and Nicole that I would take care of you, watch out for you."

What? Didn't they think I was capable of handling myself? Betrayal sliced through me. I jerked my head away from Gabe's touch and backed into the corner. Crossing my arms protectively over my chest, I wrapped what was left of my dignity around me.

"I'm sorry."

Gabe's single-word curse was succinct and to the point. He surged across the narrow space and grabbed my upper arms, giving me a slight shake. "It's not what you think."

"You don't know what I'm thinking."

"Babe, you've the look of the walking wounded." His grip tightened. "This isn't about your handling this case. You're the only one who doubts you can. This is about your friends caring that no physical harm comes to you."

I pressed my lips together. It wouldn't do to tell him about my suspicions that someone had been in my home last— My God, was it only this morning?

He gave me another shake before releasing me. He ran a hand through his hair. "Hell, Red's going to have my ass for the garage attack."

I sniffed. "My money's on Nicole."

"You'd win." He stepped back and grabbed a towel. "Let's get you dry before you get sick." He draped the large white bath sheet around my shoulders before taking another to wrap it around my hair. My eyes widened when he expertly tucked the ends in.

He grinned. "I have five younger sisters."

"Five?"

"Yeah, but being the oldest and the only male, I didn't have to wear hand-me-downs."

"Lucky you."

"I didn't think so while fighting for bathroom rights, but the experience made me the mean, dirty fighter that I am." He picked up a steaming mug from the counter and wrapped my hands around it. "Here, drink this."

He had made me tea. The simple act of kindness almost did me in. Obediently, I took a few sips.

"That's better." Gabe chucked me under the chin. "You get out those wet clothes and get some rest. I'll check in with your office and let Carling and Nicole rip some skin off of me. I'll touch base with you first thing in the morning."

No way was I going to call it quits for the day, but I wasn't about to tell him that.

One moment Gabe was leaving the bathroom, the next moment he was kissing me, branding me with another blast of heat. I didn't need the tea to warm me after all, not when my blood was racing so hot.

Before I could react, Gabe lifted his head and pressed a light kiss to my forehead.

"Since you're going to fret about what happened here anyway, that's for you to gnaw on while you sleep tonight." Then he was gone.

I sighed and set the mug on the counter. Gabe was right,

but for the wrong reason. If sex could only be the simple enjoyment that his kisses promised, but it never was. Not in my life anyway. Sex was about politics, control and self-destruction, and I wasn't about to let it into my life again unless I was damn sure I was in the driver's seat.

Bar ownership on Clematis Street turned over with the frequency of failed TV sitcoms. You never knew what would be open when you came downtown. I've lost count of the number of name changes on the bar where I'd chosen to sit, but with the latest theme switch it was the bar of the moment for West Palm Beach's ever restless young professionals. Men and women packed the place.

Even though Florida's smoking ban had been in effect for a while now, smoke from decades of patrons had permeated the very walls. As the body heat increased so did the acrid odor. For someone whose stomach had been to hell and back a few hours earlier, my sitting here probably wasn't the wisest decision, but taking it easy wasn't in my vocabulary. Since this bar was the "in place" with the restoration personnel, here was where I hoped to conduct informal interviews. Liquor has a lovely way of loosening lips.

Case in point. I sipped my seltzer water and smiled encouragingly at the man whose knees pressed against mine under our minuscule table. Peter Robbins definitely ranked as a hottie on the hunk score. With his surfer's blond streaked hair, trim athletic build and model looks, Peter drew women like a Venus flytrap drew flies. As an associate in a prestigious law firm, he wore an Italian wool suit with the aspirations of making partner stamped in its very design.

And he wasn't getting by merely on looks. Intelligence glittered in his eyes and he parried questions like a champion heavyweight. We'd been at it for over thirty minutes and I had gotten nothing useful in information other than Peter thought a woman's skirt was an open invitation to slide his hand up her inner thigh. Although he had accepted my sharp rejection gracefully, he didn't accept defeat. Even now his hand found its way to my knee. With a sigh I slapped it away.

"You and Grace never went out?"

Peter winked even as he craned his head to scan the latest arrival of giggling women. "No, she wasn't my type."

"What is your type?"

His practiced smile curled my toes. "You, of course. A long, tall, cool drink of blonde."

The ease with which the compliment rolled from him made me think he had said it in every bar up and down the street. There was a gleam in his eyes as he looked at an exotic girl with her skirt up to her butt and an abbreviated halter top sashaying by. Most likely, he would be repeating the expression before the night was over.

"I heard different about you and Grace. I heard you had the hots for her."

He shrugged and took a swallow of his third Dirty Martini. "Gossip with no foundation."

I traced a drop of condensation on my glass. "You don't strike me as the type to volunteer with the courthouse restoration."

"You don't think I'd be interested in preserving old things?"

"No."

He chuckled. "You would be right. But the partners of my law firm are major supporters of the project, and—"

"You get brownie points for your civic efforts come performance-evaluation time," I concluded.

His perfect white teeth flashed. "Exactly." He leaned toward me. "As an attorney, a very gorgeous one, I might add, you understand the games we all must play to gain the big prize."

"Partnership." Yes, I did understand.

Whether it was a job with the government, a corporation or a private firm, the pressure was all the same for a fresh-out-of-law-school attorney: to advance. Should Peter's career sputter at his law firm, he would never be offered a chance to buy into the practice as a junior partner, and eventually, subtle to not-so-subtle pressure would be exerted on him to leave.

I didn't think the man had to worry. Peter was great at sucking up. So long as he generated unbelievable billing hours of thirty-six hours per day, he would be a shoe-in.

I was so glad I had my own practice. Granted, it came with its own share of problems: paying rent and employees and hand-holding distraught clients. But at least I was my own boss.

"Getting back to our discussion of Grace—"

"I'd rather be talking about you," he interrupted smoothly as he moved to take my hand.

I picked up my glass. "Why weren't you interested in Grace? She was more your type."

Peter grimaced. "Grace was a bitch."

"She turned you down?"

"I'm not exactly a senior citizen."

For an instant I froze. I lowered my glass. "Are you saying she was having an affair with Lloyd?"

"Bingo!"

Not good. His testimony could be a death sentence for my client. Still, I studied Peter's smug expression as he drank. He was actually relishing his disclosure. Was he jealous of Lloyd, or did his resentment toward my client go much deeper?

"What about Grace's fiancé?"

Peter shrugged. "He traveled a lot. Made for a number of lonely nights for our Gracie."

"Wasn't he wealthy?"

"Rich, but cheap. She put out for him, but he wasn't giving her any bling-bling beyond the engagement ring. Grace was going to cast about for better opportunities right up to her wedding day and beyond."

"And Lloyd was that opportunity? Hard to believe."

"He didn't have jack to his name." Acid laced Peter's voice. "But what he had was *Palm Beach connections.*"

Ah, therein was the problem. Two ambitious people wanting the same thing but unable to possess it with each other. It must've eaten at Peter that Grace was on a faster track to possible wealth and power.

"So Grace was after old money."

"Yeah and look where it got her."

Not even a shred of sadness colored his voice. Peter polished off his drink and scanned the bar. Time to move on, but I needed to ask another question.

"Did she ever mention if she made these connections?"

Peter checked out the girl in the invisible skirt again. "The last time I saw her she was very excited about the upcoming restoration ball at The Breakers. Her fiancé was going to be out of town again. She said she had a hot dress and a prospect lined up. Didn't mention any names."

Peter was obviously distracted. "Well, well, well," he said, staring over my head. "Didn't think Cindy had it in her to land a date."

"Cindy Overbeck?" She was next on my list. I had hoped she would also be here.

"Check out the Latin lover."

Latin lover? I turned and saw Gabe holding the hand of the weeping Cindy.

"That's my investigator," I grumbled.

"Really? Could have fooled me. Looks like you're not going to be coming to my place tonight so maybe you should join them?" He angled a predatory smile at the half-naked girl. She tossed her hair, giving him a definite come-on.

I rose and tossed a ten-dollar bill on the table to pay for my seltzer water. "Got to go."

Excusing myself, I maneuvered a tortuous path through the crush of bodies. I had a few words to say to my investigator.

Chapter 7

"Lloyd is such an honorable man," Cindy sobbed. "How can anyone think that he'd have an affair?" Gabe patted her hand.

Hmm, interesting. I stopped in front of their table. The lovesick secretary was more concerned about the scandal that Lloyd was involved with Grace than the possibility he had killed her.

"Where were you at the time of the murder, Ms. Overbeck?"

Cindy started and gasped, "Miss Rochelle!" What little color she had drained from her face.

Gabe merely smiled as he stood. "Here, take my chair." He disappeared into the crowd. I had no doubt that he would return with another chair despite the fact that the bar's seating was at a premium.

Sitting down, I angled my legs so they'd fit into the cramped space.

Swallowing hard first, Cindy whined, "Mr. Chavez and I were only talking, really."

Realization hit me with the force of a gavel that Cindy thought Gabe was my boyfriend. "Gabe's *only* my investigator. He's assisting me with Lloyd's defense."

"That's me," Gabe plopped a chair backward by the table and then straddling it, rested his arms on top. "Your beck-and-call P.I. I aim to please." He winked at Cindy.

I rolled my eyes. "Cindy, where were you the night of the murder?"

"At a paint-your-own-pottery class. I go every week."

"Where?" I removed my notepad from my bag since I saw that Gabe wasn't moving a muscle to take notes.

"The Pottery Shed on Olive and Evernia. It's great because I can go there straight from work."

It was also close enough that she could slip out to kill Grace. "What time was your class?"

"From seven to nine."

The medical examiner's preliminary approximation of time of death was eight-thirty.

"I don't have a car, so one of the students gives me a ride home."

Opportunity just shrank, but still not impossible. "What's her name?"

Cindy moistened her lips. "Do I have to involve her? She's been so nice to me. If I had to have Dad pick me up each time, I may not be able to continue the classes."

I felt sorry for her. Single, unattractive and still living at home, with no brighter future on the immediate horizon.

Gabe said, "We only need to verify that your friend drove you home at nine, Cindy. I'll handle contacting her myself."

She brightened. "Will you?"

What was I? Some heavy-handed ogre? Gabe's hand—at least I hoped it was his—squeezed my knee under the table. Okay, I could play along.

"Perfect," I muttered while I tried to flag down a waiter. The woman clad in a tropical print shirt with birds-of-paradise and khaki shorts rushed past me as if she had blinders on.

Gabe pushed his glass at me. "Here. Water. No contagious diseases."

"Thanks." I sipped as I considered my next line of questions.

"Cindy, Lloyd's told me how invaluable you were as his assistant." Actually, she had apparently been a terrible secretary, but with the salary he could offer, he had been grateful that she knew how to sit at a desk.

The woman beamed. "I did what I could to help him."

"What project was Grace working on the day she died?"

The smile disappeared only to be replaced a pinched expression. "Grace did as she liked. She only jumped when your aunt called."

"I understood she was locating old courthouse artifacts."

"That's right. Since she was so intent on making *connections,* Lloyd placed her in charge of that area."

"You didn't like her."

Cindy shrugged. "No, but the only people who liked her were men."

"No women friends?"

"No one working there. Some women did call her."

"Recall any names?"

"No, but I keep all my phone logs."

I bet she did. "Great. Can you check them and call Gabe with any names and numbers?"

Cindy's lips curved in a timid smile. "I'll be happy to."

Gabe took out his wallet and handed her a card. "Here's my number."

The woman held the paper as if it were a diamond ring. "I'll look at them first thing when I get to the office."

She glanced at the front of the bar. "I've got to go. My girlfriend is waving at me."

Gabe rose and pulled out her chair. "Thank you for your time."

Blushing, Cindy gave him a timid smile. "Anything I can do to help Mr. Silber." She disappeared into the crowd.

As Gabe sat, I arched a brow at him.

"What?" All innocence, he spread his hands. "She was upset."

"I bet your sisters have you wrapped around their little fingers."

"Every damn one of them," he agreed. "By the way, I thought you were staying home tonight."

"Well, look, Rick, if it isn't the fallen angel?"

The masculine New York–based Hispanic accent sounded like a snitch I once had, but when I looked over my shoulder at the speaker, I didn't place the man's face with the flat crooked nose and thick lips peeled back into a sneer. His skintight black polo shirt meant to display his physique only served to enhance a mad-pug look.

He sidled up to our table, closely followed by another man dressed the same but in tan to compliment his dyed-blond looks. Cute. I bet the girls swarmed over them.

Not.

Gabe barely shifted in his chair, but he went from relaxed to alert. "If it isn't Dumb and Dumber. What sewer brought you here, Tony?"

"You always were mouthy, Chavez. Now that you've been canned, maybe we'll have to teach you a lesson."

Rick the Dumber leaned forward and muttered in his friend's ear. Tony waved him off with his large hand. "We've got plenty of time." He folded his arms. "I heard you've become a dick…I mean a private investigator."

Tony's head swiveled on his nonexistent neck so he could leer at me. "Hey, babe, you a client? If you want someone good, I could do a little consulting on the side."

Despite his boorish manners, I looked past the veneer of obnoxiousness and saw the sharp, watchful eyes. Cop.

"Thanks, but I'm afraid your fashion sense would blind me too much."

Tony flushed a dark red. "Think you're so high-and-mighty, don't you, bitch? I could teach you a thing—"

Gabe's chair crashed to the floor as he sprang up to grab Tony's shirt. The force of his grip drew Tony up on his toes.

"You will apologize to the lady. Now."

Out of the corner of my eye I spotted a burly giant pushing his way through the crowd. The club's security, no doubt.

Tony's chin jutted, but Rick laid his hand on his friend's arm. "Tony, we don't have time for this."

The urge to fight faded from Tony's eyes and his lips twisted into a smile. "Right. We have hot dates. Sorry, ma'am. Didn't mean to offend."

No, he had meant to do a lot more. He had been spoiling for a fight with Gabe. However, he had enough control to back down, though I doubted prospective dates were the real reason. From Gabe's shuttered expression I could tell he didn't believe Tony either, but he released the man.

"What's going on here?" the bouncer demanded.

I rose and smiled my best smile. "Not a thing, sir. Just a slight misunderstanding that's been resolved."

He glared a warning. "Any more funny stuff and you're all out of here."

"Understood."

"Come on, Tony." Rick moved off, and after brushing against Gabe in a failed attempt to knock him on his butt, Tony followed.

"Your former colleagues are charming," I deadpanned as I sat again. "Wonderful to see the close brotherhood of West Palm Beach police in action."

Gabe remained standing, his expression thoughtful. "Did you valet-park?"

"Yes, the garage fixed my windshield. I picked it up a few hours ago. I didn't want to park it on the street and risk any more damage."

"I want you to stand in a crowd while your car is brought to the front. Don't stand alone."

"Am I leaving?"

"We're finished for the night, and you're looking pale."

"Gee, thanks. Don't go overboard with compliments."

He gripped my elbow, urging me up and tossing a few bills on the table. "Come on."

Since my head was throbbing from the cacophony of the club's sounds, I didn't offer even a halfhearted protest. I was tired and nothing more would be gained from my staying.

"Remember, stay in the crowd and lock your car doors. I'll call you later."

"Don't worry. I can take care of myself."

"I'll call." Then, like smoke, Gabe faded into the crowd. You would think such a hunk would stand out, but he had a habit of blending in. He must've made one hell of an undercover operative on the force.

After fending off a few come-on's, I made it to the front and gave my ticket to the attendant. Though I longed to stand to the side and enjoy the cool breeze, I stayed under the canopy. I even locked the doors after I slid into the driver's seat. As I drove home, I kept an eye on my rearview mirror but didn't spot any cars following me.

Parking in my normal spot on the street in front of my house, I switched off the engine. My cell rang and I pulled it out of my tote. "Kate Rochelle."

"See?" Gabe's voice held laughter. "You even call yourself Kate rather than Katherine."

"Where are you?"

"Just go up the walk and—"

"And lock my door after turning on the lights."

"Then get on with it."

Cutting the call off, I considered beating the phone against the steering wheel but thought better of it. I strolled up the walk as if it was a Sunday in the park. However, I did hit the main switch, flooding the rooms with light, and slid the security bolt. My cell rang again as I peeked out the window.

"Sleep tight, beautiful. I'll call first thing in the morning."

As I listened to static, I watched a dark pickup drive by. Whatever Dumb and Dumber had been up to, Gabe had broken off his hunt to see me home.

My Jag lurched to a final stop on the rutted dirt lot. I took a deep breath, released it and grabbed my tote. Although a few pickups in various degrees of batteredness remained parked, I saw no sign of heavy equipment. In south Florida, the construction-industry day began early, which is why I timed my arrival for seven o'clock. I knew the caravan of laborers would already be making their way to the various sites while the office staff wouldn't arrive until eight. For this first meeting, I wanted no prying eyes or ears.

I picked my way along to the single-story stucco building and opened the heavy metal door. A blast of chilled air hit me, but, as I had hoped, the outer office was empty. Framed photos of buildings and equipment lined the walls in testimony of past successful projects. Arranged on the neat desk were a state-of-the-art computer, printer and fax machine. Although the linoleum floor at the entrance bore tracks of dirt, the waiting room was spotless with gunmetal-gray utilitarian chairs.

The setup conveyed competence and dependability for any prospective customer—important qualities in the construction and restoration business.

At least the high price of my innocence had been put to good use.

The sound of a man's voice drew me down a short hallway to the corner office. Leaning against the doorjamb, I studied the interior and its sole occupant. The man sat in a swivel leather chair, turned sideways to face a large window. He held a mobile phone propped between his shoulder and his ear as he flipped through papers in a folder.

"Got it, Stan. The sod shipment's been delayed but the drywall is to be delivered around noon today at the courthouse. We need a Bobcat and spreader crew ready to go." He closed the folder. "Good. See to it. We need to be on schedule to get the next payment." He disconnected the mobile and tossed it onto the desk.

"Good morning, Juan."

He swung around and stared at me with narrowed eyes for a long moment. Then his tense expression cleared and he smiled. "Well, Princess, what an honor. What brings you out from your ice palace?"

Disgust raked its claws down my back. I knew this encounter wouldn't be pleasant, but my ex-husband's opening volley indicated it was going to be downright nasty.

Funny how two people who had once loved each other could turn into the filthiest fighters.

But Juan Delgado had never truly loved me. He had loved only my money.

I steeled myself. "The divorce was ten years ago, Juan. Can we at least be civil?"

"Sure, Princess." He rose and approached me. Years of sun exposure had weathered his once boyishly handsome face into a harder leathery mask. Lines scored into the flesh by his eyes and mouth lent him a look of perpetual discontent. But then again, he had never been a happy person. He'd always wanted more than he had.

When I saw he meant to kiss me, I turned my face so his lips only brushed my cheek. Still the slight touch of his moist mouth sent a shiver through me.

"Hey, I thought you wanted to be friends."

"Friends, not kissing buddies."

"Don't worry, Princess. I know only too well what an ice cube you are. I would never expect an ounce of warmth from you."

His insult slashed at me, and ten years ago those same words had left ugly wounds deep within me. Had I heard those words even last week, I may have believed them.

Our social orbits rarely crossed and when they did, our pattern remained the same. Juan would take his usual swipes at me while I maintained a shield of indifference, relying on Aunt Hilary's philosophy of not stooping to another's level. But today that particular advice didn't cut it.

Memories of my making out with Gabe in the shower curled like steam through me. I lifted my chin and stepped to the side.

Time to air out the past and take no prisoners.

"As far as I know, Juan, it takes two to tangle. You

weren't the only one left unsatisfied from our sexual activity. Hump, bang and not even a 'thank you, ma'am' don't constitute intimacy."

A dark flush spread from his cheeks into his neck. "No woman has ever complained about my lovemaking."

"I doubt you would've heard them if they ever did. You weren't much into pillow talk."

"You were the one who snuck out and let me take you in the pool house."

I winced. How tacky it sounded now. At seventeen with two glasses of cheap wine in me I'd thought stealing away in the moonlight to be with the gardener's attentive, handsome son was romantic. Instead, my first time had been painful, messy but mercifully short. Still the crushing disillusionment after Juan had taken my virginity hadn't been enough to open my eyes when he had proposed that we elope.

Juan jammed his hands into his pockets while he studied me. "I often wondered whether you would've come to me if my father hadn't been fired by Hilary that day. It often gnawed at me how much of your attraction was due to your feeling sorry for me."

"I don't know."

Slowly, I sank into one of the black leather client chairs. I had forgotten about Hilary flying into a rage at Juan's father because he had overtrimmed a bougainvillea. How unfair it had seemed, to fire a man who had been the gardener for years over such a minor infraction. Months later, after my divorce, I had figured out that Hilary had been concerned about my growing attraction to Juan and by firing his father she meant to remove the temptation. Her plan had backfired when we had run away.

What a miserable, expensive mistake. Even the three-day Caribbean cruise as our honeymoon—paid for by me—

had backfired. When I had stepped off the ship, I had gone only too willingly with the waiting family representative.

"Then again—" I looked at him "—did you ever see me for anything other than as a bankroll?"

His throat muscles worked before he shrugged.

"I see." I stared at my clasped hands. "Well, enough reminiscing about the good old days."

"Why are you here, Katherine?" He sat behind his desk.

"Lloyd Silber's my client."

"Still hell-bent on trying to find justice?"

"You bet."

"Justice doesn't exist, Princess. This world's about the strongest surviving."

"Another matter we differ on. I understand your company was brought in to help meet the grand-opening deadline on the courthouse project."

"That's right. So?" Juan picked up a spike that was being used for a paperweight and flipped it through his fingers.

"Who's your field supervisor on the job?"

"Stan Turow. He's been with me for eight years. Good man."

"What do you know about all the construction delays?"

He scowled. "None due to my work."

"I didn't say they were. I asked what you knew about them."

"The usual. Weather, shipping delays, unreliable labor, equipment being stolen from the site."

"Nothing to indicate sabotage?"

He slammed the spike down. "What are you getting at, Katherine?"

"You're the expert. Do you know of anyone who'd want to keep the project from being completed?"

"Hell, no. This job is costing the general contractor a

ton in overruns. He's putting the nails to all the subs' thumbs to get this restoration back on schedule. The last thing any of us want to see is another delay. If we don't get paid, we can't pay our workers and they find another job."

"Any reports from your crew of seeing or hearing mysterious things inside the courthouse?"

"You mean those rumors that the top floor is haunted?" I nodded.

"A couple workers complained of hearing the *clip, clap* of footsteps in the hallway. Stan sent them immediately to be tested for drugs and then we fired their asses. Don't want some bozo spooking the entire crew."

"Would you mind if I talked to Stan?"

"No, but don't get in the crew's way, Princess. We're on a tight schedule and I can't afford any more delays."

"Stretched a little tight?"

"Nothing I can't handle, but another major contract is bogged down in litigation. Some sleazeball attorney," he leered at me, "filed a stay against the construction because of a nest of some damn turtles. I need the courthouse contract to go smoothly. Grace isn't worth all the fuss."

I had started to rise but sat again. "You knew Grace Roberts?"

He chuckled. "She was kind of hard to miss around the courthouse. She was a real pleasure to watch."

"Did you do more than watch?"

His mouth tightened. "I'm not the one charged with her death. That old aristocrat is."

Translation: his answer was yes. Grace's list of potential lovers was growing by the yard. I stood. "Thanks, Juan."

"How about dinner?"

"Sorry, but I don't think that's such a good idea. I'll

be in touch if I need any further information about the construction."

He followed me to the door. "Be careful, Princess. You know how your nose for the wronged always lands you in trouble. A construction site is no place for you. Accidents happen all the time."

"I'll keep that in mind."

I made it to my car before I popped three antacid tablets. I stared at the half-finished tablet roll and realized it was two days old, a record for me. While the past few days had been a roller coaster, the nerve-racking excitement had been a good kind. Trust twenty minutes with my ex to reduce me to my bad habit.

My cell phone rang and I unclipped it from my tote. "Hello."

"Yo, Kate."

"Good morning, Carling."

"Jared the Weasel just called."

"What is it with you two? Did he step on your toes in court once?"

"That gutter-hack of an attorney?" Carling's snort rang in my ear so loudly that I had to hold the phone out. "There'll never be a day I can't whip his tight ass in court."

"Tell me how you really feel about Jared Manning," I commented dryly.

"Weasel left a message that Judge Rodriguez wants to see you in chambers at eight-thirty sharp about the motions you filed."

I shot a quick glance at the dashboard clock: seven-thirty. Although I had an hour to drive ten miles, at this time of the morning I-95 resembled a game-day parking lot at the Dolphins' stadium. I'd better take back roads to get to the courthouse on time.

"Thanks, Carling. I'm on my way."

"Tell your opponent to drop dead, will you?"

"Absolutely." I hung up and started the engine, keeping the Jag at a crawl. As I lurched out of the driveway, I popped another tablet for stomach insurance.

The first round of legal warfare was about to begin.

Chapter 8

I stood in the presiding judge's chambers, warily sizing up my competition as he entered the room. With black wavy hair, high forehead, and ascetic features, Jared Manning looked like a cross between a poet and a pirate. As a lead prosecutor, he brought traits of both to a courtroom. He could slash a witness to death while at the same time persuade a jury to enter a guilty plea.

Jared extended his hand. "Ms. Rochelle." But when I returned the shake, he released my hand immediately as if he couldn't stand the contact. His manner was cool and remote, but the hard expression in his glacial-blue eyes could have cut me in half.

Stunned, I cocked a brow. "Do you have a problem, Mr. Manning?"

He crossed his arms. "As a matter of fact I do. You. On this case."

No doubt about the acid in his tone. Jared Manning hated my guts. But why? "I'm sorry…" I inwardly winced. Why was I always apologizing? I wasn't the offender here. "Have we met before?"

"Not personally, but your reputation precedes you."

Unless he was an avid fan of the Palm Beach society column, how could he know me? Then a memory clicked into place.

Of course. Jared. Harold had often talked about his buddy Jared from law school days. They met every Thursday night at a bar for a beer. No doubt Harold had filled Jared's ear about what an ungrateful bitch I was for turning him in to the authorities.

Sliding my hand into my jacket pocket, I curved my fingers around my security roll of tablets. I was sick and tired of the legal community's distortion as to what had happened at the U.S. Attorney's office. With our profession you'd think whistle-blowers of unethical conduct would be congratulated with a slap on the back. Instead, I'd received nothing but distain.

"I've heard, Mr. Manning—" I likewise folded my arms "—that you're a killer in the courtroom. You have more notches on your legal bedpost than any prosecutor since the days of my godfather Paul Schofield."

He inclined his head. "I've had a few good results."

Now I knew why Jared irritated Carling so much. His half-hearted modesty made me want to smack him with my tote.

"Rumor also has it that you may be in the running for Chief State Attorney."

He shrugged.

"Then tell me. Will you hire your good old buddy Harold to be on your staff?"

A dull flush spread across Jared's cheeks.

"I thought as much. So don't sit as judge and jury as to my actions. I did what was right."

His lips twitched. "Touché. I see why you and Carling Dent are friends."

"More than friends. We're partners."

He shot me a hooded look as he twitched his jacket cuff into place. "I had the pleasure of speaking with your partner, Ms. Dent, this morning. Charming as always." Underlying his sonorous voice was a rough edge.

Oh no. Dealing with his Harold Lowell connection was more than enough for this outing. The last thing I wanted to do at this juncture was to get caught up in the ongoing dispute between Carling and Jared. My money was on Carling being victorious anyway.

"She said the same about you."

He winced. "Ouch. I bet."

The door opened and Judge Theresita Rodriguez walked in with several folders under her arm. I'd been thrilled when the luck of case assignments had given us the same judge who had handled the first appearance hearing. Judge Rodriguez was tough but compassionate.

"Good morning, counselors."

"Good morning, Your Honor," Jared and I answered in unison as we rose.

The judge sat behind the bench. "Thank you both for responding to my office's call."

"Not a problem, Judge," I said.

"Ms. Rochelle, I reviewed your motions and the State's responses. On the motion to dismiss for insufficient evidence and for failure to properly Mirandize your client, I'm going to deny them. Insufficient showing."

Tension knotted my stomach. I knew those two motions had been pro forma. From the information disclosed to me, it appeared the State had probable cause to charge my client and the police had read him his rights. If I hadn't filed the motions, the issues would have been waived. Still it never hurt to dot every *i* and cross every *t* for appellate purposes.

But I desperately needed a favorable ruling on the third motion.

The judge held up a document. "On your motion to suppress any evidence or testimony that your client attempted suicide in jail, I'm inclined to grant."

"Your Honor, if I may respond?" Jared asked.

"Yes, Mr. Manning?"

"The defendant's suicide attempt clearly evinces his state of mind from which the jury can draw an inference of guilt."

"Counter from the defense?"

"Absolutely, Your Honor. Whether my client tried to commit suicide or not is after the fact and is irrelevant to whether he is culpable of murder. Any reasonable person hearing that my client attempted suicide is going to make a quantum jump to the conclusion he murdered Grace Roberts."

"Precisely the State's point." Jared nodded.

"This is why I'm granting the defense's motion to suppress." The judge picked up her pen and signed the blank orders my secretary had attached to the motions. "I have one more matter."

I threw a questioning look at Jared and he shrugged.

The judge set aside the folders. "I've learned that I need surgery. I've put off the procedure as long as possible, but my doctor has put down her foot and scheduled the operation for mid-May. I may be out of commission for a few months."

My mind raced. The period the judge would be out encompassed the period during which, in theory, my client's right to a speedy trial should occur.

The reality was a felony case rarely went to trial within the statutory framework due to a multitude of problems, the primary one being discovery. The opportunity to obtain depositions, documents and other evidence and then exchange the discovery with the opposition never went smoothly.

"Of course, I'm granting any motions for extension of time within reason. For those who want to go to trial, I'm farming those cases out to other judges." She glanced at her notes. "This one would be assigned to Judge Marvin Stein."

Over my dead body, I thought. Judge Stein wasn't known as "Hangman Stein" for nothing. He consistently ruled against the defense. Many of his decisions were overruled and returned on appeal, but enough murder cases slipped through to death row. Too dicey to risk.

"There's a third option," Judge Rodriguez continued, looking at me.

"Yes, Your Honor?" I asked.

"I haven't received a demand for speedy trial from you."

For good reason. When a defendant filed such a demand, it meant you were prepared to go to trial on the drop of a dime. You could be called anywhere from five to sixty days.

"Due to several plea bargains, I do have time available at the end of April and early May."

My palms dampened and I swallowed. My God, go to trial within the next four weeks?

"Naturally, I would order that expedited discovery be invoked, shortening the normal due dates. Any problems?"

Jared shook his head. "None whatsoever, Judge. So long

as the court is lenient about the order of witnesses on such short notice, the State can be ready."

Sure he could be. After all, he had at his disposal a large staff to help cover.

Carling was right. Jared Manning was a weasel.

"Ms. Rochelle?"

"I'll need to speak to my client first, Judge." Good. My voice was cool and steady.

"Of course. Do so and get back to me by four today."

"Yes, Your Honor."

The judge rose and swept out of the chambers. Jared winked, grabbed his briefcase and sauntered from the room.

I stared blankly at the wall. If my client agreed to an expedited docket, I could be defending my first murder trial in a matter of weeks with insufficient discovery done.

Talk about trial by fire.

"Do it," ordered Lloyd.

I sank into the chair opposite my client in the small conference room. "Lloyd, do you understand what you're giving it up?" I'd been shocked at the change in his appearance. With every passing day he grew more gaunt, as if being imprisoned was sapping away his very essence.

"The slight chance you may find evidence to exonerate me? Highly unlikely, don't you think?"

Alarmed by the defeated tone in his voice, I leaned forward. "Right now the State's case is all circumstantial. No gun in your collection matched the bullet that killed Grace. Everything is rumors and innuendos."

"Then it shouldn't matter whether we go to trial in five or one hundred days."

I opened my mouth to explain, but Lloyd held up his hand. "Katherine, I can't afford to wait this out. Either you clear my name or you don't. But I can't stay in a jail cell one day longer. Meredith isn't doing well with the strain."

He clasped his hands on top of the table. "I need finality."

I released the breath I'd been holding. "Are you sure?"

He nodded. "Quite."

Removing a document from my case folder, I pushed it across the table. "Then I need you to read and sign this waiver, stating that you understand the rights you are giving up by demanding a speedy trial."

He took the pen I handed him and began writing.

With every stroke, reality set in. At this juncture I would be trying a murder case on a song and a prayer.

Weeks passed without incident but also without any new evidence coming to light. Depositions of the restoration committee and staff only solidified their prior statements. Gabe dug into their backgrounds without finding any earth-shattering impeachment information. His main purpose seemed to be to get under my skin. If he wasn't calling me, he was text-messaging me. If he wasn't in the office, he was appearing on my doorstep.

I didn't get mad. I got even. I made him do what most men hate: wear a tux.

Palm Beach's elite, dressed in their designer best, filled The Breakers Venetian Ballroom to capacity. Men wore various versions of black tuxedos while women preened like peacocks in haute couture's latest. Here and there clusters of non-island attendees stood self-consciously in their off-the-rack dresses along with their dates.

Long lines at drink stations interspersed along the room's perimeter kept bartenders in white captain jackets busy. The orchestra played a mixture of swing, Broadway and dance tunes on a raised platform by the ocean-side bank of windows. A few of the more outgoing couples were already twirling on the designated dance floor under the glittering lights of the enormous chandeliers.

I sipped chilled champagne from a crystal flute while I studied the crowd. From the ogling glances of the men in the immediate vicinity, I knew I'd scored a bull's-eye with my dress. Designed by the hottest New York City designer this past season, the strapless gown was a simple column of shimmering azure silk. My hair swept up in a French twist served to keep attention on the dress. My only jewelry was a pair of stiletto earrings, a marquise-cut ring, and a cuff bracelet—all diamonds, of course. A small beaded bag in the shape of a butterfly kept my basic essentials of lipstick, comb, cell phone and a clip of folded bills.

Silk, diamonds and champagne. What more could a woman ask for in such gorgeous surroundings?

Then I saw the broad shoulders of a man cutting a swath in the crowd and knew what else I was beginning to want: a man.

People weren't stepping aside because Gabe was drop-dead gorgeous in a tux or because they thought he was a celebrity. Nope, from their measured glances, they were getting out of the way because of his ill-concealed scowl.

Just like a man. Throwing a major snit because I had cajoled him into being where he didn't want to be. Actually, I amended, I had ordered him into coming.

Gabe halted before me and proceeded to take his sweet time in scanning the length of my body. His intent was to be obnoxious, but my skin heated under his gaze so that I barely resisted the urge to fan myself. However, two could play this sexual mating game. I tilted a hip, rested my hand and purse on it, and inspected him as I sipped the champagne to moisten my dry mouth.

Yum. Definitely a ten on the eye-candy scale. Gabe's fitted tux definitely wasn't a rental. A former cop who owned his own tailored evening clothes. Impressive. He'd passed on the current preference for tunic shirts and wore the traditional black silk tie and crisp white shirt, which contrasted oh-so-nicely with his dark looks. Light glinted off the subtle gold cuff links and the diamond he wore in his left lobe.

"When did you get your ear pierced?" I demanded. No way I would've missed that detail before.

Gabe's smile was downright piratical. All he needed to complete the picture was long hair tied back. "I had a little free time this afternoon so I went with a whim. Don't worry," he winked, "I don't have any urge to raid your jewelry box."

He reached out and with a light touch sent my earring swaying. "I love the way those show off that elegant neck of yours."

I flushed. "My neck? Elegant?"

"Like a princess."

Princess. That word forever and a day had been tainted by my former husband. I stiffened.

"I can see the chill in your eyes." Gabe lowered his hand to cup my shoulder. "What did I say to piss you off?"

"Katherine."

Spinning, I found Hilary and Colin behind us. Colin looked at Gabe with unconcealed curiosity, but Hilary's very pointed glare at Gabe's hand could have cut a lesser man's arm off at the wrist. I stepped away from Gabe.

"Uncle Colin, Aunt Hilary," I murmured as I pressed a light kiss to both their cheeks. "You look very striking tonight."

"Didn't you bring a wrap?" Hilary asked.

"I'm not cold, not in this crush."

"I think you look gorgeous, sweetheart, like a fairy-tale princess." Colin beamed.

Just slap a tiara on top of my head, but I knew Colin meant well and, as he had done his entire life, was placing himself between his wife and me. "Thank you, Uncle Colin."

"Aren't you going to introduce us to your friend?" Hilary continued to examine Gabe.

"Certainly. This is—"

"Gabriel Chavez," Gabe interrupted, smoothly taking my uncle's hand and shaking it. "I'm a work associate of Kate's."

I rolled my eyes. Not even Carling dared to call me Kate in my aunt's presence.

"Her name is Katherine."

Gabe flashed an irrepressible grin. "And a lovely name it is, but don't you think *Kate* suits the woman she's become?"

"No."

One thing about Hilary. She sure knew how to put a stopper in any conversation. "I wasn't aware the girls had taken on a male attorney in the firm."

"The women still rule the firm. I'm the private investigator they use."

"Oh really." Hilary shot me a look. "Weren't you with the police department?"

"In my former life I was a detective."

"Fired, weren't you?"

"Made front-page news," Gabe agreed cheerfully.

"Your family's from Cuba, correct?"

"That's right." Although Gabe's voice remained pleasant, his expression became guarded.

"Chavez." Hilary arched a brow. "Does your family run the restaurant on Southern Boulevard?"

"Yes."

"Humph."

The single-word expression held classic Hilary disdain. The conversation had nowhere to go but downhill. If she held true to her course, she'd next be implying that Gabe had no right to be here. Hilary's sense of class had never changed with the times. She believed Palm Beach belonged to the elite.

I had to intervene before she said something that I would regret.

"Gabe." I placed a hand on his forearm. He looked at me. I could see dark storms raging in his eyes. He knew damn well Hilary's intent was to put him down.

"Would you please get me a seltzer with lime? The heat in here is making me thirsty."

I could see his silent debate. To stand and defend his family or go in response to my unspoken plea for no scene.

"Sure. Can I get anything for you, Mr. and Mrs. Wilkes?"

"No, we're set for now, Gabe." Colin smiled with relief. "I'm going to steal my niece for a dance while you're gone."

Gabe nodded and made his way to the nearest drink station.

"Really, Katherine. Bringing someone like that as your escort."

The band began to play a slow dance tune. "Excuse me, dear, but they're playing the one song I think I can manage to dance to. Come on, Katherine."

We joined others on the dance floor and Colin tucked my hand in his. "That was a close call."

"Thanks, Uncle Colin."

"Anytime. By the way, I like your young man. Something very solid about him."

"We're only business associates."

"Really? I suspect Gabriel has something more on his mind by the way he looks at you."

Flustered, I looked back at where we had left Hilary. I didn't want Gabe to have to fence with her while we were gone.

With a start, I saw my ex-husband, in a white tuxedo jacket standing close to her, talking.

"Uncle Colin, she's with Juan."

"Yes, they've actually become friendly during the restoration. He attends some of the same meetings and they got to talking. I'm afraid it's too late in terms of what happened to your marriage, but it gives me hope."

"Hope for what?"

"That she'll learn to accept others so that when you do meet someone else, like your private investigator, she'll accept him with open arms into the family."

"Open arms? That'll be the day."

"Hilary's not a bad person, darling. She's had a hard life.

"Money, prestige, family. That's a tough life."

"Not everything is about the tangible. She's had a rough go of it in the emotional department."

True, my aunt's parents had been cold, loveless people. What little love they had in them they expended on Jonathan. Hilary had tried everything to win their respect, even competed on the Olympics team, but they didn't bother to attend the games. Bit by bit, whatever soft emotions she had were covered up behind a tough veneer.

"Then when Jonathan disappointed his parents, going into public service by becoming a judge," Colin continued, "Hilary stepped in, overseeing the family's holdings. It wasn't what she wanted to do with her life, but it was what she had to do.

"The family name. That's what drives her, gives her life value. If you can understand that, Katherine, then you can go a long way to forgiving her."

"And what about you, Uncle Colin? Do you have enough love?"

His shoulder moved underneath my hand. "I have what I deserve. That's enough for me."

The song ended. For a moment, I stood looking at the sad, resigned man who had been my buffer for all of my life. Had I ever thanked him? I gave him a hug. "I love you."

"Thank you, my dear. I love you, too." He held out his arm. "I see your young man with your drink standing over by the window. Let me escort you to him."

When we reached Gabe, Colin flashed a smile and left. Gabe handed me a glass of water. "Who's the guy your aunt is falling all over? I had the distinct impression that she'd shun anyone with dark skin color unless it came from a sunlamp."

"You would've been right except according to my uncle, she's actually become friendly with my ex."

"So that's the infamous ex-husband. What's he doing here?"

"His construction company was the one brought in to help meet the deadline."

"And you didn't think that detail important enough to tell me?"

"That it was my ex? No. The only germane fact was the name of the company."

"I just love it when you go Palm Beach on me," he murmured as he lifted my hand and pressed his lips to my knuckles.

The tingle zipped all the way to my Christian Dior pink nail-polished toes.

"Don't you think it's peculiar your aunt and ex have formed a liaison after all these years?"

"Very."

"Do you want me to rough him up a bit?"

"Why?"

"For hurting you."

A different type of warmth unfurled deep within me. "No, but thank you. I may have different plans for you and Juan, depending how tonight goes."

"So what now?"

"We split up and work the crowd."

"What are we looking for?"

"The man who, according to Peter Robbins, Grace was so anxious to see tonight."

Two hours later my feet ached from being trampled on during a dance with Derek Jones, and I still didn't have a clue as to Grace's targeted subject. I had spoken with a number of contributors and government officials but had gleaned very little new information.

"May I have this dance with the room's most beautiful woman?"

"Paul! I didn't know you were here!" I beamed with joy at my godfather.

"I got here a short while ago. I had a function to attend before this." He led me onto the dance floor.

"I don't know how you do it." I searched his face, noting the faint lines of fatigue. "You look tired."

His lips curved. "I am, but the alternative would be to rattle around my house."

Sympathy filled me. Paul's wife had died from cancer three years ago, and his children had long ago moved on with their lives.

"I heard you had some trouble that day I saw you in the old courthouse. Are you all right?"

Startled, I shot a look at where my aunt and uncle stood talking to another bored-looking couple.

"No," said Paul with a smile. "I haven't told them you were attacked in the courthouse garage, and I doubt if they read the police blotter in the local news."

My tension eased. "I'm fine."

"I understand your drive to defend Lloyd, but don't you think you should leave the investigation to that Chavez fellow?"

"You don't miss a trick, do you?"

"Not when it comes to my favorite goddaughter."

"Your only goddaughter," I teased.

"All the more reason you're precious to me."

Maybe Paul was the one I could talk to about my grandfather.

"Paul, do you believe my grandfather was in with the mob?"

His mouth tightened. "Of course not. What brought that on?"

"All the connections to him in this case."

"What connections?"

"The fact that Grace Roberts was collecting his memorabilia for the museum, that she was murdered in his chambers."

"She was also working on other judicial memorabilia, honey. In fact she was putting together my collection."

"Oh, I hadn't realized that."

"The room bearing my name is also going to be on the fourth floor. It's just a coincidence, Katherine, nothing more."

"But what was Granddad like?"

"He was a man of honor and principle, unbending in fact. More than likely some criminal he had sent to jail killed him."

"But what about Grandmother?"

"She probably was at the wrong place at the wrong

time." His hand tightened on mine. "They loved each other very much. They would've wanted to be together in death, remember that."

I fought back a sudden lump in my throat.

"Thanks, Paul. No one will ever talk about them to me."

"You remind me so much of Jonathan. That same quest for justice. Someday soon let's get together for dinner and I'll bore you with my reminiscing about the good old days."

"I'd like that very much."

The music ended and we walked off the dance floor. "In the meantime, I want you to be careful. I can't lose my only godchild."

"I'll be careful."

"Good." Paul kissed my cheek. "Now I must circulate."

"Of course."

After Paul left me, I realized I was by the ocean side of the room. I began to wind my way to the bar. As I reached the bank of windows, someone gripped my elbow.

"You think you're so much better than everyone else, just like he did."

Maybe in court I had to be respectful, but this was my turf. I twisted around. "Judge Winewski, I suggest you let go of me. Now."

Although his evening clothes were immaculate, the judge's cheeks were flushed and his eyes held a wild expression. When he lowered his head to me, I could smell alcohol on his breath. Oh brother, he'd had one too many. I had never heard any rumors of him having a substance-abuse problem, but he wouldn't be the first judge. I glanced around but saw no one I knew in the immediate vicinity. I was on my own.

Since Winewski hadn't removed his hand, he obviously needed further persuasion. Rolling my diamond ring facet-side down, I gripped his hand so that the stone ground into his flesh. He cursed but released me. "You stinking bitch!"

"Would you care to tell me why you hated my grandfather so much?"

"I see him looking out of your eyes."

"I get that."

"Well, get this." He leaned so close that I prepared to stomp his foot with my heel. "You have the same long nose for trouble too." He wagged his finger. "If you don't watch out, you'll end up dead like him."

I stiffened. "What do you know about my grandfather's death?"

Was it panic that I saw in those alcohol-glazed eyes? Was he threatening me?

"Jonathan played with fire and paid for it. If you want to live, you'll leave well enough alone." He turned and wheeled off into the crowd.

Drawing a shaky breath, I rubbed my throbbing arm. All at once the room seemed too noisy, too warm. I had to get out of here. I located the door that led to the beach and slipped out into the night.

Chapter 9

On the hotel's loggia, I drank in a deep breath of fresh air. After removing my sandals, I made my way down the short flight of steps leading to the beach. The tide was out, so the ocean was a flat shimmering disk under the moonlight. A balmy breeze cooled my warm face.

Once I reached the hard-packed sand by the edge of the water, I turned and walked away from the hotel. Gentle waves lapped and sucked at my feet. Tension ebbed from me, carried away by the ocean.

I loved the beach at night when only the occasional lovers strolled it. Growing up, I had often stolen down to be alone. Because of the Palm Beach police department, crime was a rarity on the island, limited to the sordid scandals the rich and famous managed to get themselves in. But the season was almost over and with its end, the snowbirds would be heading north to their next seasonal home. Palm Beach would lie dormant, populated by only the locals.

Gradually, the hotel's blazing lights dimmed to only a glow in the night. With distance I relaxed even more, allowing my thoughts to flow with the rhythm of the waves.

What was the deal with Kurt Winewski?

I knew from the legal gossip that he had served on the circuit court bench for only a few years. Then inexplicably he had accepted a demotion to the county court. When he'd grown dissatisfied, Kurt had applied repeatedly for vacancies for higher seats, but every time the Judicial Nominating Committee had passed him over.

On the other hand, with his name, community standing and zeal for the law, my grandfather had been appointed then elected to the circuit bench. Within a year he had risen to chief judge. Had Winewski so resented Jonathan Rochelle that the years hadn't erased his hatred? Would it be worth a shot to approach him during the day, when he was sober, to question him? While others sought to protect me, maybe Winewski would be willing to talk about my grandfather.

In my path something gleamed like a gigantic pearl and I picked it up, brushing off grains of sand. It was a sand dollar, perfectly round. I would add it to my growing collection in the Waterford vase on my coffee table. My bid for freedom had driven me inland, far enough away from the island so people couldn't just drop in on a whim. But I missed the comfort of the ocean's waves, so much that I had bought one of those sound machines in order to sleep at night.

A dark shadow joined mine against the sand, and a sense of awareness tingled through me. I was no longer alone. I spun around.

Gabe loomed over me, the night carving deep shadows on his face. "Are you nuts coming out here all by yourself?"

Although part of me relaxed, another part went on high

alert. On this moonlit beach, I was in a different kind of danger.

"I needed to be alone for a moment."

He placed a finger under my chin, lifting my face to the moonlight. "What spooked you?"

I have to admit, Gabe's ability to read me was disconcerting. All the years of finishing school had taught me to present a mask to the world, yet this man within a short time of knowing me had stripped it away. Why him, when neither Juan nor Harold had ever bothered?

Off balance, I managed to shrug. "I had a run-in with someone who wasn't a fan of my grandfather."

Gabe's gaze lowered and his jaw tightened, but his touch was tender as he ran a gentle hand along my upper arm. "Did he do this to you?"

Puzzled, I glanced down and, in the moonlight, saw dark spots the shape of fingertips marring my arm. One of the many curses of having a fair complexion. Burning easily in the sun insured I kept a gallon of forty-five proof suntan lotion on hand at all times. However, no commercial preventive measure for bruising existed. The one time I had donated blood, my arm had been black-and-blue for over a week.

"It looks worse than it actually is, Gabe. I bruise on the drop of a dime."

"Someone gripped you hard enough to do this."

"Too much alcohol."

"Never an excuse." Gabe bit out the words, each one loaded with reproach. Or was it self-loathing I heard?

I thought about the other night at the bar, and tonight, and Gabe's preference for water. Not once have I seen him with an alcoholic drink in hand. I wondered how long he had been in recovery.

"Kate?"

With a start I realized Gabe had been talking. Normally, I didn't zone out like that. "What did you say?"

"I asked who did this to you?"

"Judge Winewski."

"Winewski? What does he have to do with all this?"

"I'm not sure. He was a judge at the same time as my granddad and without question hated him. When I first appeared before Winewski in court, he lectured me about appropriate behavior and took a verbal swipe at my grandfather." It would be the last time, I promised myself, that anyone would be able to denigrate Jonathan.

"Do you think he's the one Grace wanted to meet here tonight?"

"I don't know." I shook my head. "True to the male's innate fear of attending a function alone, every man here tonight has a date. With all that wealth and power centered in one room, it's hard to imagine who might have been her target. One thing for sure, Grace would've been in heaven."

"You want me to check into Winewski?"

"Yes." I didn't mention that I planned to confront the judge. Gabe would insist on accompanying me and I desperately wanted Winewski to talk to me about my grandfather. No matter how tainted his words would be, his account would be more than anyone else has been willing to give me.

I was tired of having cotton batting wrapped around me because of the old family scandal. But I had to be careful to maintain my objectivity. My instincts screamed that somehow my grandfather's disappearance was connected to Grace.

"I'll start looking into his background first thing tomorrow." Gabe's arms slipped around my waist, drawing me closer to the heat of his body. Funny, I hadn't noticed I had become chilled in the night air.

"I thought you were upset about your ex being here."

Gabe didn't miss a trick.

"No. Only surprised to learn he and my aunt have arrived at a truce."

"Did she have the same problem with him that she did with me?"

I didn't pretend to not understand the point of his question. "Let me put it this way. Hilary's an equal-opportunity bigot. If your bloodline isn't society blue, she doesn't take to you, no matter what your heritage is."

"Your marrying an Hispanic must have caused quite a stir."

"A hotline crisis. My relatives sent out an all-points bulletin to anyone who would help. They didn't have to worry."

"What did Juan do to you? Did he hurt you?" Gabe asked in a voice that held deep stillness.

"Not in a physical sense. Though..."

Memories of the last night I had been with Juan lashed at me. Sex had been very abbreviated, almost painful, lasting hardly a minute before he had...well, lost his erection. He had pulled himself free and lit into me. "Making love to you is like making love to an ice cube. How can a man feel like staying inside you when you're so unresponsive?"

If I hadn't swallowed my pride and run that night, if I had stayed married to him, would I now be one those victims of spousal abuse? Could I break free from a pattern of selecting men who made me frozen inside?

"What?" Gabe was intense as he studied my face. "Tell me what happened?"

"Nothing important."

"No, Kate, I think that bastard hurt you terribly."

"Not all his fault. I have a bad habit of picking the wrong man."

"And who is the right man, babe?"

"Don't ask me. I used to think a lightning bolt would strike announcing his arrival. I thought it was something I would know with crystal clarity. But this is real life and wolves come wrapped in all degrees of sheep's clothing."

"Too much pain," Gabe murmured, drawing me closer. "It's too beautiful an evening to have so much pain. Listen."

"To what?" Damn me, I wanted this intimate moment to go on forever. To have him just hold me.

"The music of the night."

We were too far away from the hotel to hear the band. "I don't hear anything."

He pressed a finger across my lips. "You're listening with your head. Listen with your heart. Hear it? The ocean."

The waves hissed as they lapped upon the beach, before retreating. Like an ancient melody, their throbbing cadence seeped into my blood.

"Dance with me."

Before I could reply, Gabe began to move. Of their own volition, my arms stole around his neck. Together we moved to the rhythm of the night. With the stars as our lights and the sand our dance floor, I wouldn't have traded the place for all the exclusive nightclubs in the world.

I sighed and pressed my face against his neck so I could inhale his musky scent. A sense of languidness stole all the tension from my body, replacing it with a different but more delicious throbbing.

When Gabe's breath feathered against my ear, I tilted my head. His mouth rained light kisses across my face until they reached my mouth. The first kiss was slow, soft as the night. When his tongue traced the outline of my mouth, I opened to him.

When he didn't enter at my invitation, I opened my eyes and found him intently looking at me.

"Take me," he whispered.

Take him? What did he mean?

I pressed closer so I could feel his erection against my lower body. His answering smile was so hot that I felt emboldened. He kissed me again.

Desire was now an insistent undertow deep within me. I needed more. Framing his face with my hands, I thrust my tongue into his mouth. The sensation of the various textures of his mouth fused my brain.

I moaned under the impact. Gabe returned the assault.

Skin. I needed to feel his skin. I fumbled at the tuxedo shirt's studs.

A woman's shrill, drunken laughter split the night's stillness, reverberating through my sexual haze. A man answered the woman, and she laughed again. Their voices were close, too close.

My hands stilled, and Gabe gave me one last kiss before raising his head. His hands rubbed my shoulders as he looked down the beach.

"They're coming our way. We should head back to the hotel."

I drank in a calming breath, trying to force my raging hormones back into their closet.

"You okay?"

"Fine, I'm fine." Taking a step backward, I stepped ankle-deep into the rising tide. A wave slapped at my legs, nearly sending me sprawling.

Laughing, Gabe caught me. "Looks to me more like you've been swept off your feet."

"And you're all wet." Indignant, I tried to push him away but it was like trying to topple the Rock of Gibraltar. His smile was self-deprecating as he steadied me.

"If it makes your pride feel any better, I'm not fine either. I've got a hard-on that's going to require a cold, cold shower."

My lips twitched. "I'll take a swim as soon as I get home."

His expression was intense. "You know, babe, at some point we're going to have to take that final step."

"We have a case to solve."

He threw back his head and laughed. Before I knew what was happening, he lifted me up and swung me around in a circle.

"Ah, Kate. You kill a man's ego."

I stiffened and tried to pull away, but he only hugged me tighter.

"I'm going to enjoy the chase, but when you finally catch me—"

"What? Me catch you? You arrogant—"

His hard kiss cut off my protest. "Oh yes, beautiful, I'm going to let you do the catching. And when you do, I'm going to make love with you until we both either die of exhaustion or starvation."

"Sex more than once?"

He lowered me until my feet touched the beach. "Once? Babe, you definitely have been picking the wrong men."

He whispered something hot in my ear and then grabbed my hand and began to pull me along the beach.

I couldn't have heard him right. Surely a man couldn't have sex for that long and that many times in one night, could he?

From their closet, my hormones broke out, singing "Anticipation, baby!"

* * *

Stan Turow, Juan's field supervisor, yelled at me over the noise of a Bobcat scooping up a load of dirt. "There's no problem." He spoke into his walkie-talkie and strode toward the on-site construction trailer across a field of dirt.

The sod Juan had been worrying about when I had been at his office had finally arrived. Just my luck.

I looked down at my Bruno Magli shoes, consigning them to the trash, and followed Stan. For weeks on end I'd been trying to speak with the elusive foreman, so I wasn't about to lose him now. But landscaping being done around the courthouse meant the finishing touches on the restoration were drawing to a close.

The window of opportunity to find out who had killed Grace Roberts was quickly slamming shut in more ways than one. That morning the judge's office had called, advising me trial would begin next week.

My heels sank into the soil as I matched the foreman's stride. Although it was only noon, the sun already packed a punch. My black Irish-linen jacket clung to my back, driving home the irony of wearing breathable fabric in a color that soaked up heat like a magnet. Next time I came to a construction site, practicality would win over chic.

"You said there's no trouble, Mr. Turow, but what about all the delays? Late shipments? Men quitting?"

"That's not trouble, ma'am, that's construction. Happens all the time." Stan was a testament to Florida tattoo shops. Colorful designs covered every inch of his exposed flesh, including his shaved head. I shuddered to think about what tattoos he had on the body parts covered by his clothing.

"More than usual on this project?" I tried not to stare at the snake slithering over one bulging bicep or the dragon writhing over the other.

He shrugged a massive shoulder. "Been a pain in the butt, but we've managed."

"What about the crew working inside the courthouse? Have you had a high turnover there?"

"Julio, not there, over there!" He waved at a worker on a backhoe before speaking tersely into his walkie-talkie.

When he looked down at me with irritation, I persisted. "The courthouse interior. Have any workers been spooked, reported anything strange?"

"Haven't paid any attention. Laborers come and go."

"What do you do when a large number don't show?"

He flashed a grin. "We go to the labor-supply companies."

"And I bet if I checked your roster, I would find it doesn't match up with your declaration for workers' compensation."

His smile faded into a scowl. In south Florida construction companies often sent supervisors with pickup trucks or vans to street corners in heavily Haitian and Hispanic populated communities. For a day's pay in cash they would get cheap labor that wouldn't be reported, thus saving on their insurance and tax overhead.

"What do you want to know?"

"Any rumors of strange things happening inside?"

"A few men complained of hearing the clip-clap of shoes in the fourth-floor hallway, but when they went to look, no one was there. Then there have been a couple of accidents."

"What kind of accidents?"

"One man claimed he was pushed down the stairs and after he fell, he saw no one."

Stan swiped his brow with his forearm. "Immediately the workers leaped to the conclusion that there's a ghost on the fourth floor. People feeling cold spots, like someone is watching them. Things like that. The gossip's gotten so bad that I can't get anyone to work on the top floor. In fact Juan and I plan to do the finishing work ourselves over the new few weeks."

Juan hadn't done grunt work for years. He was into being the head honcho, dealing with clients. The pressure to complete the restoration by the scheduled grand opening had to be great. I wondered if the company's finances were as strong as Juan made them out to be.

"Heard anything that goes bump in the night yourself?"

Stan hesitated for a fraction of a second before shaking his head. "Nah."

"Did you know Grace Roberts?"

"I don't deal with the restoration folks other than to yell at them. They're Juan's department."

Stan didn't actually answer my question but his walkie-talkie erupted again. He answered and then swore in a way that would put any sailor to shame. "Look, I gotta go."

"One more question. Any men who got spooked still on the crew?"

"Francelus. Haitian. Doesn't speak English. Over there." With a jerk of his thumb, Stan strode off toward the courthouse.

I watched his back for a moment, debating whether I should follow to see what the latest crisis was. But a long, drawn-out whistle accompanied by catcalls drew my attention to a crew of men by a truck. I gathered they were supposed to be unloading it, but they were having more fun calling out lurid suggestions in various languages. Fortunately or rather unfortunately, due to my years abroad, I could understand them.

"Hey, baby." One man, speaking with a heavy Spanish accent and wearing a red bandanna, broke apart from the others and swaggered a few steps toward me.

His smile was a flash of white against his dark skin. His sweat-drenched armless T-shirt revealed bronzed muscular arms and a broad chest. Snug, worn jeans showed strong, toned legs.

Hot, hot, hot. He was primal male to the core.

"You and me—" he pointed "—later?"

I cocked a hip and planted my hand on it as I gave him a long, slow survey. The other men hooted and hollered. Then I shook my head.

"No."

He clasped his hands to his chest. "*Dios! Por qué?* Why not?"

"Because you don't do it for me, baby."

The crew howled and the man touched his hand to his forehead in a salute. He turned and sauntered back the truck. I swallowed, hard, while I admired the view.

I had to admit, Gabriel Chavez had one major cute butt.

Looked like our plan had worked. He must not have had any problem in being picked up as a laborer this morning. The strategy was that I would rattle people by being on-site today, asking questions, and maybe he in his undercover role could shake free some useful information.

Time for me to do more rattling. I turned and went to the area that was going to be the courtyard. Several groups of laborers were working on the landscaping. On one side was a towering pile of topsoil. Right next to it was…a canvas-covered gigantic penis pointing at me.

I came to an abrupt halt and stared at it. A halfhearted breeze stirred the edges of the draped cover and I caught a flash of metal. Of course. The infamous statue "Fallen Justice" donated by a renowned abstract artist.

His work was abstract all right. It lacked any resemblance to a woman. One end was narrower than the other, but whether that signified Lady Justice's head or feet, no one knew, and the artist wasn't telling because he was getting a lot of news coverage about his contribution to the old courthouse.

Carling had dubbed the distorted piece of six-foot-long metal set on a massive pedestal base "The Flying Sperm." Amazing how a piece of cloth transformed the monstrosity from being the ejaculation to being the ejaculator. Carling would die laughing if she saw it now.

Reluctantly, I tore my attention from the statue and approached the man closest to me. "Francelus?" He shook his head and gestured to the next group. I approached them. "Francelus?"

A man raking dirt paused and looked up.

"I'm Katherine Rochelle. Your boss Turow said you were on the crew working on the courthouse fourth floor?"

He shook his head and flashed a gold-tooth filled smile. "No speak English."

I repeated what I had said in French. "Understand me?" He nodded.

I continued in pidgin French.

"I'm a lawyer."

At once Francelus's expression became closed. Lawyer, law, police, authority. They were all synonymous to many immigrants from the turbulent island of Haiti. After years of brutality, those who had fled to America remained a tight-knit group. They lived together, often eight to ten people in a small apartment, patronized Haitian-owned businesses and went to church together. Outsiders were not welcomed and looked at with suspicion. As for any authority figure, forget it. The group clammed up tighter than Florida's coastal borders.

But they loved to bargain and dicker. I held up my hand.

"Five dollars if you tell me about what you saw or heard on the top floor of the courthouse."

"Fifty," said Francelus in English.

"You understand English?"

"Fifty dollars." This time he spoke in thick Creole.

So we had a game going. Let's jerk the little lady around.

"Ten," I deliberately said in English.

"Forty-five."

After a few minutes of intense negotiations, we arrived at a deal for twenty. Francelus extended his hand and I got a crisp new bill out of my tote. He pocketed the money and leaned on his rake.

"What do you want to know?" He was back to Creole.

"Anything unusual you saw or heard on the fourth floor?"

"A restless spirit. I consulted the priest, and he told me a man walked the hallways, searching."

"Searching for what?"

"Revenge. His is a lost soul trapped on that floor because of his sudden death."

"The priest told you all that?" The priest and probably a slaughtered chicken or two. Unless I was way off, Francelus practiced a form of Santeria.

"Yes, but I also saw the man's spirit walking the hallways. Very upset with our disturbing his peace. I told him that if he didn't bother me, I wouldn't work there anymore."

"Anyplace in particular he haunted?"

Francelus shrugged. "He walked between the machine room and the great room."

Great room? For a moment I was stumped. "Do you mean the large courtroom?"

"Yes, but of course."

One of the architectural points of interest in the old courthouse was a two-story courtroom that was being restored, adjoining my grandfather's former office. I assumed the machine room had to be the air-conditioning and other equipment installed in the later years.

The men around us laid down their tools and moved off. One called out to Francelus.

He looked at me and pointed at the sun. "Time off."

"It's time for your break?"

He nodded.

"Thank you. If you think of anything else, here's my card."

He pocketed the card and slowly followed his buddies.

Standing in the now empty courtyard, I tried to fit the newest information into the puzzle. I swiped at a bee dive-bombing at my ear. Behind me I heard the increasing whine and growl of a Bobcat.

All right. I had done my job and stirred the pot here. I needed to go back to the office and return a few phone calls before tackling the next batch of witnesses.

The Bobcat's drone was quite close. The ground vibrated under my feet. The hairs on the back of my neck prickled. The ground wasn't the only thing vibrating.

I spun around. The mountain of topsoil stirred, as if coming to life. Then dirt began to slip and slide, gathering momentum—toward me. The Bobcat was driving into the mound.

"Hey, someone is over here!" I yelled, but the soil continued to shift.

When I had skied in the Switzerland Alps, my instructor had told me that if I was ever caught in an avalanche to pray. As the top of this mountain began to spill toward me, I prayed but I also turned and began running.

The air turned brown, cloying. Dirt spattered over my

head, clogging my nose. Sharp stones stung my back and the gathering force of the landslide flung me forward as if I were a limp doll. In desperation I stretched out into a headfirst dive, sliding for all my life like a major league baseball player. The earth trembled, the air roared and everything went pitch-black.

I was buried alive.

Chapter 10

Disoriented, I stirred. Good, I could move the upper part of my body, despite the weight pressing against my legs. Although grit still stung my eyes, I opened my eyes and blinked. I was in a dark cavelike space, though the far side was backlit and fluttered slightly. The faintest breeze wafted against my face.

Of course. I was under the penis statue. In that last burst of desperation I had flung myself at it. My grinding belly flop had carried me under the canvas. From the air and sunlight, the dirt hadn't spilled over to the other side. If I could drag my legs free, I could get out.

I first tried a flutter kick but no dice. Couldn't move my feet an inch. With a grunt I raised myself on both elbows and then extended one hand. There. Warm metal. Curling my fingers over the edge, I tugged as hard as I could. I moved forward an inch.

Sweat trickled down my face. Taking another deep breath, I reached farther along the metal surface, gripped and tugged. I could swear I moved at least two inches. Even the pressure on my legs felt lighter. Another foot and I should be clear. Taking another grip, I paused. The ringing in my ears hadn't stopped but I could swear I heard voices.

"Here!" My shout came out a muffled croak. I swallowed and tried again. "I'm here!"

I thought I was louder this time, but the effort sapped my energy. I dropped my head and willed myself to try again. This time I needed to say where I was, okay? Have to shout out where I am. On the count of three.

One, two…I drew in a shaky breath.

"Kate?"

The canvas flapped up, allowing sun to flood the area under the statue. I narrowed my eyes against the blinding light and saw the silhouette of a man's head. Arms reached forward and strong hands gripped mine.

"Gabe," I managed to gasp. "My legs. Trapped."

"Hold on to me, babe," Gabe said as he pulled. Inch by inch, I slid forward. When I saw the gleam of metal, I ducked my head so I wouldn't conk myself out on the statue.

As I finally felt the sun on my skin, Gabe dropped my hands and gripped under me under my arms. With a grunt he dragged me clear, falling on his butt. I sprawled half on, half off him.

I was alive. I was free.

When I regained my strength, I was going to have to do something celebratory, such as kiss Gabe. For now, I was content to lie on top of him.

"What the hell happened here?"

I managed to twist my head and look up. Stan the tattoo man stood towering above, his hands fisted on his hips.

"What were you doing fooling around with the topsoil, lady? You could've been killed."

Below me I felt Gabe tense. I patted his arm in a silent warning. He levered up and for the next few moments we were a blur of flying elbows and knees as we sought to untangle ourselves. Finally, Gabe helped me to my feet but kept his arm around my waist.

"*Señorita,* your knees." He pointed at my ripped pant legs. "You okay?"

For a second I stared at him, wondering why he was speaking in broken English, before I remembered he was undercover.

I quit leaning into his side and stood. My legs, though wobbly, held. There wasn't an inch of my body not aching or covered in dirt, but I didn't appear to have any major injuries…nothing that a hot shower wouldn't cure.

I nodded at Gabe. "Thank you."

"It is nothing," he murmured.

"Gonzalez, isn't it?" Stan asked.

"Yes, *señor.*"

"Well, we're not paying you to stand around and flirt with the ladies."

"Oh really." I stepped forward and got into Stan's face. "Listen up, Mr. Turow. Someone on a Bobcat pushed that load of dirt on top of me—after I yelled that I was standing here. I would still be lying buried if this man hadn't helped me out."

A muscle flexed along Stan's jaw. "Look, Miss Rochelle. No one was working in this area. They were on break."

"Are you suggesting the avalanche happened all by itself?" I demanded indignantly.

"Señor Turow," Gabe called out. He had moved around the spill area.

"What?"

"The machine that moves the dirt." Gabe made a gesture indicating the Bobcat. "It's not here."

"What!" Stan rushed over and, after looking in all directions around the yard, stood scratching his bald head. He jerked out his walkie-talkie. "Someone call the police. One of the Bobcats is missing."

He glared at me. "I don't suppose you can describe who the driver was."

"Never saw him. The bucket was up."

"Great. And since you're a lawyer, I imagine you'll march right across the street and file a lawsuit against us."

The idea had its merits, particularly since it would be Juan's pride-and-joy company that I could sue, but our marriage had been my mistake, not his. He had known what he was doing; I hadn't. Sometimes revenge meant accepting your part in a disaster and moving on.

"No," I answered. "But you might want to consider securing your equipment when it's not in use." I turned to leave.

"Where are you going? The police will need to speak with you." Stan moved to block my path, but with one cool look from me, he stepped aside.

"Give the police my name and they can call me."

I looked at the statue gleaming under the sun. Carling was correct. Without the canvas it was back to resembling a silver sperm. "I should go thank an artist for that work of art."

Stan spat. "That ugly piece of crap?"

"Ugly it may be, but it saved my life."

He shrugged and called out orders to get the dirt cleaned up. Through the thinning crowd, I caught a glimpse of

Cindy Overbeck, hovering at the edge. Limping, I made my way to her. I didn't want her to get too close to the disaster area. She had been infatuated with Gabe and could recognize him.

"I was just on my way to see you," I said.

She darted a nervous glance around, but the few people remaining were intent on the dirt pile. "I have something for you."

Since Cindy appeared reluctant to hand it over in public, I gestured toward the street. "Let's head toward my car." This morning I had parked on the street, shunning the garage. I suspected it would be a while before I would park there again, if ever.

She nodded and accompanied me to the sidewalk. Once we were in the throng of people heading to lunch, she relaxed. She pulled from a denim bag a crumpled envelope.

"I made a copy of Grace's phone messages that Gabe asked for. You'll make sure that he gets them, won't you? He told me they might help Lloyd."

I resisted rolling my eyes. Instead, I smiled and took the envelope. "Thank you. I'll make sure Gabe sees them." Only after I was finished with them.

I placed the bundle in my tote. "I'll also make sure Lloyd knows how much help you've been."

A smile lit Cindy's face. When animated she was almost pretty. With different clothes and hairstyle and confidence, she would be attractive.

"Thank you. I have to go now before I'm missed."

"Don't you get a lunch hour?"

She blushed and shook her head. "I brown-bag it and eat at my desk."

Translation, she had no friends to meet. I said goodbye and watched her walk away. In a hurry to be somewhere, people flowed around Cindy, but no one noticed her. She was invisible on the streets of West Palm Beach. When this case was over, I was going to change that. A makeover and hairstylist would do wonders for her.

Two hours later I gimped into the cool, large foyer of an office building on Flagler Drive. Although a hot shower and change of clothes had gone a long way to restore my appearance, my knees hurt like hell.

While I had given consideration to calling up Armando's Spa and Retreat for an afternoon of massage and pampering, a message from my office had alerted me that my quarry had landed back in West Palm Beach. I crossed the green marble floor around the huge water fountain and checked the directory. After stepping into the glass elevator, I watched the ground floor recede as it whisked me up three flights. The curving hallway took me to the last bank of offices.

As I entered, the receptionist behind a security enclosure was chattering in Spanish on the phone. She waggled her fingers at me, which I interpreted to mean she would be with me shortly. "Shortly" turned out to be five minutes. The conversation, punctuated often with exclamations and the waving of an arm covered with bangles, was about her friend's no-good husband. When the receptionist hung up, she gave me a practiced smile.

"May I help you?"

"I'm here to see Mr. Chase."

She glanced down at a sheet of paper and frowned. "Do you have an appointment?"

"No." I handed her my ivory embossed business card. "Tell him it's about Grace Roberts."

The receptionist's mouth tightened but she dialed a number. Turning away, she spoke on her headset. When the conversation concluded, she looked at me and pushed a buzzer. "Mr. Chase will see you."

I opened the door and she escorted me down a short bank of offices before gesturing at the corner one. I thanked her and entered a spacious office outfitted with black leather and chrome. A man rose and came around a massive glass table set on a diagonal.

"Ms. Rochelle." He extended a hand. As we shook, I had to admit, Charles Taylor Chase, no hyphen, was not what I had expected of Grace Roberts's fiancé.

Dark-haired, medium height and slender, he came across as a somber man. Not a lot of laugh lines around his mouth or brown eyes. Although dressed in an Italian-made wool suit and leather shoes, his overall appearance was discreet, no flash. Even his Rolex watch was a mere glint of gold on his wrist. Nothing ostentatious.

His mouth twitched as he observed my study of him. "Not what you would expect of Grace's boyfriend?" He gestured for me to take a client chair.

Boyfriend, not fiancé. "To be honest, no."

Chase resumed his seat behind his desk and propped his elbows on the arms, his hands forming a steeple. "We were the classic case of opposites attracting."

At the smell of money, Grace would have always been attracted, but why set her sight on Chase in particular?

He swiveled his chair so he could look out on his view of the Intracoastal Waterway and the boat traffic moving up and down it. "Grace was a vibrant woman. So alive. I was immediately attracted to her."

"Did she have any enemies?"

"Enemies?" His mouth pursed as if he found the word distasteful. "How do any of us know that until murder is solved?"

Good point. "Did she ever complain about anyone, seem apprehensive?"

"Complain? Yes, Grace did that a lot. She tended to be jealous of others. She was a bit insecure."

Grace insecure? "Anyone in particular she was jealous of?"

"You for one. That's why I agreed to see you. I can see why now."

"Me?"

"Cool sophistication. Class. Family name. Qualities Grace strived for but never could obtain."

I pointed out the obvious. "She could have married into a family name."

"True, but apparently she decided 'Chase' wasn't good enough."

"Excuse me?"

"Grace broke off our relationship while I was out of town on business. Not only did I return to news of her death but also a message on my answering machine telling me it was over, that she had bigger fish to fry since I couldn't trust her."

I opened my mouth to ask my next question, but he held up his hand. "I've already given the police the answering machine, and yes, I can verify I was in San Francisco. I'll be happy to give you the same names of the people I was with that I gave to the State Attorney's office."

One didn't need to actually be present to commit murder. With his resources he could've hired someone to do his dirty work for him.

Chase rose and went to stand by the window. The filtered sunlight threw his features in stark relief, showing his tormented expression.

"You did care for Grace, didn't you?"

His body jerked as if he had taken a blow. "Yes."

"What did she mean that you didn't trust her?"

But he didn't appear to hear my question, lost in staring out the window at a yacht churning north.

"Charles?"

He looked at me with a troubled expression. "What difference would it have been to me, to give her the things she wanted? The exotic trips, the jewelry? I could've afforded it."

"Then why didn't you?"

"Because I wanted to make sure she cared for me, that her affection didn't have a price tag attached."

"I can relate to that one."

His smile was bitter. "I bet you can. Grace used to complain you and I were like two peas in a pod, so distant and self-contained. If it wasn't for her interest in your grandfather, she would have washed her hands of both you and your aunt long ago."

"My aunt?"

"Yes. Grace hated her. They had quite a fight the week before her death."

Here Grace had always given the appearance that the sun rose and fell in Hilary.

"Do you know what it was about?"

"No, Grace called up and apologized even though she didn't want to."

Grace only did what would advance her, so why did she make up with Hilary? There was one sure way for me to find out. I stood. "Thank you for your time."

He came over and stared at me. "Grace was right on one account. I think you and I do have a lot in common. Ever wonder why we fall for those all wrong for us?"

I had asked myself that same question a thousand times and still had no answer. "Maybe because we can't judge who's right for us? We're so afraid of trusting that we doom ourselves to being hurt."

He nodded. "Perhaps."

I touched his arm. "I'm sorry for your loss."

"Thank you."

"I'll show myself out." I turned and left. By the time I reached the foyer my stomach was churning. Next stop, The Club.

Forty minutes later, after changing in the clubhouse dressing room, I found Hilary on the skeet-shooting range. I nodded at the attendant, accepted a gun and took up the station next to my aunt's.

The Club, so exclusive that its membership roll was top secret and kept under tight security, catered to the wealthy and famous. Whatever a member's recreational interest, it could be satisfied here from the mundane, such as golfing and tennis, to the more exotic such as skeet shooting or fox-hunting during the season.

With the northward migration poised to begin, this section of the grounds was fairly deserted. I watched as Hilary smoothly finished off her current tray of disks.

Pull, fire, hit. Pull, fire, hit. Hilary's eyesight was still eagle sharp. Along with all her swimming trophies, she also possessed a number of skeet-shooting awards. Last year she had topped the competition in the senior class at Nationals.

Switching on my machine, I followed the disk's arc. I fired and smiled with satisfaction as the disk disintegrated against the blue clear sky. With rapid pulls, I finished off my tray with a clean slate of direct hits.

"Haven't lost your touch, I see." Hilary stood watching,

her rifle cradled in her arms, while the attendant filled her machine.

"Thank you. Neither have you. Are you planning to enter the competition again this year?"

"I doubt it. My schedule's rather heavy right now."

That startled me. Hilary loved competing with fellow athletes. With a flash of insight, I realized it probably was a treat for her to be with others like her.

"Do you miss it?" I asked.

"Miss what?"

"The training and the races from when you competed in swimming?"

Astonishment flickered in her eyes. "Yes, I do," she simply said. She turned and began another round of shooting. When she finished, she motioned the attendant away. Well trained to cater to the whims of the membership, he moved a discreet distance away. Hilary looked at me.

"I assume this isn't a social call."

"No, it isn't. Some questions have come up with my investigation."

"Is it going well? Does Lloyd stand a chance?"

"I think so. I think there's more about Grace's death than a simple motive of jealousy or rage."

"Such as?"

"What did you and Grace argue about right before her death?"

Hilary's mouth thinned but she answered, "Grace unforgivably insulted Colin."

Whatever my feelings were about Hilary, I'd always admired her pit bull–like defense of her husband. Whether she loved him or not, she stood by him. I often wondered if he realized how much his wife protected him.

I cradled my gun. "That doesn't sound like the society-savvy Grace." Very clumsy of her to push Hilary's hot button by insulting her husband.

"Yes, Grace did know how to kiss ass when need be, didn't she?"

My jaw dropped. Hilary had known all along Grace's motive for being her beck-and-call assistant?

"Why do you look so surprised? Grace was very transparent."

"But useful?"

"Of course. She was also quite talented and amusing, so one could ignore her fawning."

Huh.

"However, because of her aspirations to use her connections, Grace called and apologized for her comments. I accepted, for which I'm grateful. I wouldn't have liked having harsh words to be our last."

Double huh. This was another Hilary I wasn't used to hearing.

"Did she ever mention finding anything strange or exciting of Granddad's?" Was it my imagination, or did Hilary's face whiten?

"No. As far as I know, the extent of my brother's collection was what I donated."

"What about Grandmother's family? Would any of them have their belongings?"

"Why the sudden interest?"

I shrugged. "Because Granddad may be tied to Grace's murder. There are too many coincidences, too many connections."

"Nonsense. His disappearance was only of momentary interest to the press until the next scandal came along. He's of no importance to anyone living now."

She meant herself, but what about me?

"Judge Winewski warned me off Granddad at the ball."

"Kurt?" Disgust dripped from Hilary's voice. "That drunk."

"Was he friends with my grandfather?"

"No."

"But wasn't he a judge at the same time?"

"Yes, but they didn't like each other. In his typical fashion Jonathan sneered at Kurt's incompetence."

Even if it was in the negative, this was the most Hilary had ever talked about her brother.

"What about Uncle Colin? Were he and Kurt friends?"

"Of course not!" she snapped, swinging toward the clubhouse. Then she hesitated and turned back to me.

"Look, before you bumble about and dig up pain and bad memories better left buried in the past, let me tell you how it was back then. The legal community was small, informal. It was a different way of life. Practices would close down for the summer even. Everyone knew everyone. Prosecutors, defense attorneys and judges would all meet at a local bar and discuss cases, work out deals." She frowned, remembering.

"There were nights when your grandmother and I almost sent out search parties because Colin and Jonathan were out so late with others at these 'bar' meetings."

"Did Granddad drink too much?"

"My perfect brother? Of course not. Jonathan was the master of control."

I always sensed Hilary had hated her brother, but the strength of her overt jealousy after all this time surprised me.

"Why did you hate him so much?"

"I did not hate him." Queen of denial, she drew herself erect as if the rifle she held was attached to her spine.

"But he was spoiled. Our parents allowed Jonathan to

do whatever he wanted, regardless of the consequences, because he was the boy, the heir apparent. He wanted to go to law school so they let him. He wanted to be a judge instead of going into the family business so they backed him with dreams of his becoming President dancing in their heads. Jonathan could do no wrong while I could do no right."

I could relate to that part. With Hilary I had never been able to do right. But since she had never known support, how could she know how to give it in return?

Wait a minute. Was I having an epiphany about Hilary after all this time? Why did that make me feel so uncomfortable? Did I prefer to hate her rather than reaching some plane of understanding? My path stretched before me and suddenly I saw I had been following the same one chosen by Hilary.

"That must have been tough for you," I observed.

Surprise registered on her face. "Not as tough as watching Jonathan garner all the limelight while Colin struggled to make his mark."

"Which he did."

"Yes, Colin was a superb attorney general even though he served only one term." She glanced at the diamond-crusted watch on her wrist. "I must be going. I have a meeting in an hour."

She looked at me. "Leave the past alone, Katherine. You might not like what you find."

Watching her tall proud figure walk toward the clubhouse, I let out a long, slow breath. When I was young I had possessed the intrinsic child gene that, when told not to do something, I had done it anyway. Looked like that gene hadn't dissipated.

Don't touch the past? I had to. For the case, for myself.

A twig snapped.

I whirled but saw no one. The attendant had disappeared and the shooting range was empty. Here and there were carefully planted sections of palm trees and tropical vegetation to screen this range from others. A slight breeze rustled the palm fronds.

Even as I listened for the sound of another person, the hair on my nape stirred. Deliberately, I changed the angle on the disk machine, lifted my rifle and triggered the machine. The disk flew over the nearest bank of trees and I pulled the trigger.

Bam!

I reset the machine and tracked the disk over the next section of trees. *Bam!*

I paused, listening with all my senses until I was sure the watcher was gone. Satisfied, I cradled the rifle and walked up to the clubhouse.

Chapter 11

That night when I got home, the red light on my answering machine was doing its annoying blink. After changing, I fed Willy, grabbed a container of yogurt from the fridge and pushed the play button.

First up was a message from my secretary and then a long pause before a low raspy voice began to speak. I thought possibly the caller was male, but it was hard to tell from the static reception.

"You're in danger. Leave well enough alone. Don't go digging into the past. Please." The soft sound of a disconnection and then my machine fell silent.

I popped the tape out and replaced it with a blank. I considered the tiny spool in my hand. Clearly a warning but a friendly or threatening one? The word "please" suggested the former, but maybe I had a polite killer. I placed the tape in a white business envelope, marked the outside as to the contents and then sealed and put it in my safe.

Enough was enough. There was only one past the caller had been talking about. The red neon sign on the wall was flashing the word "Grandfather."

Going to the hall closet, I found an old cardboard box at the back. I set it down in the center of the living room and sat cross-legged. Within minutes I had its contents spread across the plush champagne carpet. Carefully I unfolded yellowed newspaper clippings.

Before Hilary had caught me, I often had stolen into the small room at the mansion where my grandparents' possessions had been stored. One rainy afternoon I had discovered this box containing the clippings and several scrapbooks. By the feminine handwriting I had deduced that they had been my grandmother's.

Fortunately, since Hilary was such a stickler for respecting others' privacy, I was able to cart the box to my room, hiding it in the darkest corner of my closet. When I had moved out, I'd brought the box with me, meaning to go through it with an adult's eye but never had taken the time. Until now.

Many of the articles detailed Jonathan's days as a state prosecutor and then his unexpected appointment to the bench when a judge had been killed in a car accident. Also, snippets from local news about criminal cases he had presided over, and coverage of his assuming the position as chief judge several months before his disappearance. Then nothing.

The doorbell rang and I grimaced as I rose. The day had taken a toll on my body. I needed a massage overhaul. I gimped a few feet to the door. After checking through the peephole, I groaned and opened it. "I wasn't expecting company."

Gabe gave me his pirate's grin as he walked in. "I can see that."

His eyes went a liquid chocolate as he gave me a thorough once-over. My hand self-consciously went to my hair. I'd pulled it into a ponytail the moment I'd arrived home. I was wearing cutoff jeans and a midriff-bearing sleeveless top. Suddenly, I felt too exposed.

To give myself something to do, I sidled past Gabe and went into the kitchen. After grabbing a glass, I filled it with cracked ice and water and handed it to him.

"Thanks." He studied it with bemusement.

"It's only water," I said.

"I know, but I'm not used to it being served in a crystal glass except at weddings."

Frankly I wasn't crazy about plain water and thought it tasted better when served in crystal. Besides, all I had was a Baccarat set Hilary and Colin had given me. I hadn't had the time to go out buy a normal set of glassware.

I edged toward the counter, intending to hide the platter of chocolate-chip cookies I had set on a bone-china plate, but he reached out and snagged a cookie without comment. He gestured at the chaos in the living room. "What's all this?"

"That—" I took a cookie and left the kitchen "—is a box of all I have belonging to my grandparents."

I settled onto the sofa and scowled when Gabe sat beside me. I scooted into the corner against the stack of pillows and didn't miss his smug expression.

"You don't look too whipped after a day of hard labor." In fact, he looked down right yummy, although I had to admit to a tinge of regret. He had changed out of his construction worker's getup into blue jeans and a black T-shirt.

He took a swig of his water and shrugged. "I worked construction to help pay for college."

That explained the way he had blended in so easily today. "Learn anything of interest?"

"What you suspected. Your ex is way overextended on projects, hurting bad financially. The laborers talked among themselves about the pay being poor and erratic."

I stretched out my legs and contemplated the pink nail polish. Maybe I should switch back to red polish my next manicure visit. Red was more daring, sexier. I said absently, "Juan's backer won't be pleased."

"He has a backer?"

I nodded. "Not that you'd find the name on any documents, I would bet. The Castillo family does business on the basis of a word."

Gabe didn't break out of his slouch, but his sudden interest radiated in waves from him. "Your ex is a Castillo associate?"

"Yes. He and his father went to work for them after my aunt tossed them out. Why's that important?"

"Did you ever meet Marcos Castillo?"

"Yes, once." I suppressed a shudder at the memory. "I didn't like him."

Marcos, in his thirties when I had first met him, had been starkly handsome and overtly charming, but even as a naive eighteen-year-old, I had taken an instant dislike to the man. His appearance and personality had run only skin-deep. Deep down I had sensed a still coldness in the man. I had told Juan that Marcos was like a viper waiting to strike. Juan had laughed nervously and then made sure I never again saw Marcos or any of the other Castillos for that matter.

Gabe considered me. "Your reaction to him is pretty surprising considering the swath Marcos's cut through women over the years."

"He lacked…" I hesitated, uncertain how to describe how Marcos had given me the creeps.

"Any shred of humanity? That he could kill without shedding a tear?"

"Yes, that's it."

"Not surprising since he comes from a family who ran a crime ring in Cuba until Castro tossed them out to land here."

"The Castillos are a drug cartel?"

Gabe set down his water on the coaster on the side table. "Drugs, guns, racketeering, you name the crime and if there's a profit to be had, the Castillos have both hands in it."

"I don't recall ever hearing about them on the news."

"Because they run a very tight ship. They keep the local Cuban community terrorized on any given day. We've been trying to catch them for years, but any time we get a witness who might testify, that witness disappears or ends up dead. Their payoffs run deep."

"How deep?"

"Police, prosecutors, judges, who knows?" Gabe's voice was tight with anger and bitterness. "All I know is any time I thought I had a decent case, something went wrong. Evidence destroyed, prosecution dismissed on a technicality."

"Are the Castillos the reason you punched out your chief?"

Gabe's grin was vicious. "Among other reasons." He rose.

"What next?" I asked.

"Now that I know your ex's connected to the Castillos, I'm going to do some digging in that direction."

"Be careful."

He bent over and, grabbing the front of my blouse, drew me close, practically nose-to-nose. "You're the one who has to be careful, babe. I don't want you sticking your head out of your office tomorrow."

No one could tell me what to do. Not anymore. I narrowed my eyes. "There's too much work to be done—"

His kiss was hot, searing, and mind-numbing. He took total possession of my mouth and before I could respond, it was over. I blinked at him.

"In case you haven't gotten it through your thick skull, Kate, someone either wants you dead or scared off of this case. You're a walking target. If the Cuban crime family is involved, they play for keeps."

Gabe shook his finger at me. "I want your word or I'll handcuff you here and now to the sofa."

My mouth dried at the incredibly sexy image of Gabe having his way with me while I was handcuffed.

Something in my expression must have alerted him to the direction of my thoughts for he cursed a blue streak and hauled me close for another assault on my lips. "You keep that image in your mind, babe, for the next time."

He gripped my chin. "Your promise, Kate."

"I promise I'll go into the office tomorrow."

"Good." With a heated look that stripped me bare, he was gone.

I dragged a shuddering breath into my heated lungs. Of course, what I hadn't mentioned to Gabe was that I planned to make one or two stops on the way to the office. At max.

Eight-thirty the next morning found me in the outer office to Judge Winewski's chambers. I had chosen that time because there were no motion hearings scheduled and the judge's first case wasn't until ten o'clock.

I had stayed up late, reading every newsletter article on my grandfather several times, so my system whined for another cup of coffee. The disgruntled judicial assistant, who had found me waiting outside in the hallway, also appeared to be in dire straits of caffeine so I went downstairs and bought two cups from the courthouse café.

Although somewhat mollified with a shot of java, Winnie, a huge black woman with long painted nails that could do some serious damage, kept shooting me glances. I wondered if the judge had few visitors or if Winnie simply had an antenna for trouble.

"You aren't here to yell at him, are you?" She finally broke the silence.

"I don't plan on it."

"Because if you are, he's been feeling poorly."

"Do many attorneys yell at him?" I asked out of morbid curiosity.

"Oh sure, but usually right after motion hearings. They come up here to bitch their heads off over his rulings. Don't do no good, I warn you. Once he's made up his mind, it's made until the appeals court overrules him."

"That happens a lot?"

Her snort flared her nostrils quite a bit. "Does the sun shine, honey?"

I smiled and glanced around the office again. A framed document caught my attention. It wasn't the usual diploma or certificate, so I rose and crossed the room to study it. Faded but preserved beneath the glass was a newspaper clipping about a murder trial. As I read the account I was startled to see both my uncle Colin's and godfather Paul's names mentioned. I looked for the date and saw that it was two months before my grandparents disappeared. My pace quickened.

I heard movement in the next office. Winnie must have heard it as well for she picked up her phone, murmuring that I was there to see the judge. She hung up and said, "He'll see you in a bit."

A bit could be a while but I'd wait all day if need be. I nodded at the framed clipping. "Was this a famous case of Judge Winewski's?"

Winnie cackled. "You might call it that. The judge calls it the case that sent him to purgatory here on county court. He keeps it there to remind him of his downfall."

From the inner office I could hear footsteps receding as if the judge had been at the door and then the sounds of a desk drawer opening and closing.

I glanced at my watch. It was eight forty-five. I took out my notepad and copied information from the article.

Bam!

Winnie and I looked at each other for one frozen minute and then she was on the phone, calling security. I swallowed and crossed to the door. Although I knew what the sound meant, I had to be sure.

Steeling myself, I slowly opened the door and looked in. Just as slowly, I closed it. The acid taste of coffee burned my throat and I swallowed. Hard.

Winnie looked at me, her brown eyes huge with horror, and I shook my head. The better part of Judge Winewski's head was splattered behind the chair where he had sat and pulled the trigger. He was beyond any help.

Winnie pressed her lips together and then said, "He's finally moved beyond purgatory. Maybe, with all his penance, he's with the angels now. I can only pray."

"You do that, Winnie."

I walked out into the hallway to wait for the police and to drink a deep breath of air not tainted with blood and death.

Fifteen minutes later I could have smacked myself on the forehead, but I was too busy keeping my head between my knees as I sat in the courthouse corridor.

Why did I think I could get away with coming here without telling Gabe?

Two tall dark-haired men strode with purpose down the

hallway from the elevator banks, and I didn't need my twenty-twenty vision to recognize the one man.

Gabe.

Groaning, I flipped through a mental chart of excuses. No, I was rotten at being pathetic or forgetful. I was never any good at batting eyelashes and enchanting a man. I'd better suck it up and take it on the chin.

I sat up, ignored the queasy twist of my stomach and waited. First up was a man similarly dressed as Gabe but with the addition of a sport jacket. He looked familiar but I couldn't place the context. Probably the homicide detective.

He flashed a killer smile. "Katherine, I don't know if you remember me. I'm Lieutenant Sam Bowie."

Uh-oh. Of course. Texas drawl, dangerous looks. It had been over a year since I'd last seen him. My law partner Nicole wouldn't like this run-in with Sam one bit. The mere mention of his name in her presence was forbidden. The two were like oil and water.

"Lieutenant." I acknowledged him with a slight nod.

"Brr." He faked a shudder. "Dang, it's cold in here."

I suppressed a smile. If you gave Sam an inch, his humor would take a mile and then some.

"You've become quite the topic of conversation at the station." He rubbed his chin. "I took this call because I had to see the infamous Katherine Rochelle."

"Infamous?" I asked.

"You've become the crime-scene queen lately."

I flushed and cast a guilty glance at Gabe. Uh-oh. He had on his cop face.

"I may have a few questions for you," Sam said amiably. "Can you stick around?"

"Of course."

He nodded and went inside the chambers.

Ignoring Gabe as he sat beside me, I stared at the opposite wall. "How—"

"I was having breakfast with Sam when the call came in. The moment I heard Winewski's name, I knew."

Hmm.

"Why did you lie to me, Kate?"

That got my attention. Indignant, I swung to face him. "I-did-not-lie," I enunciated each word carefully.

"Really? Didn't you promise to go into the office?"

"I was. Right after I stopped here. I simply omitted this little detail."

"Not telling me something isn't lying?"

"No, it's the fine art of lawyering."

"What you're telling me is the next time you promise me anything, it's meaningless."

My temper flared. "How many promises have you broken as a cop or a P.I.? How many lies have you told?"

A deep red flush stained his cheeks. "That's different."

I poked his chest. "No difference. Omissions, misstatements, misdirection. In our professions, we both must use them to at times to accomplish the end."

"This is different."

"Baloney. It's not. If you were hot on the trail of the Castillo family, I bet you would do anything to bring them down, correct?"

"Yes, but—"

"No buts. No out clauses between us, Gabe. You were trying to keep me from doing my job, which is proving my client innocent. I won't stand for it. You want me to be honest with you, then stop trying to put me in a corner like a bad little girl."

The thing about stress, it can trigger the stomach, and

mine had had enough. Nausea slammed into me. I lurched to my feet, barely muttered an "excuse me" and ran to the ladies' restroom by the elevators.

Inside I made it to the first stall only a second before I prayed to the porcelain goddess. Ten minutes later, after rinsing out my mouth and taking a good dose of breath mints, I emerged. Gabe stood right next to the door, his shoulder propped against the wall.

"Feel better?"

I nodded. "Do you ever get used to it?"

"Used to seeing dead bodies? No, but you build up defenses to deal with it."

"I need those defense mechanisms. Fast."

He looped his arm around my shoulders. "Since I can't stop you, I'll tell you about them."

"Thanks."

We walked toward Judge Winewski's chambers and saw Lieutenant Bowie waiting, his sharp gaze taking in Gabe's arm around me. He grinned and in that moment I realized how similar both men were. Dark, fit and edgy tempered with a sense of humor, albeit at times perverse. I wondered how deep their friendship ran.

"It's about time you got it right, Chavez," Bowie commented. "Katherine, are you ready to answer some questions now?"

"Sure." I was already running through what I could say and couldn't say.

"Uh-oh." Sam's brow arched. "I can see the lawyer in you already strategizing."

I lifted my chin. "Damn straight."

Gabe gave me a warning squeeze and then dropped his arm. "I have to go."

I turned and planted my hands on my hips. "Where are

you going?" If I had to account for my actions then so should my private investigator.

Gabe's eyes darkened and he lowered his head to whisper in my ear, "Remember? I'm undercover. I have to change before returning to the construction site. I'm already late." Then he nibbled my ear, slowly, deliberately.

My breath shortened and adrenaline-fueled lust spiked through me. It was all I could do not to reach out and grab him.

Sam drawled, "I think there's an unoccupied broom closet down the hallway."

My bones jelled. I pulled away from Gabe and shot Sam a glare glacial enough to freeze the Texan out of him.

"Ouch!" he said, rubbing his chest. "I've been shot."

Gabe tugged my braid. "Be nice, Kate. Sam here can't handle a real woman." He then hooked his hand around my waist and drew me close for a quick, mind-numbing kiss. "I'm off. Look after her, Sam."

Gabe and Sam exchanged one of those mysterious male glances, and Gabe sauntered off. Although my brains were a bit scrambled by the kiss, they weren't so fogged that it didn't strike me how odd it was that Sam and Gabe had been having breakfast this morning.

Secrets. Ones I held, ones he held. Weren't they an intrinsic part of both our jobs? Mine because of the attorney-client privilege, his because of the life-and-death dictates of his former job?

You could slap the title private investigator on him but at heart Gabe was still a cop. How could two people with so many secrets build a bridge of trust?

As I watched Gabe disappear around the corner, I asked quietly, "You'll watch his back while he goes after the Castillos, won't you, Sam?"

During the time he and Nicole had circled around each other, I had often thought Sam had been the master of being immutable, but he looked at me with a stunned expression. Then he laughed. "Boy, you're one sharp lady. Gabe's going to have his hands full with you and it serves him right."

He cupped my elbow. "Don't you worry, honey. Gabe was the best cop I've ever known and he knows what he's doing. Now," he opened the chambers door, "I do have a few questions for you, lady lawyer, such as how come in recent weeks every time there's a dead body in West Palm Beach, you're involved?"

An hour later I entered the offices of the circuit court clerk. Since technically I was still in the same building, I didn't see the point of calling Gabe.

After studying the index of court documents, I filled out a request form, took a number and waited for a harried clerk to call on me. Years ago when the paper volume had grown overwhelming, and storage and maintenance of court documents had become a real problem, the government, at enormous taxpayer expense, had undertaken the massive project of copying all old court filings onto film.

The young, overweight clerk huffed her way to the microfilm bank and punched in a sequence of codes. The machine growled as the bins spun. Finally, one bin opened and the clerk flipped through the stack of microfiche.

Pausing, she frowned. "Someone must have misfiled it." She kept flipping through the rest of the film and then went through the section one more time.

She shook her head. "I'm sorry but the film you wanted isn't here."

What were the odds that film for cases thirty-five years ago would be misplaced? Slim to none.

"Do you have a record as to who last requested it?"

"Yes, but I can't give out that information."

I gave her my best pleading smile. "Please." I handed her my business card. "It's important. I needed that information for a murder case I'm defending."

On a hunch, I added, "I suspect that the film was taken out within the past month."

She looked doubtful but then she shrugged. "What can it hurt? If you find the film—"

"Of course, I'll notify the clerk's office and return it."

I followed her to the desk where she flipped through the record of people who had requested film. She ran a pudgy finger down the column of film numbers. Her lips moved as she silently read the numbers. She flipped through a couple of pages and then stopped.

"Here it is." She scrunched her face as she tried to read the handwriting. "The last person who looked at the film was Grace Roberts." She closed the book. "I'm sorry, I can't give out her phone number, but I'll call her about returning the film."

"Don't bother calling her." I hiked the strap of my tote bag over my shoulder.

"Why on earth not? There's a fine for taking the film."

"She won't be able to return it. Grace Roberts is dead."

I left the office with the clerk staring at me with her mouth open.

Chapter 12

At the family mansion, Edwin let me in with only the merest lift of his brow. I told him in the iciest Rochelle tone that I would announce myself to my uncle. At this time of the day there was only one place he would be.

I walked down the hall and paused outside the den that also served as his office. Startled, I heard through the thick carved walnut-paneled door my uncle arguing. I could count on the fingers of one hand the number of times I'd heard him speak in a raised voice. Was he fighting with my aunt? Maybe I'd better eat crow and return to the foyer so Edwin could announce me.

Then I heard the muffled sound of a phone receiver being slammed down. Counting to ten, I rapped on the door. "Uncle Colin?"

I heard the sound of a desk drawer being shut and then the door swung open.

"Katherine! What an unexpected surprise." Looking unruffled except for the ruddy tint of his cheeks, Colin kissed my check. "And to what do I owe this honor of a visit by our town's illustrious defense attorney?"

I rolled my eyes and followed him as he led me into his office. Although my uncle hadn't actively practiced law for nearly twenty years, not since his stint as the state's attorney general, he used this room to run his various business interests, including his duties as consulting counsel to Rochelle Enterprises. Out of the twenty-six rooms in this mansion, this one room was his alone. Privately I had always thought he had latched onto the excuse of this office to keep Hilary at bay. It had worked. We all had honored his retreat.

I took one of the worn burgundy club chairs while Colin sat in his custom-designed black leather chair behind his desk.

"How goes Lloyd's case?"

"It's taken some unexpected turns."

Colin chuckled. "They always do."

"Were you friends with Kurt Winewski?"

His smile faded. "Hardly friends. I had trials before him when I served as a public defender."

"Have you heard that he committed suicide?"

Coin's face whitened. "That's terrible, but hardly unexpected. I had heard through the years how despondent he had become due to being passed over for promotion."

"I was in his outer chambers when he did it."

With an expression of half horror, half concern, Colin rose. "Are you all right?"

I motioned for him to sit again. "I'm fine, Uncle Colin." I wasn't about to tell him that dead bodies were rapidly becoming a way of life for me.

"You say that now, sweetheart, but being in the presence of violent death can often come back to haunt you. Promise me you'll come to me if you start having problems. I know a superb psychiatrist."

I wondered how Colin would know about this aspect of life, but then I realized he must have seen quite a bit during his days as a public defender. Were those horrific images the reason he started down his drinking path?

I managed a reassuring smile. "Of course, I'll call you." Not. But I didn't want him to worry about me.

"All right, my dear." He leaned back in his chair.

"Up on the wall in the outer chambers where I was, Judge Winewski had a framed newspaper article about a case you were involved in before him."

Suddenly, Colin had a stilled, watchful quality. "Oh? I guess I should be flattered."

"What do you recall about the Lopez case?"

"The what case?"

"State versus Lopez."

He shook his head. "I'm sorry, but I don't recall—"

"You were the P.D., Paul was the state attorney and Winewski the judge."

"Katherine, the criminal legal community was small and tight-knit back then. Paul and I had any number of cases together. It's how we became friends."

"Lopez was a Cuban recently immigrated who was charged with the murder of another Cuban."

"Oh, yes." Colin rose and walked over to the bank of windows facing the ocean. "Manuel Lopez. It's coming back to me. The victim, highly regarded, owned a market that catered to the Hispanic community on Southern Boulevard. Right? Brutal murder. If I remember correctly, someone beat the owner to death, and the bloody bat was found in the garbage can at the house my client and his wife shared with eight other family members."

Despite myself, I was intrigued. "What was Lopez's connection?"

"The owner had only hired him the week before to clean the store at night. It was his first job. He didn't even have enough money to take a bus. He had to walk to the store at night."

"How far?"

"A mile."

I was incredulous. "You mean your client carried a dripping bat all the way from the store to hide it at home?"

Colin beamed. "You always did have a quick mind. Exactly the point I argued."

"What was the motive?"

"Money, of course. Paul's theory was the owner caught Manuel stealing from the till."

"And Lopez killed him with a bat in the store? Where did he get it?"

"Several witnesses reported the owner kept one under the counter for security purposes."

I could understand that, given the break-in at my house.

Colin sighed and rubbed his forehead. "Open-and-shut case for the prosecution. The jury took only long enough to select a foreman and cast one vote. Guilty."

"What happened to your client?"

"I'm not sure. Someone came up with money to get him a new attorney, and I was fired. I think there was a series of motions and then an appeal was filed until a deal was worked out where he only got a life sentence rather than the death penalty."

I frowned. It sounded like a typical murder case. What was I missing? "So why would Winewski choose that trial to single out on his wall?"

"God knows. Maybe the old goat's conscience finally

woke up. He certainly ruled against me enough during that trial or any others I had with him. I couldn't get a win for the life of me."

"Ouch. That must have been tough."

Colin's lips twisted into a bitter smile. "It made plea bargaining a bitch, if you'd pardon the expression." He flushed. "But Paul knew he had a sure thing when Winewski presided."

"Katherine, I didn't know you were here."

I twisted in the chair and saw Hilary in the doorway. Although her cream silk pant suit was exquisitely styled, she appeared to be losing weight. I didn't like her ashen skin color either. "Aunt Hilary. Are you all right?"

"Of course." She stepped inside and walked to where Colin stood.

"You look thinner."

"Thank you. I've been trying a new low-fat diet. Was I interrupting anything important?"

Colin brushed a light kiss on his wife's cheek. "Remember Kurt Winewski?"

Hilary shot me a sharp look. "Of course."

"He committed suicide. Katherine was at his office today when it happened."

What little color my aunt had drained from her face. "How perfectly dreadful! Are you all right?"

"Yes. I was in the outer office."

"Katherine saw a clipping about an old case on Kurt's wall and was curious about it."

"Case?"

"Yes, one I was the public defender on and of course Paul was the prosecutor."

"How bizarre," she murmured.

"That's what I thought. I had a lot of cases and that one certainly wasn't memorable except for the fact I lost."

She patted his arm. "Kurt always did have it in for you."

"True."

"Judge Winewski told his assistant he wanted the article on the wall to remind him of the day he entered purgatory."

Hilary's laugh was short and bitter. "Obviously, the poor man had been in desperate need of mental attention for a long time. A tragedy, yes, but hardly a noteworthy mystery."

She glanced at her watch. "Colin, we have that testimonial dinner for Paul at six. You need to get ready."

"Certainly, my dear. I'll just walk Katherine out."

Hilary didn't look happy with the notion, but Colin crossed the room. I stood and walked with him into the hallway. As we went toward the foyer, I used the opportunity to ask him a few more questions.

"Uncle Colin, did my grandfather have an assistant?"

"Of course. Every judge had a secretary and bailiff assigned to him."

"Do you recall the names of Jonathan's court staff?"

His brows furrowed. "The secretary was a spinsterlooking woman. Sue…Susan. Something ordinary like that. I believe the bailiff's name was Stewart."

"Do you know if either of them is still alive?"

"No, can't say that I do. I lost contact with them after I became attorney general. Why do you want to know their names?"

"I thought they might be able to tell me what cases Granddad was working on when he disappeared."

Colin halted and placed his hands on my shoulders. "Honey, let the past go. I'm sorry that you had such a hellish childhood, though God knows, Hilary and I tried to fill the place of parents to you."

"I know you did," I gave him a quick hug.

"I'm worried that you're becoming obsessed. Jonathan

and Marguerite vanished without a trace all those years ago. It destroyed your mother and it can destroy you, too, if you're not careful. It's too late to do anything about it."

I shook my head and broke away. "I'm sorry, Uncle Colin. I can't do that. There have been too many secrets in my life, too many situations where I've chosen to look the other way rather than act. I've never believed that Grand-dad was on the take." I lifted my palms. "I just can't. I need to find out the truth. Somehow I think what happened in that courthouse thirty-five years ago is tied into Grace's death."

"I don't want to lose you, too, Katherine."

"You won't."

I turned and left Colin standing in that great foyer, looking lost under the glittering chandelier.

Why was I not surprised when lead prosecutor Jared Manning emerged from the patrol car along with a uniformed police officer in front of the town house Grace Roberts had rented? When I had called yesterday, the assistant prosecutor had sounded astonished at my request, pursuant to the discovery rules, to be allowed to search the decedent's premises. She had put me off until this morning.

"Good morning, Ms. Rochelle," Jared called out as he and the officer walked toward me. As I returned the greeting, Gabe's truck pulled up behind the patrol car.

Oh goody. A full house. Gabe had been downright surly last night when I had called him and told him where I was going today. However, he had seemed satisfied that I wouldn't be alone during my inspection. I hadn't really expected him since he seemed to be all wrapped up in his pursuit of the Castillo angle, trying to help out Lieutenant Bowie.

Unlike Jared's brisk energy, Gabe sauntered up while

the officer unlocked the door. I merely arched my brow and he smirked.

Jared handed me a document. "Here's my final disclosure list."

Pursuant to the discovery rules, the prosecution is obligated to furnish the defense with a list of witnesses it anticipates calling at trial along with any witness statement. I had already received one such list so I scanned it looking for the changes.

One name in particular stood out: Isabella Montoya. My mental folder on Grace's friends flipped open. Isabella, owner of an antique store on Southern Boulevard. She had called Grace at least four times in the week before her murder. So far Isabella had failed to return my phone calls, but apparently she had spoken to the prosecution.

Hmm. I removed a manila folder from my tote and carefully tucked away the list. Jared gestured and I entered the house. For a moment I stood in the postage-sized foyer, allowing my vision to adjust to the dim interior. Then I entered the living room.

Standard South Florida town house with two bedrooms, a bath and a half, conjoined living-dining room with a door leading to a small courtyard, and combined kitchen and utility room. White walls, beige carpet. It was a rental all right.

Grace's furniture, though, was on the expensive side and not from one of those mass-market places. She favored the contemporary style except for the huge floor-standing mirror in the corner, which was more along the baroque lines. No photographs were displayed anywhere, only framed uninspiring prints. One thing for sure, Grace hadn't bothered to acquire any tastes in the arts.

"If you would tell us what you're looking for, Ms.

Rochelle, perhaps we can help you." Jared studied me with curiosity. Gabe had already taken his cue and disappeared into the first bedroom followed by the officer.

Jared's office had furnished me with a transcript of the tape removed from Grace's answering machine and an inventory of the house's contents. In this day of high tech she hadn't owned a computer; at least one hadn't been found.

"Microfilm," I offered as I went to the sideboard in the dining room that appeared to be the only place that offered storage.

"Microfilm?" Clearly, I had managed to surprise Jared. Score one for the defense.

"Yes. Before her death Grace was in the clerk's office and took a microfiche of court cases from thirty-five years ago."

Jared shook his head as I opened one drawer. "I don't get the connection."

"You don't have to." Credit receipts and bills jammed drawer number one. Taking a handful, I sorted through them. No black square. I continued the process until I had reviewed everything in the drawer. Drawer number two contained the same. I sighed and began to flip through them. Gabe called out that there was nothing in the master bedroom and headed into the second one.

One receipt leaped out at me but I didn't pause over it even though I about gagged over the price. The mirror came from The Old World Antique Store on Southern. I'd bet my last dollar that was Isabella Montoya's place and she sure knew how to gouge people. Why had Grace splurged on something so not her style unless...

I turned and studied the mirror. "What's the matter?" Jared asked, but I ignored him. I crossed the living room to the corner. Gabe, wearing latex gloves, materialized at my side, and, without a word, moved the mirror so that I could see behind it. I squinted and, with a grunt, he handed me a small high-powered flashlight. Switching it on, I panned the beam up and down.

There. On the left side was the faint gummed markings left by tape. Whatever had been taped there had been removed, but at one time something had been hidden behind this mirror. Or was I jumping to an assumption? Had simply a sales ticket been tacked there so as not to mar the mirror side?

"Kate, pan down toward the other side," Gabe said. I moved the light and saw a small dark outline. My pulse quickened. Gabe said to the officer, "Tim, would you give me a hand here?"

The officer took the mirror from him, and Gabe removed the item. It was the microfiche. Before I could even enjoy the victory, Jared stepped forward with a plastic bag.

"If you would drop that in here, the officer will take it back to the station to be analyzed."

Hang on. I planted my hands on my hips. "That's my evidence I found."

"And pursuant to the rules, you will be given a copy."

"When? Trial begins on Monday."

"My office will have it ready by tomorrow."

Not nearly enough time, but there was more than one way to skin a prosecutor.

"I'll be at your office first thing in the morning."

"I'll look forward to it. Was there anything else you needed to look at?"

I flashed him a brilliant smile. "We haven't checked the kitchen or courtyard yet." I could hear the silent groan inside all three men, but they followed me into the kitchen.

Rochelles are thorough, if nothing else positive can be said about us.

* * *

"I don't have nothing to say to you." Isabella Montoya glared at us from behind the small counter in her antique shop. Not even Gabe's charm, turned on full blast when we had introduced ourselves, had had any effect on the hostile store owner. Gabe and I had made a beeline here after leaving Grace's town house.

"You spoke to the state attorney's office," I pointed out.

She picked up a cloth and swiped at a pewter plate. "No, I haven't. I told him I didn't know nothing about Grace's death and still the bastard subpoenaed me. I've a business to run. I can't afford to be stuck in court."

I glanced around her shop while I tried to place what I was hearing in the tone of her voice. She was spitting mad, but another emotion was at play here. Fear?

Her store overall was on the low end of antiques, if one could call a 1960 Danish-style dresser or a black velvet Elvis an antique. Poor quality, outrageous prices.

I turned my attention back to Isabella, a petite darkhaired woman dressed stylishly enough in a vivid red blouse and black slacks. "That baroque mirror you sold Grace doesn't seem in keeping with your inventory here."

The woman started. "I didn't sell Grace anything." Was sweat beading on her temples?

"I saw both the mirror and the sales receipt at her house, Ms. Montoya. If need be, I can request the State have those on hand for when you testify."

"I didn't sell it to her. I bought it on her behalf from an auction in Palm Beach."

Semantics. She was trying to toy with us.

"What color was the backing?"

Isabella flashed me a startled look. "Regular cardboard stapled onto the frame, which is why I was so surprised by the price. But Grace insisted that I get it, no matter what the cost. She said it once belonged to someone important."

Cardboard. At the house the mirror had had no backing, just the coated glass. Had something been hidden, covered by the cardboard? Did that account for the outline of tape?

"Did Grace mention who the mirror belonged to?"

"No. Just that it had changed hands a while back and the current owner had recently died. His widow auctioned off a few of their things so she could sell their house and move up north."

Wait a minute. Excitement buzzed through me. Perry Wentworth had died at the beginning of the year. Hilary had mentioned with a sneer that his wife was closing down their mansion next door. If I had their ages right, Perry would have been a contemporary of my grandfather's.

The mirror had been my grandparents'. It all fit; it had to.

"Kate, are you all right?" Gabe asked, placing his hand on my arm.

"No, I'm fine. I just realized who the original owner of the mirror was." I composed my racing thoughts.

"Was Grace blackmailing anyone?"

A closed expression slammed down on Isabella's face. "We weren't girlfriends, you know what I mean."

The woman was one of those people who couldn't lie directly so she would beat around the question. A funny odor wafted into the store, but I ignored it. However, I sensed Gabe going into alert mode. He moved toward the rear of the store.

"I didn't ask you that. I asked if you were aware of Grace's blackmailing anyone? Did she find something attached to the back of the mirror?"

Isabella's jaw bunched. A crashing sound came from the back of the store where I assumed her storage was.

Gabe ran to me, grabbed my elbow and yelled, "Everyone get out of here. Now!"

I didn't need an engraved invitation, not after the past few weeks. I ran. Out of the corner of my eye, I saw a white-faced Isabella move from behind the counter.

Gabe and I zigzagged around the antiques and burst through the front door. We were almost across the street when I heard a *whoosh* followed by an ear-shattering *boom*. Next thing I knew I was airborne. The ground rushed up at me and I tried to tuck and roll. Pain shot through my shoulder and then I saw stars above, with the ocean rushing in my ears.

Through the din I heard someone's voice. "Baby, talk to me. Are you hurt?"

I blinked and the whirling sky stilled. Gabe's face hovered over me. The roar in my ears dulled to a drone. Then my brain clicked into action.

There had been an explosion.

I struggled to sit up and Gabe's arm came around my shoulders. Pain seared through me, bringing tears to my eyes. "My shoulder!"

He dropped his hand and moved to my right side. "You have one hell of a red mark." Although I heard sirens wailing closer, Gabe dug out his phone and called 911 requesting an ambulance.

"I don't need a doctor," I protested. Now that the first wave of pain had receded, I gingerly tested it. This time the pain was less.

"Like hell you don't. You're lucky it wasn't your head that hit the ground."

For the first time I noticed that I was sitting on a grassy slope before a small bungalow that housed a hair salon. When I saw the sidewalk was only a foot away, I closed my eyes and swallowed hard.

The ear drone dulled to a buzz.

I reopened my eyes and viewed the circle of curious on-lookers. Through a gap I could see flames leaping high from the antique store.

"Isabella! Where is she?"

"I don't know if she made it out." Gabe ran a hand through his hair. "I was too busy having nine lives scared out of me when I saw you lying here."

"We've got to find her." I struggled to stand. With a string of curses, Gabe put his arm around my waist and helped me. The crowd parted and we walked into the street. I saw a body covered by a coat lying closer to the store. "Oh no!"

Gabe released me and, after kneeling beside the body, lifted the edge of the coat. A muscle bunched along his jaw. "Damn fool. Her purse wasn't worth risking her life."

I then saw the small black leather purse lying beside Isabella's body. It made no sense. Why had she gone for her purse?

Averting my gaze from the damage done to the woman's face, I crouched by the bag, using my body to block any observer's view. I lifted open the flap and checked out the contents. Compact, lipstick, mascara, wallet, brush… What was that tucked in the corner? I removed a battered envelope, yellowed with age.

The sirens were louder. "Kate, the emergency response will be here any second," Gabe warned in a low voice.

"I know. This won't take me but a second." My fingers trembled as I opened the envelope and drew out a typed document. I frowned as I scanned the faded writing.

"What is it?"

"It's a hearing schedule." My heart was pounding so hard that my chest hurt. "It's a calendar of my grandfather's hearings. Grace must have given it to Isabella for safekeeping."

Gabe let out a low whistle as tires screeched nearby. Fire rescue was here. Hurriedly, I slipped the envelope and schedule into my jacket pocket. He helped me up and then held me still.

"Don't tell me you're removing evidence from a crime scene."

Gabe's police face was on so that I couldn't read him. I bit my lower lip. "Technically, since the schedule was my grandfather's, it belongs to me."

He stared at me for a long moment and then he grinned. "Works for me."

I let out a whoosh of breath.

"Well, well, well. There's a dead body so Katherine Rochelle must be around."

I sighed and faced the scowling Lieutenant Bowie. "Hey, Sam. I can explain—"

The lieutenant held up his hand. "Stop. I don't think I can handle hearing it right now." He arched a brow. "From the looks of you, the medics need to check you both out. Where can I find you later?"

"At Kate's house," said Gabe.

"What?" I glared at him and he winked.

"After the day you had, I think you at least deserve me cooking my famous paella."

I smiled. "That works for me."

Chapter 13

Leading a life of privilege can be a double-edged sword. It can either enhance your strengths or aid your weaknesses.

For example, patience has never been my strong suit. With a large staff at the Rochelles' beck and call, I never had to wait for anything. Only during my years at the private school and then college and law school did I learn that not everything could come to me with a snap of my fingers.

Despite all my arguments, the paramedics bundled me into an ambulance to take me to the local hospital to have my shoulder checked out, with Gabe following behind in his truck. Why did he come through the exam with flying colors while I had to be treated like a porcelain doll? If I didn't know better, they gave him a clean bill of health simply because he was a former cop.

The ride did nothing to help my simmering temper. All I wanted to do was crawl into a hole somewhere and think.

Pieces of information were being hurled at me like debris in a hurricane, disjointed, disconnected and all hinting at a larger picture that I still didn't comprehend. My client's trial was upon me, and all I had was a rapidly rising body count with one dead judge and two murdered women.

My mind skirted around another truism—someone wanted my body to be included in that count.

When the driver set the siren to wailing, I scrambled off the gurney and ordered, "Turn it off." My well-trained voice with its proper chilled degree of haughtiness had him instantly complying. I sat back down, crossed my arms over my chest and fumed.

Sadly, by now I was becoming a real expert on the aftereffects of a crisis on a person. The adrenaline that pumped through my body during the explosion was turning into something more potent. I needed a release but I was going to have to wait until I was home and could swim a few laps, oh say, about a thousand. If I couldn't use my shoulder, then I would have to find a substitute to burn off the aftermath of violence.

However, when I saw the teeming waiting room at the hospital, the harried emergency staff, and the doctors who didn't even look my age, enough was enough. I whipped out my cell phone and called the Rochelle family doctor.

Thirty minutes later Dr. Young had whisked me through X-ray, located the on-call orthopedic specialist, and ordered an MRI of my right shoulder. Through all the poking, prodding and testing, Gabe silently shadowed me. Dr. Young took one look at his set expression and didn't force the issue of Gabe waiting outside the examination room.

Inexplicably, Gabe's tight-lipped presence pissed me off. Damn it, I could take care of myself. I didn't need him. As the orthopedic surgeon with an unpronounceable name asked me to raise my arm for the fiftieth time, I glared over the doctor's head at Gabe. "Don't you have anything better to do, such as investigate something? Like who just killed Isabella Montoya?"

"It can wait." Gabe could have been a slab of granite propped against the back wall for all his reaction.

"You're just hoping to catch a glimpse of my backside in this gown."

"And a very lovely butt you have. You must like to tan in the buff."

From the corner of my eye, I saw Dr. Young's lips twitch. My jaw set.

At that moment the orthopedist found a particularly sensitive spot on my shoulder socket to drill his finger into. I gave up on responding to Gabe and focused on not screaming and knocking the doctor on flat on his ass.

But my medical torture wasn't over. Heck no. Next up, the magnetic resonance imaging machine, otherwise known as an MRI. The technician led me into a ghastly white room barren except for a chair and a large machine the shape of a cube with a hollowed center. The air was so cold that you could have kept frozen meat in here. The tech gestured for me to lie on the patient table that would slide into the tube. Gabe straddled the chair backward. The tech secured a belt around my middle and showed me how to operate the panic button. Great.

As I slid into the mechanical equivalent of a coffin, I decided it was a good thing I wasn't claustrophobic. Then the sound of flying bullets erupted.

"Let me out of here!" I pushed the panic button and the noise stopped as the tray slid out. Before I popped out completely, I fought to loosen the restraining band across my stomach. The technician rushed in from the control panel. "Pleáse, Ms. Rochelle. The test only lasts twenty minutes."

"And that's twenty minutes too long."

Gabe reached out and took my hand. Can people truly be linked through touch? If so, then his calm flowed into me. I felt strangely comforted. "You can do this, Kate."

I drew in a long, deep breath before I nodded and let the tech maneuver me back into the machine.

Over the echoing racket of the MRI I could hear Gabe talking to me. I couldn't hear his words, but the rumble of his voice gave me something to focus on.

And worry about.

Where exactly was I heading with Gabriel Chavez? The sparks and heat of sexual attraction I welcomed. Yes, even wanted. The desire that lay coiled in me every time I was around Gabe meant that my two previous lovers were wrong: I wasn't cold.

I wasn't the Ice Princess.

I knew that what had happened between Gabe and me on the beach and in the shower would lead to the bed, although I wanted it to be on *my* timing. Even the thought of being naked with him sent a rush of heat through me, despite the chill of the air-conditioned room. The tug of desire was even more frustrating, as I couldn't move because of the scan underway.

I then knew I would have to have sex with Gabe soon.

Very soon.

But at what cost?

Wanting, desiring, or craving was one thing. But needing? That was another ball of entanglements.

Such as I needed Gabe's hand enclosing mine right now. Needed his thumb stroking soothingly over the back of my hand to get me through this hellacious clacking machine.

To need someone. To depend and rely on another person. I had no experience with that. I had no personal barometer by which to gauge how to handle my emotions.

For also included in that snarl was trust.

Except for Carling and Nicole, I had no one else I trusted. I had affection for both my aunt, uncle and godfather, but I had always known their ultimate loyalties lay elsewhere. You can't trust someone who will sacrifice you.

Could I trust Gabe?

The noise abruptly ceased, and I had no more time to think. The machine thrust me back out into the room. Gabe gave my hand a final squeeze and I once more was whisked back to the room where I could change clothes.

I'd had enough. More than anything else, I needed to be alone to sort out my feelings for Gabe. My shoulder was tender but not painful unless being tortured by the doctors. The results of the MRI wouldn't be immediately available, so I wouldn't learn if I had a rotator cuff tear until tomorrow at the earliest.

I poked my head out. No sign of Dr. Young or Gabe. Good. They probably were waiting for me back in the examination room. Spotting a young nurse, I muttered a prayer of thanks. An older or more experienced nurse probably would drag me kicking and screaming to Dr. Young. I called out in a low voice, "Nurse."

She paused. "Yes, ma'am?"

"Would you give Dr. Young a message for me? He's in the last room on the right. Give him my apologies and tell him that Katherine Rochelle has gone home. I'll call him in the morning."

"But—"

She was speaking to my back as I rushed down the hall.

After a few more twists and turns, I was outside the hospital and flagging down a cab.

Fifteen minutes later I was home. My home. I was almost giddy with relief. I opened the door and almost fell inside. I tossed my tote onto the sofa and headed into the kitchen. I half expected the silence of my house to soothe me like it always did, but instead the tension still lay coiled inside me, waiting. Waiting for what?

I poured myself a glass of ice tea and polished it off. There was no sign of Willy; he must be outside stalking a gecko, a small lizard that abounded in this part of Florida. Fortunately, all he would capture would be the tail, which would break off, allowing the lizard to run off and hide.

Tick, tick, tick. Swinging around, I stared at the grandfather clock in the hallway. Why had I never noticed how loud it was before? Its sound mirrored the beat of the MRI machine. I had to put a stop to that. I placed my glass on the counter and as I walked toward it, my doorbell rang

"Kate, I know you're in there." So much for avoiding Gabe. I opened the door and he stalked into the foyer. "What the hell do you think you're doing?" Anger darkened his eyes.

I propped my hands on my hips. Good. A fight. I could use one. "I came home for a little peace and quiet. Do you mind going out the way you came in?"

Glowering, he stood so close to me that I could smell the warm sandalwood note of the cologne he favored. "After you dragged Dr. Young from his other patients to the hospital like some prima donna, the least you could've done was to thank him in person rather than sneaking out."

I winced but jerked my chin up. "I'll call and apologize to him in the morning."

He advanced and I backed up until my heel struck the

wall. Trapped. He braced his arms on either side of my head. "What? You think as a Rochelle all you have to do is apologize for your bad behavior and it will be all right?"

Shame ripped loose a few bands of control. "No, I don't, but that's between Dr. Young and me. I don't have to answer to you."

"Oh, you don't, huh?" Gabe moved closer. "You left me high and dry as well. Since working for you, I've been shot at and nearly blown to bits. Seems to me an apology is in order."

Yes, but not today. The vortex deep inside me swirled even more.

"Back off." I pushed at his chest, an exercise in futility. It was like shoving a mountain.

"No." When his body pressed against mine, I realized how aroused he was, but not as aroused as I was. The controls were off, and all was fair in war.

I hooked my foot around the back of his leg. "Last chance."

Gabe lowered his head. "Or what?" His warm breath feathered my face.

"Too late." I framed his face and brought him closer. Then my mouth fused against his. I could eat him alive, he tasted so good.

Oh boy. All my nerve endings singed, all the tension that had been building exploded.

Sexual meltdown.

But as good as Gabe's tongue warring with mine was, I needed more. I needed skin.

I gripped the edge of his T-shirt and pulled it up. Gabe straightened only long enough to drag his shirt over his head. Then I was running my hands over the smooth muscular planes of his chest. His flat nipples tantalized me and I lowered my head to lick one.

Gabe muttered a low oath and then ripped away my silk blouse. He didn't bother to unfasten my bra, plunging his fingers into the lace and freeing my breast for his mouth. When he suckled, desire ignited.

I had to get him inside me. Now.

I released my lock on his leg so I could squeeze my hand between our bodies to unzip his pants. I curled my fingers around his erection and died a small death of pleasure. He was hot and heavy and throbbing.

For me.

I wrapped my arms and legs around Gabe and tried to climb up him. He grabbed my waist to steady me. With a half groan, half chuckle, he pressed a kiss against my damp forehead.

"Babe, hold on. You need to lose a few clothes and I need to add some protection."

Some of the haze cleared from my head. "Sorry."

God, I was acting like a sex-starved maniac—which I was of course—but Gabe didn't have to know that. Embarrassed, I lowered my legs and tried to squirm free, but his grip tightened.

"Hold still, will you?" Gabe pulled down my pants along with my lace panties and the air-conditioning chilled my heated flesh. He handed me a foil packet. Oh wow. He wanted me to put on the condom. I tore open the package and then focused as I slowly rolled on the thin elastic.

"You're driving me crazy." Gabe ran his hand over my stomach to between my legs and fingered me. I shuddered and closed my eyes.

"Kate, look at me." I opened them and then I was airborne. Gabe lifted me until I could wrap my legs around his waist. With one thrust he drove into me. Gasping, I tightened my legs around him. I looked down to where I saw our bodies joined together, my pale skin contrasting with his tanned skin. It was the most erotic sight I had ever seen.

He gripped me under my buttocks and I began to ride him. The tension increased and I met his thrusts, seeking something I knew only Gabe could give me.

When my release came, I cried out his name and gave myself to him.

I didn't have a bone left in my body. The muscles and tendons were shot as well. Never in my life had I felt so languid, so relaxed.

Of course, never had I experienced such sexual satiation. If you had asked me yesterday, I would've emphatically stated that no way a lover such as Gabe existed except in the wistful imagination of women.

I tried to count the number of times Gabe and I had made love, but couldn't. At some point over the course of the evening Gabe had carried me into the bedroom where now we lay together in spoon-fashion on my bed, the duvet and sheets a tangled mess on the floor.

Was it still nighttime? I cracked one eye open and peered out. Nope. Judging by the pale light spilling through the cracks of the plantation shutters, dawn was upon us.

I stretched cautiously, exploring the degree of soreness of unused muscles. Gabe's arm around my waist tightened and I snuggled closer to his body heat.

As I lay there quietly, enjoying the simple sensation of being with a man, the floodgates opened, freeing thoughts and images. Like a water globe the events of the past few weeks bobbed to the forefront. I tried to see a pattern, but it kept eluding me. Just when I thought I had a concrete idea, it would slip away.

"I can hear the wheels of your mind turning," Gabe murmured as he nuzzled my neck.

I smiled and turned to face him. I circled my arms around him. "Sorry, I didn't mean to wake you."

He pressed a kiss to my forehead. "How are you?"

I knew what he was asking and felt strangely touched. No man had ever asked me how I was after sex. Their comments had always centered on their needs.

"I'm fantastic." Pausing, I gathered together the edges of my courage. "And you?"

A simple but loaded question.

"Died and lying in paradise right now."

Tension I hadn't realized had formed dissipated. I slid down so I could rest my head on his chest and listen to his heart beat. We lay in companionable silence.

Questions formed, coalesced. I saw the incongruity.

I bolted up and stared down at my lover's bemused expression.

My lover.

The words coming out of the blue derailed me from my train of thought. Pleasure that had nothing to do with the physical variety rushed through me. I wanted to throw myself back into his arms, but the emotional abandonment to do so was merely a seed inside me. I needed to nurture this new development.

Coward. What I really wanted to do was maintain the titanium walls built between me and the male species in order to protect myself from any more hurt.

"Kate, what's wrong? You have the strangest look on your face."

With an effort I pulled myself back to a safer topic.

"Gabe, I know why this case doesn't make sense. It's like several different forces are at work. The explosion yesterday doesn't match up with my assailant in the parking garage or the Bobcat incident or the person who shot at us in the courthouse."

"I know," he agreed quietly as he sat up and leaned against the headboard.

"If it's the same murderer, why didn't he simply shoot Isabella?"

Gabe's eyes darkened as he reached out and lightly stroked my bandaged shoulder. "Because explosions are a trademark of the Castillo family."

My jaw could have scraped the bed. "I know financially they may have been involved with my ex's construction company, but what's the connection to Grace's murder?"

He shrugged. "A blackmailer normally doesn't stop with one victim."

"True, but everything points to the fact that Grace was digging around my grandfather's disappearance. So far we have nothing to indicate she had any connection to the sabotage of the courthouse restoration. Since the Castillos are behind the financing, you'd think they'd want the construction to finish as soon as possible."

"What if the Castillos are linked to your grandfather?"

For a moment time stood still as pieces shifted like a kaleidoscope and fell into a pattern of clarity. I scrambled off the bed and raced out into the hall where I had tossed my tote bag. I dug around its depths and came up with the paper I had taken from Isabella.

"What's going on?" Rubbing his chest, Gabe stood in the doorway of the bedroom, apparently without a care in the world that he was totally nude.

Wait a minute. I didn't have anything on either. Score one for another step for the new, improved Kate Rochelle. I unfolded the faded sheet of paper.

"This is a page torn from my grandfather's docket calendar. I didn't get a chance to read it earlier." I ran my finger down the neat entries of case names. Given the time allotments, I gathered this day had been booked for evidentiary motion hearings.

My finger halted at the last motion scheduled that day. Excitement coursed through me. My throat tightened so much I could barely speak. "The purgatory case."

Gabe walked down the hallway and knelt beside me. "You mean the case Judge Winewski called his downfall?"

I smiled. Sometimes I forgot Gabe had a cop's attention to detail.

"Yes."

"Why was this case on your grandfather's calendar when Winewski presided at trial?"

Several scenarios whipped through my mind, none of them pleasant. "I don't know, but I'm going to find out. I need you to dig into the Castillo connection."

"With pleasure."

At Gabe's grim tone, I glanced over and placed my hand over his. "I'm fine. Really."

The phone rang and I rose to answer it.

"Kate, it's Carling. How are you?"

I could tell immediately her question wasn't an "I'm concerned about you," but rather "are you well enough" query.

"I'm fine, Carling. What do you need?"

After she told me, I shook my head. "You have to be kidding."

"Can you handle it?"

"I wouldn't miss this one for anything," I assured her. I hung up and looked at Gabe. "I've got to shower and get dressed. Carling needs me to cover a new client's first appearance in an hour."

A smile tugged at the corner of Gabe's mouth. "That's enough time…" He walked toward me but, laughing, I circled around him.

"No, it's not. I need time to prepare."

"What's there to prepare for? First appearance should be a piece of cake for a savvy criminal defense attorney like you."

I reached the bedroom and made a mad dash for the bathroom, with Gabe close behind me. "Not this one. Assault with a deadly weapon."

"So what?" Gabe leered at me, motioning toward the bed with his head. "That should be a no-brainer."

"Our client tried to beat his wife with a live alligator." I grinned at his blank look and shut the door.

Chapter 14

"Counselor, you can't be serious." The first-appearance judge glowered at me. Behind me, I could hear the buzz of people in the crowded courtroom. Out of the corner of my eye I saw one and then another TV reporter slide onto the front bench seat.

Great. News at five o'clock. The alligator wife-beater.

Beside me stood my client, swaying in an orange jumpsuit, his head bowed. Probably a good thing as the man's eyes were still bloodshot. In my brief meeting with him before court, I had learned Joey Gore was a native Floridian who lived out in Okeechobee. Short and stocky, he ran a car-repair shop during the day and drank himself stupid every night. During these binges he liked to take potshots at his wife.

So it was no small wonder that yesterday Joey, after a beer pit stop at his favorite bar, had come home and found another man in a pickup pulling out of his driveway. Since they didn't have a pool and nothing was broken, he had concluded the man wasn't there for business, especially when he found his wife in the kitchen clad only in her thong panties.

Instead of doing the reasonable thing, such as yelling or calling a divorce attorney, he had run into his bathroom and grabbed the four-foot-long gator he kept in the tub.

Fortunately for the wife, the bathroom was closer at hand than the bedroom. According to Joey's police record, he kept a shotgun under the bed, which he liked to shoot off into the air every Fourth of July—and Labor Day, Christmas and New Year's Eve.

The arrest report stated that Joey had grabbed the alligator by the tail and chased after his wife, hitting her twice with the gator, before she had managed to flee from the house and run to the neighbor's for help. When the first officers had arrived on the scene, they had found Joey sitting on the kitchen floor, crying and crooning baby talk to the gator cradled in his arms.

The gator was fine, but his owner wasn't.

With my court face on, I calmly answered the presiding judge. "Yes, Your Honor. I'm serious. This is an *ore tenus* motion to dismiss the charge of assault with a deadly weapon. The basis is that an alligator is not a weapon by statutory definition." I ticked off my fingers. "The statute lists guns, knives, shotguns, even knuckles, but not animals."

The judge glared at me. "Response from the State?"

Although the prosecutor was another wet-behind-the-ears law school graduate, he turned out to be quick on his feet. "Your Honor, the intent of the statute is to cover those items that can harm a person. Certainly, given the number of deaths caused by alligators every year in Florida, the use of an alligator by Mr. Gore to attack his wife can be viewed as use of deadly force."

I countered. "The alligator was a family pet. The arrest report states the officers found my client holding his gator."

"I read the report, Ms. Rochelle." The judge narrowed his eyes. "It also states your client's shirt was ripped and bloody and he had several puncture marks on his shoulder."

There was that slight damning detail, I had to admit silently. But one had to argue every possible nuance.

The judge shuffled papers. "I'm reserving for now on the issue and will set this for an evidentiary hearing. I suggest counsel be prepared to brief the issue thoroughly. I would note that the lesser offense of assault is encompassed within the charge of assault with a deadly weapon, which the jury could consider. I also would note, Ms. Rochelle, that you tread a dangerous path with your argument as the other charge is reckless endangerment of an animal."

True, but that charge could lead to a much lesser penalty, such as a fine, while assault could mean jail time. I simply nodded. "Understood, Your Honor."

"In the meantime, on your request for bail, the bond is set at twenty thousand dollars." He banged the gavel. "Next case."

After the sheriff led my client out, I left the room and went out into the hallway.

"Hey, Alligator Lady!"

I sighed and turned to face the reporter. "Good afternoon, Jim."

Jim Grabkowski was a lesson to any fledgling reporter: be careful of how far you reach for a story. Years ago, in his bid for a national broadcasting spot, Jim had manufactured a report on a drug gang and been caught in the lie.

Fired, he had faded into obscurity and, if rumors were true, onto skid row, until a new local station had given him the grunge duty of first-appearance reporting. His air of dissolution actually made a great fit with these surroundings, and he was now a fixture at the Gun Club facility.

With his wiry white hair in disarray and shirt rumpled, the reporter halted, his long, thin notepad poised and ready. "How about a statement about your plans for defending Joey Gore?"

"Not now, Jim. This is actually my partner Carling Dent's case. I'll let her field any questions from the press."

The gleam of avarice in the reporter's eyes only intensified. "What about Lloyd Silber? After all, trial is next week."

As if I needed the reminder.

"Word is the prosecution has an open-and-shut case against Silber."

"That's the State's viewpoint based on flimsy circumstantial evidence. I'm confident the jury will acquit my client."

He snorted. "Good luck."

I studied him. Jim had spent years in the underbelly of life of West Palm Beach, first as a newspaper reporter and then on TV. Maybe…

"Off the record, Jim?" I couldn't trust him to honor the request, but if I was careful, I might get lucky and get a few quick answers. It was a risk I was willing to take since I was running out of time.

He ran the tip of his tongue over his lips. I checked to see if his fingers were crossed, but they merely tightened on his pad. "Sure, Kate. Got a scoop on the prosecution?"

"This isn't about the Silber case." *Well, not directly anyway,* I told myself.

The reporter's intense expression switched to irritation. "Then what? I need to get back inside."

I couldn't pussyfoot around with a graceful way to ask the question. "Did you cover the courthouse thirty-five years ago?"

He flushed. "There are days I feel like I've spent my entire life on this beat." His gaze sharpened. "This about your grandfather?"

Jim may have fallen from grace, but one should never underestimate him. Once a reporter, always a reporter.

"Yes. I was curious—"

"About damn time that someone from your family cared enough to investigate his death."

"But I'm not—"

"That rumor Jonathan Rochelle was on the take was pure bull."

Finally. I stepped away further from the courtroom. Couldn't risk anyone overhearing our conversation. "Why do you say that?"

"Your grandfather was a straight shooter." He rubbed the back of his hand across his nose. "Then there was your grandmother, whom everyone overlooked in the scandal. If a crime family wanted to send a message, why not a car bomb or a public shooting of your grandfather? The traditional Mob element doesn't like complications so why did she disappear?"

"She was in the wrong place at the wrong time," I said.

"Exactly." Jim looked pleased, like a teacher with a pet student. "You've got some brains. Maybe Silber's trial isn't so cut-and-dry."

I fought a rush of pleasure at the unexpected compliment. "I think I can guarantee that."

"Hmm." He slapped his notepad against his thigh. "Maybe I can pull in a favor to cover the trial." He shrugged. "Anyway, I did check into your grandfather's disappearance."

"What did you come up with?"

Jim grinned. "A reporter never reveals his sources. I still may get a story after all these years."

"What did you suspect?"

"Your grandfather was investigating a dirty judge."

"Winewski?"

The reporter whistled softly. "Now I'm definitely re-opening that file. Yes, according to my sources, Rochelle was checking into an allegation Winewski fixed a trial."

"Did you interview my grandfather's staff?"

"Sure."

"Could you pull your file and tell me their names?"

He tapped a gnarled finger against his forehead. "Don't need to. I have the information right here. The bailiff, Stewart McKee, died several years ago."

Damn. "And his judicial assistant? Is she dead, too?"

"Called them secretaries back then. Shirley Cameron's still alive."

My pulse quickened. At last I had the name.

"If you call where she's at living. Personally, I'd call it hell."

"Why's that?"

"She became a drunk after your grandfather's death."

Shock flashed through me.

Giving me a shrewd look, he said, "Jonathan Rochelle has to be dead, you know." His voice held a trace of kindness.

"Yes, but it's the first time I've ever heard it expressed out loud." Of course, my grandparents were dead. This wasn't some novel where they had been spirited off to some exotic Caribbean island to spend the rest of their lives.

I shook off the wave of grief that crested through me. "Has Shirley been institutionalized?"

"No, she's on the streets. Actually, she haunts the alleys

around the old courthouse and Clematis." He rubbed his chin. "Got a fax?"

"Yes." I gave him the number.

"I'll fax you a picture of her if you agree to give me the story."

"It's a deal."

"I've got the rest of the hearings and then I'll dig up the photo for you." He turned.

"Thanks, Jim."

Pausing, he glanced over his shoulder. "No, thank you. I'd almost forgotten what it was like to be on the hunt for real news."

As I walked along the hall, I turned on my cell phone and listened to the one terse voice mail message from Carling. My euphoria trickled away. I jammed the phone into my tote and stalked toward the stairs as opposed to the elevator. Maybe by the time I reached the jail cells, my anger would burn off. Otherwise, tomorrow's headlines would read, Lawyer Kills Client!

"You lied to me, Lloyd." I braced my hands on the table. "You were paying Grace Roberts off."

My soon-to-be-fired client flinched but didn't say a word.

"My office just received exhibits from the State. Do you want to know what they contain?" I didn't wait for his answer.

"Grace's bank records showing deposits on the same day and in the same amount you made cash withdrawals from your account." I paused, fighting to keep my voice level. "The account you kept separately from you and your wife's joint checking account."

I leaned closer to him. "Do you know what this means? The State has more than a circumstantial link between you and the victim. Before it merely had gossip and innuendos. Now it has a solid motive. Blackmail."

Lloyd rubbed his face.

"Why didn't you tell me?"

"Because I was afraid you wouldn't believe me," he said in a low voice.

"Me? I think the issue is what a jury believes." I straightened. I was so going to be out of there in the next minute.

Lloyd shook his head. "You don't know your own power yet, do you?"

I almost rocked back on my heels. Me, power? "I don't know what you mean."

"I've watched you. When you believe in something or someone, you glow with intensity. You make a person want to believe. That's why I wanted, no, needed you to represent me. I knew you would care if you had faith in me, while to any other attorney, I'd only be a dollar sign."

I folded my arms. "So what am I to think?"

"That I'm foolish, desperate, but not a murderer."

Lloyd's quiet resignation tugged but didn't convince me. "So what did Grace have on you?"

"She discovered I was receiving kickbacks."

"Wait a minute." I held up my hand. "As projects go, the courthouse restoration isn't a Taj Mahal development, not in the grand scheme of Palm Beach County."

Lloyd shrugged. "I know. But someone was willing to pay me to look the other way for the construction delays. I was in a financial crunch. I had an investment opportunity, but I needed cash up front."

"Who paid you?"

"I don't know."

I was incredulous. "How can you not know?"

"I got a call from a man who said a good-faith gesture

would be forthcoming if I didn't raise a fuss about problems concerning any restoration delay. The next day I had a large deposit in my account. The money was a boon from heaven. I thought, what was the harm? We'd been ahead of schedule, so what did a few months' delay mean?"

He sighed. "So I took the money. I looked the other way. When I got messages about my benefactor needing night access to the premises, I left the security code and keys in an envelope near the construction trailer and continued to look the other way. I even mentioned hearing strange noises to the staff. It seemed so simple, and I had a second chance to recoup my stock market losses. To start my life again."

He leaned forward. "Katherine, I was stupid, but I'm not a murderer. You have to believe me."

God help me, I didn't know.

Lloyd's skin turned a chalky tone. "How can you represent me if you're not convinced I'm telling you the truth?"

"Because apparently your versions of the truth contain shades of omission." I grabbed my tote. "Lloyd, I need to think on this. I'll let you know by tomorrow. If I withdraw, the judge will have to grant you a continuance."

Lloyd closed his eyes briefly. "I guess I'm hardly in a position to ask for more."

Outside the client conference room, I leaned against the wall and fumbled in my suit pocket for my antacid tablets. How in the hell could I represent a client with a crystal-clear motive for murder?

I was still agonizing over the question that surely must plague every criminal defense attorney as I gunned the Jag along Okeechobee Boulevard.

How could I represent someone who was guilty of murder? whispered my morality.

But hadn't I taken an oath? Wasn't our judicial system based on the premise that everyone was presumed innocent until proven guilty? My job was to defend, wasn't it? Not to sit as judge and jury?

I pulled into the office parking lot with a squeal of brakes, headed straight into my office and slammed the door shut. After tossing my tote onto the nearest chair, I paced back and forth.

I had been so sure that I was on the right path in structuring my defense. Now this. Lloyd not only had been paid off, he had also been paying off the murder victim.

Open-and-shut case for the prosecution while all I had was a string of suppositions and dead bodies.

Who was I kidding? I wasn't up to this mess.

My door opened and Nicole strode in. "The staff said you looked like a sick dog slinking in, and I guess they were right. What's wrong?"

"This." I spread my hands. "Me."

Nicole coolly sat in the chair and crossed her legs. "I'm sorry. It's a little late in the day for me to interpret disjointed sentences. Could you please elaborate?"

"My being in this partnership. It's a sham. I'm a sham."

Nicole's brow rose. "What brought on this bout of self-pity?"

Hurt slashed through me. "Gee, thanks. Sorry to have burdened you and Carling so much."

Nicole's eyes flashed blue fire. "Grow up, Kate. We're your friends, not your nursemaids."

"I've never asked either of you to carry me." Pride stiffened my spine, indignation iced my voice. Self-preservation was paramount.

"No, but you've got to learn to trust in yourself again. So what if your taste in men sucks big time? Join the club. But you're letting your past affect your professionalism."

She rose, walked over and took my hands. "Carling and I didn't become your friends because you were the perfect Palm Beach debutante. We're your friends because you're smart and hardworking and have a heart of gold."

My throat tightened and tears formed.

"What's got you so off balance?"

"Lloyd Silber was being blackmailed by Grace Roberts. She found out that he was being paid off for construction delays."

"That's a bump, not an unmitigated disaster. Blackmail is only a motive for murder. It doesn't mean Lloyd killed Grace."

"But I'm not sure I can defend him if he's guilty."

Nicole squeezed my hands before releasing them. "Kate, while an innocent client is a pleasant bonus for a defense attorney, it's not the most important thing."

"What is?"

"Justice."

"But—how can we serve justice if our client is guilty?"

"Remember the story of John Adams representing the British soldiers accused of shooting the colonists?"

"Yes."

"He believed the soldiers had certain rights." Nicole smiled. "If one of this country's forefathers thought the protection of the accused was paramount to the pursuit of justice, then—"

"How can we do less?" I nodded.

"For every person who is guilty, somewhere out there's a person who is innocent, who needs our help to keep the system honest so he or she will have their fair day in court."

"Criminal Law One-O-One," I said.

"Exactly."

True, but did I buy into that concept hook, line and sinker? Nicole looked at me expectantly.

I drew in a deep breath. "Okay, I see your argument."

"But not fully convinced?"

"Not totally, but I've got plenty to think about. Thank you."

Nicole gave me a hug. "Welcome to the hood, Kate. Attorneys don't grow old. They drop dead at a young age from worrying." She crossed to the doorway. "Catch you later."

Sitting behind my desk, I leaned back in my chair. Was justice a black-and-white concept or were there gradients of gray? If so, how did an attorney ever find the right path without being trapped in a quagmire of uncertainty?

For comfort I wrapped my fingers around the locket containing my grandparents' pictures.

Always I had envisioned Jonathan Rochelle as being a pursuer of the pure form of justice, but had he actually been more a realist like a John Adams? Able to set his personal opinions aside in order to preserve another's rights?

I frowned. The reporter Jim Grabkowski had said my grandfather had been investigating a rumor of a fixed trial. A man had been convicted, but Jonathan Rochelle had sought the truth, no matter what the cost. Could I do less?

Did I have the strength to do more?

I could hear Aunt Hilary's voice as clearly as if she were standing in front of me. "Rochelles never waiver, Katherine. We always do our duty."

Talk about guilt trips. The Rochelle brother and sister team knew how to work in tandem—even if the former was dead.

I straightened, pushed up the sleeves of my silk blouse, and grabbed a stack of mail to review. Time for moping was over. It was time for action. I had a client to notify that I was still on the case.

During the next hour, in between calls and dictation, I drove the staff crazy by sticking my head out every fifteen minutes to check on whether a fax had arrived from Jim.

Murphy's Law of bathrooms: if you go, the fax will come. As soon as I left the ladies' room and walked toward my office, I spotted the paper lying on the fax tray. I rushed over and snatched up the blurred photograph. A half sigh, half giggle from the receptionist warned me Gabe was in the building even before she greeted him.

Hormones warred with the attorney in me and the latter won by a narrow margin. I studied the photograph of the woman, probably mid-thirties at the time of the shot. I let out a sigh of frustration

"What's wrong?" Gabe leaned against the wall next to me.

This time the female side of me came out on top and I surreptitiously sniffed the masculine scent that was all Gabe. Deep inside me desire stirred.

Get a grip, Kate, I ordered. It's only been…

Nine hours and forty minutes.

Boy, was I in trouble.

"Kate?" Gabe nudged me. "What's wrong? You have the strangest expression on your face, like you just stuck your finger in a socket.

Small wonder. It wasn't every day it occurred to me that the mere presence of a man could unsettle me.

Focus. Time is of the essence. I cleared my throat and held out the sheet.

"Ever hear of a reporter by the name of Jim Grabkowski?"

Instantly Gabe's expression became inscrutable, but he

shrugged a shoulder. "Who hasn't? What has he to do with the case?"

"Jim had the court beat at the time my grandparents disappeared. He investigated the scandal but turned up empty. However, he recalled having a picture of Jonathan's judicial assistant and faxed it to me."

"So?"

"According to him, Shirley is now a drunk on the streets. But her picture…" I waved it. "She's so ordinary. If a movie director needed a background shot with extras, she would be your woman. Not ugly, but not pretty. No distinguishing marks other than a mole by her left eyebrow, dark eyes."

I pinched the bridge of my nose. "She's going to be hard to find."

"I'll look for her but not tonight."

"Why not?"

"Because." Gabe wrapped his arm around my waist and drew me close. I swear my partners Carling and Nicole must have been standing in their offices, their ears pressed against the doors, for at that moment they both chose to appear in the hallway.

"Hey sport," Carling greeted him with an all-too-brilliant smile. Nicole followed with a more sedate greeting.

Gabe winked at both of them but didn't release his hold on me despite my wiggle.

"Ladies, I need a favor."

Nicole lifted a sardonic brow. "Looks like you already have all the favors you need."

My face felt so hot that the overhead smoke alarm should have been wailing.

"Not nearly enough," Gabe said. "I have a lead on the Winewski 'downfall' case. The wife of the man convicted for the storeowner's murder is still alive."

I twisted around. "Then I need to go with you."

"No, you can't."

"Why not?"

"Because she's Cuban, old Cuban. If I show up with you, a non-Hispanic, she'll clam up. She lives in Port St. Lucie so I need someone to keep an eye on you until I get back."

Carling's green eyes gleamed with speculation. "Sure, Gabe. We haven't had a girls' night out in a while. I'm sure we have loads to talk about." Her pointed smile reminded me of a panther bearing down on helpless prey.

"Great. I should be by your place around midnight." Gabe turned me around, gave me a furnace-blast of a kiss and then walked away.

As the sound of the front door slamming shut echoed, Carling and Nicole folded their arms in unison.

"Katherine Rochelle," said Nicole, "you have a lot of explaining to do."

I thought about my options and decided to make the best of the limited one. "Tonight is 'Thursday on Clematis.' How about dinner at one of the street restaurants?"

While my friends gave me the third degree, I could at least hunt for my grandfather's assistant.

Chapter 15

Shrugging into my jacket, I left my office and walked toward Carling's. Time to get this girls' night out started. I spotted a piece of paper lying under the receptionist's desk and bent to pick it up. The fax machine was forever overshooting its tray. I froze, staring in disbelief.

The document was a receipt slip for the picture of my grandfather's secretary. At the bottom of the sheet was a confirmation the fax had been transmitted to a number that was not our office's—thirty minutes after I had received the original.

I heard the swish and creak of the restroom door and stood up. Jennifer Acosta, our new receptionist, appeared, clutching her purse and patting a curl into place. She looked toward her desk, saw me holding the paper and blanched.

"Jennifer—"

She spun and ran down the hallway leading to the parking lot.

"Hey, come back here!" I yelled.

Naturally, Jennifer paid me no heed. The back door slammed. I ran outside only to watch her careen away in an old Chevy. In frustration I picked up a small rock and aimed it at the tailgate of her car.

Carling and Nicole came rushing out. "What's wrong?" Carling asked.

I showed them the fax. "Jennifer made a copy of the picture and faxed it. I found this on the floor."

Nicole's brows furrowed. "I gather you didn't ask her to send it to someone."

"No."

Carling folded her arms. "Damn. I guess we'll have to fire her ass. Good, cheap bilingual receptionists are so hard to find."

My lips quirked. "I guess so."

"Really, Carling. The issue is why Jennifer did this."

"I think that's obvious, Nicole," I said. "She was paid. The issue is how long has she been working as a hired spy in our office?"

"Get out! A spy?" Carling was incredulous.

Certain pieces of the puzzle clicked together. I paced back and forth. "Look, it makes sense. Remember when my briefcase was grabbed in the parking lot?"

"What has that to do—"

Nicole snapped her fingers. "Someone wanted your file notes."

"Exactly. When they failed again after breaking into my house—"

Carling's voice rose. "When did that happen?"

"Shortly—"

She grabbed me. "And why didn't you tell us?"

"Being shot at and buried alive plus being nearly blown to smithereens somewhat superseded in importance a break-in," I commented wryly.

Carling hugged me before turning. "Come on. We can't let Jennifer get away."

I stopped her. "It's okay. I know where she's going."

"You do?"

"Yes." I turned and went back inside to get my tote and car keys.

Nicole was the first to follow. "Do you want to clue in your poor befuddled partners?"

"Not now." I glanced at my Gevril watch. "I'll meet you at Joey's Bar and Grille in an hour."

Nicole grimaced. "Can't we eat at Ramone's? The food's better there."

But not its location, I thought. Joey's was the latest eatery trying to survive on the Olive and Clematis. The restaurant would afford a clear view of the entrance to the alley that ran between Banyan and Clematis.

"Another time. I'm dying for a cold burger."

"And warm beer," Carling added with a grin. She would be a happy camper wherever there was a large screen TV with a game on.

"If I must," groused Nicole.

"You must," I said as I headed out.

I took the Royal Park Bridge into Palm Beach, driving north along Country Road past The Beach Club before turning into a long curving driveway. After being cleared by a security guard, I pulled in front of a mansion created by an architect who had aspired to be another Mizner but never had obtained any recognition beyond Palm Beach. Still, its clean, masculine lines mirrored its owner.

I got out of the Jag, resisting the urge to kick the tire of the Chevy parked beside me. I strolled up the stairs and smiled at the butler who opened the door. "He's expecting you in the parlor."

"Thank you, Ramon." I went through the special foyer and entered the second room facing the Atlantic.

My godfather Paul stood by the French doors. A few feet away was Jennifer, looking pale and apprehensive.

"Hi, Paul. Has your paid flunky been filling you in on the latest details of my investigation?" I brushed my lips against his weathered cheek.

"Now, Katherine. Don't be upset with me."

I was damned if I'd show him how angry I was. I sat in the nearest wingback chair. As the guilty parties remained standing, I was afforded the unique position of being judge and jury. I braced my elbows on the chair's arms and bridged my fingers.

"Why would I be upset, Paul? How did you think I'd react seeing your phone number on the fax? Didn't you trust me to do my job?"

My godfather gestured to Jennifer. "Thank you, Ms. Acosta. My aide will pay you. Your services are no longer needed."

She nodded stiffly. "Thank you, Judge." She avoided looking at me as she left.

Paul sat in the chair across from me and leaned forward. "Katherine, I'm sorry if I've hurt you. I never meant for you to know. But you have to understand. Your aunt and uncle were frantic for you. You've been through so much that they didn't want to see you hurt any more."

"Spying on me was the solution? Really, Paul, you expect me to buy that?"

He spread his hands. "I thought if I could keep Hilary

and Colin apprised of your movements, of your progress, that I could give them peace of mind."

I resisted the urge to chew on an antacid tablet.

"Having a man steal my briefcase is peace of mind?"

He had the grace to grimace. "I'll never forgive myself for that or your house being broken into. The aide I first gave the assignment to totally overstepped all limits of reason. I'm afraid he had seen one too many crime dramas. When he told me what he'd done and the thugs he had paid, I was the angriest I've ever been. To risk my Supreme Court appointment for such tawdry actions."

Paul reached out and took my hands. "On my honor, Katherine, I've dealt with the matter. And if I ever find out who's behind the attacks on you, I'll deal with them as well."

For a split second I envisioned myself being in a TV show about a crime family where the head of the family has just ordered a hit. I suppressed a shudder at my hyperactive imagination.

"I swear. Jennifer only sent me your calendar so I could keep track of your appointments. Her sending me that picture was on her own initiative."

"That's rich." My tone was as brittle as aged glass. "Now everything's supposed to be all right again?"

"No." Paul slightly shook my hands. "I can't undo the mistake."

"Mistakes," I corrected.

For a moment I thought the expression in his eyes hardened, but then he smiled. "Mistakes," he agreed quietly. "Blame my foolishness on wanting only the best for you because I love you like my own daughter."

No fair. Destroying a good outrageous mad by pushing my buttons. But then again, Paul hadn't been a top-notch attorney and judge by being a poor politician. He knew the right things to say.

I nodded.

"Forgiven?"

I managed a weak smile. "Working on it."

"That's all a foolish old man can ask." He kissed my forehead.

"You're hardly old."

"There are days when I am and this is one of them."

"No more interference?"

"No more," he promised. "I have to say, I've been really impressed."

Praise from a man of his stature was golden. "Thank you. That means the world to me."

He gripped my elbow as I stood. "I think you stand a real chance of getting Lloyd off. I wouldn't be surprised if the prosecutor tries to work a deal with you on a lesser charge. I suggest you discuss the possibility with your client ahead of time so he can be thinking about it."

"Thank you, I will."

Paul escorted me to the door. "Please be cautious, Katherine. I know Hilary isn't good about expressing her feelings, but she does care."

I never doubted my aunt cared. It was the things she cared about that I disputed. However, I didn't argue with my godfather. His loyalty first and foremost had been to my family.

"I'll see you, Paul. Good luck with the appointment."

Heeding the speed limit this time, I drove back over the bridge to West Palm Beach. Parking in one of the city garages, I walked along Olive to Joey's. Twilight had taken some of the edge off the heat so Carling and Nicole were sitting at an outside table.

I slipped into the cushioned chair, flagged down a waiter and ordered a glass of Pinot Grigio.

"Well?" Carling asked as she shot a look over her shoulder at the TV inside. "Who's the culprit?"

During my ride here, I had already decided not to tell my friends about Paul's involvement. I knew how important the Supreme Court appointment process was and how tight the scrutiny continued to be. While I could trust Carling and Nicole with my life, I had no right to extend that trust on Paul's behalf.

"I can't tell you right now."

Nicole studied me over the rim of her Cosmopolitan. "Must be family."

"In a manner of speaking."

She sipped her drink. "All right." She set the glass on the table and propped her chin on the palm of her hand. "Then what should we talk about?"

Carling mimicked Nicole's position and tapped a fingertip against her mouth. "Oh, I don't know. How about…"

"Gabriel Chavez," Nicole finished.

I rolled my eyes. Let the inquisition begin.

And so it did with a barrage of questions coming at me with the machine-gun rapidity.

"When did you two get it on?"

"What's he like as a lover?"

Soul-baring warred with years of proper behavior drilled into me, not to mention a latent tendency toward being a prude. However, these were my friends.

I opened my mouth, but Carling and Nicole were on a roll.

"Does he wear boxers or briefs?"

"Or nothing at all?" Carling waggled her brows.

I took a deep breath and nearly shouted, "He wears briefs!"

Naturally, the game on TV chose that moment to go to commercial break. In the sudden quiet my voice reverberated down the street and into the restaurant. My face burned as people around us laughed.

My embarrassment didn't deter Carling one iota. She waved a hand. "Tell us more."

Amazingly, I could. While I drew a line at the bedroom door, I did talk about everything else. How he made me feel. My doubts and insecurities.

Together we laughed, cried and cursed at men.

As I looked at my friends, words welled up, words I had to say.

"I love you guys."

Carling paused midstream in eating, dangling a French fry. Nicole set down her glass of water with a sharp clink. They looked at each other.

I grew irritated. Now, I didn't expect responding declarations…or maybe I did. But a polite thank-you would have been nice.

"You're obviously embarrassed." I folded my napkin and laid it beside my plate. "Forget I said anything."

Carling let out a *whoop,* sprang up and threw her arms around my neck. Nicole rose in a more sedate manner but also wrapped her arms around me.

I could barely breathe, but I wasn't about to break up this group hug. It felt too wonderful, almost as if I were part of a family.

Wait a minute, I was. While Nicole and Carling may not be my blood relatives, they were the sisters I'd never had.

I patted the closest arm. "Thank you for being my friends."

"Oh God," Carling sniffed, let go and plopped down in her chair. "Stop. I can't take any more or I'll start bawling."

Nicole's eyes looked suspiciously damp as she resumed her seat. "Carling, you cry every time the Marlins lose."

"Do not."

"Do too. I've seen you in the bathroom."

"Pul-ease. You insult me." Carling sounded indignant. "I only cry when the Miami Hurricanes lose."

"Especially when they can't win the national title," Nicole teased.

"At least they've had a shot at the title unlike your Gators."

Uh-oh. I'd better nip this state intra-rivalry fight in the bud or we'd be here all night.

"Isn't it strange?"

They both looked at me. "It's strange, all right," Carling said, "how an intelligent woman can support University of Florida football."

I smiled and shook my head. "No, I was thinking what a small world it is. Here I'm defending a case that both your ex-boyfriends are involved—"

"What are you talking about?" demanded Carling.

"Why the prosecutor is your Jared Manning—"

"Jared Manning is not *mine,* never was."

Surprised by the vehemence in her tone, I held up my hand. "Fine."

Nicole leaned forward. "And let's be clear. Lieutenant Sam Bowie is history as far as I'm concerned."

"That's what I said…'ex.'"

"Good."

She leaned back.

"Wait a minute." I drummed my fingers on the table. "You two just gleefully gave me the third degree over every aspect of my love life with Gabe and all my exes."

"Which questions you were all too happy to answer." Nicole's smile was a tad too saccharine sweet.

Carling gave a slight snort. "I still can't believe Harold Lowell is a minute man."

My face flamed. Maybe I shouldn't have had that glass of wine. Somehow it slipped out that sex with Harold had been abbreviated. Very abbreviated.

"*A* minute man?" I arched a brow. "Sounds like you've known a few yourself."

"Who me?" Carling rose. "Excuse me a second. I think the Marlins have just scored." She rushed inside to the bar.

Nicole sighed. "We're a screwed-up lot, aren't we?"

I raised my water glass. "As to men, yes. As to the court of law, no."

"Salute!" She lifted her Cosmopolitan just as a plump waitress squeezed between the tables, knocking Nicole's elbow. Liquor spilled over the front of her emerald-green suit.

"Oh!" The woman gasped. "I'm so sorry."

Nicole rose. "That's all right. I'll run into the restroom and rinse it out."

The restaurant manager rushed up. "Miss, we'll pay to have the suit dry-cleaned."

Nicole held the damp fabric out from her chest. "Let's first see if it will rinse out. If you would excuse me."

The waitress and manager trailed after her as she wound her way inside. I sat back to wait. In the distance I heard the band begin another set. Tonight was reggae and my blood stirred with the beat of the music. If only Gabe was here…

No, don't go down that path. Take each moment with him as it comes.

But I could wonder how his interview was going. Normally a criminal trial is fixed to get the defendant off. Thirty-five years ago someone paid Judge Winewski to find a defendant guilty.

A fall guy. Somewhere out there a powerful person got away with murder.

Mulling over this idea, I glanced across the street at the alley for about the hundredth time and saw the shadows stir. Someone moved in the dark. I went on alert. A form shuffled to the sidewalk: a woman carrying a stuffed bag.

I grabbed the waiter walking by and thrust a hundred dollar bill at him for the tab. "Please let my friends know that I'll be right back. Tell them it's about the case. They'll understand." I then snatched my tote and crossed the street.

Murphy's Law said I was looking for a needle in a haystack, but maybe, just maybe, this was my lucky night.

Chapter 16

In my rush I dodged a few cars, horns blaring, but by the time I had reached the opposite side, the woman had reached Clematis. For all that her bent shape indicated she was at least sixty-plus, she was booking it. But then again, I cringed as a slight breeze loaded with odors of rotting garbage wafted from the alley. Who would want to linger here?

I made my way to Clematis and looked eastward into the crowd. Every Thursday night the city of West Palm Beach shut down vehicle traffic for this section for a street party. Tables from busy restaurants spilled onto the sidewalks. Retail stores put out racks and tables of clothes and other merchandise. Tucked everywhere were food and drink carts. Center stage was the band playing by the fountain built at the cross section Clematis and Narcissus. The weekly affair had grown so large that it now ran all the way to the Intracoastal, where a floating bar barge was moored and in full swing for next week's SunFest, the city's biggest party of all.

Tourists were already flooding into the city for the large jazz festival, judging how crowded Clematis was. Who was I fooling? I'd never find the woman in this throng. Besides, it could've been someone foolishly taking a short cut through the alley. I simply wanted the woman to be Shirley Cameron.

I halted in the crush. Ahead of me, bright pulsating light spilled from a nightclub. A woman by the club turned slightly as if she were looking inside. The light captured her profile and I held my breath. Weathered and aged beyond her years, yes, but the shape, the mole.

She could be Shirley Cameron.

A burly bouncer appeared in the doorway and yelled at her, motioning for her to move away. The woman disappeared into the crowd again.

Biting back an oath, I pushed my way to the street so I could move parallel. Big mistake. The band broke into singing "Red, Red Wine" and the crowd went into a jostling frenzy. I lost sight of my subject, but I kept moving forward because that had been her direction. At last I reached the fountain and fisted my hands in frustration. Talk about confusion corner. The fountain sat at the hub of intersecting streets and sidewalks. She could be anywhere.

A drunk middle-aged man grabbed me around the waist, "Hey, baby, you're too pretty to be alone."

I leveled an elbow into his stomach and left him bent over in a groan. I had no time to be polite. Stepping to my right, I peered down one street leading to Flagler Drive. My pulse quickened. The bent form of a woman was walking toward the bar barge. She stopped a couple who immediately waved off her begging attempt. She shrugged I set off, skirting a group of giggling, stumbling teenage girls who obviously had managed to beat the alcohol limitation law in some establishment.

Although the night was clear, the moon was only at quarter stage so that the Intracoastal Waterway ran like a glossy black ribbon, with only the occasional sparkle of light on its surface. While the floating bar was an explosion of noise and action, darkness surrounded it as a number of streetlights were out as a result of last week's night fair. According to the newspaper's report, a group of rowdy drunks had dared each other as to how many lights they could bust. The count had been at twenty when the police had put a stop to their fun.

I crossed Flagler to the seawall, littered with abandoned bottles. Tethered to the bar were a number of assorted boats, bobbing in the wake of any passing boat. A movement to my left caught my attention. A woman was walking along the wall, picking up bottles and drinking their contents.

Eeewww. Just think of the germs. Maybe all the alcohol in her system would kill them.

I walked toward her and called out, "Shirley Cameron?"

"Don't know her," she muttered, letting a beer can clatter to the ground.

"I'm Katherine Rochelle."

The woman froze. "Jonathan's daughter?"

"No, his granddaughter."

She pressed trembling fingers to her mouth. "Granddaughter?" She blinked her eyes as she struggled to focus on my face. "Yeah, you have the look of Jonathan."

"I'd like to talk with you about him."

"I've nothing to say." She stepped away.

If I had to lead a devil to… I gestured toward the bar. "How about something cool to drink on this warm night?"

She wet her lips as she glanced around. "You buying?"

"Sure." If the owner wouldn't let us in—a strong possibility given Shirley's body odor—I'd pay him off to serve us on the sidewalk.

"Maybe just a small toddy to tide me over."

I let her pass so I could follow. I wanted to keep an eye on her at all times. I could feel the waves of nervous energy rolling off her. If anyone would bolt at the drop of a pin, it was Shirley Cameron.

Were her jitters something beyond a street person's natural avoidance of society?

As we reached the landing, two familiar-looking men stepped from the deep shadows cast by the barge. As they moved to cut us off from the barge, light glinted on the guns they both held. Somehow I didn't think Officers Rick and Tony, aka Dumb and Dumber, were here on official police business.

Shirley whimpered and then stumbled as she tried to turn and run. I caught her arm to steady her.

Behind me I heard the hiss of tires. Thinking I could flag the driver down for help, I looked but saw a dark sedan, its headlights off, pulling to the side of the road.

Right, no help there. Clearly we were about to be forced inside that car.

I tightened my hold on Shirley's arm. A roar of laughter caused our would-be abductors to turn. A group of partyers leaving the bar teetered along the pier. The men hid their guns and tried to blend in with the seawall.

Opportunity beckoned. "Come on." I urged Shirley forward. I rushed to the pier before half lifting and half throwing her into the first boat. She shrieked and the partyers stumbled, halted, thus cutting off the thugs.

"Whatsa going on here?" One man, his tie askew, asked.

I untied the lines and prayed the engine was well tuned. It was. It roared to life on my first attempt. I gunned the motor, spraying the crowd. Shouts rose as I sped off. Shirley struggled to sit upright, but the rocking motion kept her off balance.

"What was my grandfather working on at the time of his death?" I yelled at her.

"Don't know."

I heard another boat motor kick in and knew that pursuit was on the way. I didn't have much time.

"Yes, you do. Secretaries know everything. Jonathan was checking into a crooked judge, wasn't he?"

"Yes." Shirley drew her knees to her chest. "A lawyer came to him, claiming his new client's murder trial had been rigged. Jonathan was very upset."

"Why?" I spun the wheel and veered toward Palm Beach. I knew that side like the back of my hand, and I needed every advantage. A quick look over my shoulder had shown me that the men had shanghaied a faster speedboat than I had.

"Don't know. Jonathan warned me not to say anything, to anyone."

Which meant Shirley did know something more. "What didn't he want you discussing?"

"Nothing."

"Listen, we have two men chasing us and it's not to wish us well. They want to kill us. Tell me what you remember about his investigation."

She wiped her mouth with the back of her hand. "The defendant didn't kill the store owner. His murder was a hit."

Out of the corner of my eye, I saw the nose of the other boat. They were going to try to cut in front of me. I spotted the dark form of the anchored barge from which the SunFest fireworks would be launched.

Let's play a game of water chicken.

I throttled up, asking the engine for all the power it would give me. Water stung my face and wind tore at me, whipping my hair free from its braid. I steered straight at the barge. The other boat overshot me and then righted to run parallel.

Game on.

"Who ordered the hit?" I shouted above the engine noise.

"A Cuban crime lord. Diego something." She made a cross.

"Castillo?"

"Yes, yes." She pointed her hand and screamed. "You're going to crash!"

"No, I'm not, but they will."

All those summers of boating all over the world—from Cannes to Hawaii—were paying off. I had the feel of the boat now and a good handle on what it could and couldn't do. While it may not be the speedster the thugs were driving, this baby had maneuverability and rode well in the water.

As the dark sides of the barge loomed ahead, I began a mental countdown. I heard the other boat hot on my stern and smiled. Three, two, one.

I spun the wheel at the same time I throttled down. The engine roared its protest as the boat sharply veered to the right. A plume of white spray rose high to our side.

"Come on, baby," I cooed as the boat jolted and careened. For a moment I wondered if I had misjudged the distance but then the boat held the water and zoomed around the barge.

My pursuers weren't as fortunate. An explosion erupted as light flashed through the night like lightning. I glanced over my shoulder and saw another boat racing to the crash scene. A powerful beam spotlighted the area, and I saw two men thrashing in the water, waving for help. They must have bailed at the last moment.

Relieved, I eased back on the throttle. I didn't want more bodies to be on my conscience. Instead of the other motor shutting off, it increased in noise. Startled, I swung around. The boat was making a beeline toward me.

The sedan on Flagler.

Cursing, I poured on the power. Fortunately, every square inch of this part of the Palm Beach shoreline boasted a pier. I planned to hide in the warren of boats. The other boat's light wasn't powerful enough to catch us in its beam so I stood a chance at being able to lose them.

Not the first pier, not the second, but the third...

I cut the engine and threaded through the outer series of anchored yachts. There, a spot between *Bahama Mama* and the *Dolphine*. I eased in the narrow slip with barely an inch to spare on either side. Good. The yachts were so large that a passerby could mistake this smaller boat for one of their tenders.

I scrambled over the quivering mass that was Shirley and tied the boat up. "Come on," I said, grabbing the woman's arm. Thank God, she didn't protest. On the dock I removed my shoes and gestured for her to do the same. I then pulled her along in my wake. If I remembered this dock, a dense tropical garden lined the drive to the road.

Yes! I dove into the nearest outcrop and wormed my way as deep as I could, pulling Shirley with me. Although Shirley wasn't the person I would nominate to share a bush with, given her smell, she was wearing dark clothing. I sent a quick prayer of thanks that I had picked out my black wool crepe suit this morning instead of the ivory.

The new hunter didn't bother to mask his arrival. The hum of his engine grew louder and louder as he coasted along the pier. Through the foliage I watched the light pan over the moored yachts. Then the light arced, grew fainter. The engine noise lessened.

Good, he was heading out. I whispered to Shirley, "We'll give it another minute and then we'll head toward the road. At this time of the night, I should be able to flag a taxi doing the Worth Avenue circle."

Vehicular traffic followed a square through town to hit the famous fashion avenue plus the other hot spots. At this time of the night, the flow should be constant if not downright heavy.

Shirley rasped, "You shouldn't have done this. Risk yourself for me. Jonathan would never have forgiven me if harm came to one of his own."

Would. She knew he was dead.

"Do you know who killed my grandfather?"

"No."

Her denial was too quick. "Try again."

"I don't, not really." She shifted beside me.

"But you have your suspicions?"

"Who's going to listen to the ramblings of a jealous old drunk?"

That set me back on my heels. "You were in love with my grandfather?"

"He never noticed. Too wrapped up in that wife of his." Her voice was bitter.

Criminal Law 101: Jealousy was a prime motive for murder. "Did you kill him?"

"No!" Her voice rose, and I laid my hand on her arm and squeezed a warning. I listened, but the motor continued to grow fainter.

"I would never hurt him," she continued.

"Who would?"

"He put lots of people in jail."

Great. That was helpful. "Any threats in particular before he disappeared?"

"No." She shrugged. "All he could think about was that trial."

"Did you work late the night he disappeared?"

"No, he sent me home early despite the fact he was working on a decision. He always handwrote his first drafts you know," she confided.

"Why did he let you go home?"

"He had a meeting and didn't need me."

Didn't need her or didn't want her to be a witness, I thought.

She reached into her coat pocket, pulled out a small bottle and drank until she polished it off. From the odor I would say it contained the cheapest gin made.

Wiping the back of her mouth on her sleeve, she patted my hand. "Jonathan was kind like that. He said I didn't need to hang around for The Family."

During my research, I had learned the Castillos were often referred to as "The Family" in Cuban society. I frowned. "Do you mean the Castillos?"

She struggled to stand up. "I want to get out of here."

"Wait. Let me make sure they're gone." Inching forward, I could see the length of the pier. No sign of the boat. The breeze kicked up and I thought I could hear the engine moving to the south of us.

"It's okay for us to move." I turned. "I'll call—"

Shirley was gone. I scrambled clear of the brush but saw no one and no movement. I listened but heard no sounds.

I smacked my forehead. How stupid. I should've remembered that years of living on the streets would've honed her hiding ability to the max.

Sighing, I pulled my phone from my bag. Shirley may have declined a ride in an air-conditioned taxi, but I was so ready. Then I would call Carling and Nicole. The phone's screen lit up indicating I had a text message. It was from Gabe stating he was on his way back. I glanced at my watch.

I needed to get back to my house. Quickly.

I was right. Getting a cab was a relative breeze. During the short ride into West Palm Beach, I called Nicole and brought her up to speed.

Once home I rushed straight into the bedroom, ruined clothes flying. I gathered and thrust them into the deepest recess of my closet. I changed into a crisp pair of shorts and midriff top. Since I needed to set the scene, I didn't take time for my hair, other than tucking a few strands behind my ears. Back out in the living room, I laid out notepads and my case file.

There. I switched on a table lamp. The picture of someone working at home. Maybe I had time for a quick makeup and hair fix....

I heard a knock at the door and sighed. Or perhaps not.

After checking through the peephole, I opened it. With a duffel bag slung over his shoulder, Gabe sauntered in and hauled me close for a long, lingering kiss before releasing me, breathless.

"I need a key if I'm going to be staying here."

His request blindsided me. A door key. Free access to the haven I had created for myself.

Be logical, Kate. Our schedules were all over the place.

"Of course." I went into the room that served as my home office and headed to the wall safe. Unbelievably, my fingers trembled as I dealt with the lock.

Why was I acting like this was such a momentous occasion? Gabe wasn't moving in with me permanently. This wasn't a step in our relationship, if we had one. Giving him a key was simply an expedient.

I took a deep breath and opened the safe. The contents included important documents, a few pieces of valuable jewelry and my gun. I pulled out an envelope containing extra sets of house keys, removed one and handed it to Gabe.

He slipped it onto his key ring and stuck it in his pocket. "Thanks. I'm hungry. Got anything in the fridge?"

So much for significant milestones. I bit back a smile and said, "Let me see what I can find."

On cue my cat appeared in the doorway and yowled loud and plaintive. "I'm sorry, Willy. It's way past your dinnertime. I'll feed you."

I skirted around Gabe to enter the hallway, but he looped his arm around my waist. "Hang on, Kate."

He pulled me close, so close his breath feathered my ear. Hmm, maybe Willy could wait. I turned and placed my hands on his shoulders. "Do you have something better in mind?"

"I might." He nipped my earlobe, sending a luscious shiver down my spine. "But first, I want to know…" He trailed kisses along my neck.

Sighing, I arched slightly to give him better access. "Yes?"

"Why is Willy so hungry and why do you have a twig caught in your hair?" He released me only to brace his hands on the wall, caging me. "What have you been up to tonight? And don't tell me you've only been hanging out with the girls. Carling called me earlier, frantic, when you disappeared."

Betrayed and trapped. Damn. No way to waffle out of this one.

I folded my arms and leaned against the wall. "If you must know, I was playing a game of water chicken with your buddies Dumb and Dumber."

"What do you mean?"

"I spotted my grandfather's secretary tonight on Clematis. When I followed her to Flagler, guess what two creeps crawled out from the shadows?"

Cold fire lit his eyes as he cupped my face. "Babe, did they hurt you?"

"No." I covered his hand with mine. "But they had quite a bath, though I doubt if it was enough to wash away all their dirt."

"I'm almost afraid to ask."

"When a car pulled up on Flagler, I gathered that Shirley and I were meant to be bundled inside by your friends. I gave them the slip and borrowed a boat."

"Borrowed?"

"I've already called a friend who will return it to the rightful owner tomorrow along with a filled tank and a note promising to cover any damages," I replied in a prim tone.

"So what happened?"

"I took off with Shirley, but Dumb and Dumber grabbed a faster boat. I decided to see if their balls were as small as their minds."

Gabe's lips quirked. "That small, huh?"

"I would say so. When I steered at the fireworks barge—"

My teeth rattled together as Gabe first gave me a shake and then hugged me. "Have you lost your mind? You could've been killed!"

I found it hard to talk with my face smothered against his chest, but I didn't mind. "Not really, Gabe. I've spent a lot of time around boats. I know how to handle one. I figured that gave me an advantage over your friends."

"They're dead. I swear to God they're dead."

I wiggled free. "I'm pretty sure you may get your chance."

He groaned and pressed his forehead to mine. "Finish it while I still have a mind."

I bit my lip but decided now was not a good time to tease him. Quickly, I told him the rest, trying not to notice how Gabe's jaw resembled granite. "So I'm fine, though I would love a massage and hot shower. How did your meeting go?"

"On a scale of one to ten in comparison to yours? Oh, I say about a minus one hundred."

Disappointment jabbed through me. "You didn't learn anything from the widow?"

"Yes, but…" Gabe knelt. Before I could react, he lifted me into a firefighter's carry over his shoulder.

"What are you doing?"

He headed down the hall to my bedroom. "First I'm going to check you head to toe to make sure you're really all right." I shrieked as he dumped me onto the bed. He dropped on top of me, bracing himself on his outstretched hands. "Then I'm going to make love to you until we're beyond exhaustion."

I smiled. "Oh really?"

He lowered his head. "Really."

Expecting hot, bone-melting sex, I arched up, ready for the onslaught. Gently, he pushed me back. "Not so fast." He slid down and gripped my foot. Slowly, he slipped off my sandal and then began to massage my foot.

I bit back a whimper as pain flared before dissipating as the abused muscles relaxed. He repeated the process with my other foot. When I could've curled my toes into the mattress, he slid his hands over my left calf. I clenched my fists as inch by inch he kneaded both legs, moving tantalizingly closer.

At his urging I lifted my hips and he removed my shorts.

Next came my top. The breeze stirred by the ceiling fan cooled my heated flesh. I was more than ready and reached to draw him closer, but he shook his head.

"Turn over." With only a slight protest I obliged. Gabe straddled me and, when he stretched to rub my neck, his erection pressed against me. His fingers stroked, caressed and found every tight muscle in my back.

Coiled within the languidness was with a growing sensual tension. I bunched my buttocks and bucked slightly against Gabe.

"Hey—" Gabe gave me a slight swat "—stop that."

"But…" I rolled over.

Gabe palmed one breast, rolling my nipple to a hard peak. "But what?"

"I want."

His teeth flashed in the dark. "Tell me what you want.

"Your mouth on me. Everywhere."

"Your wish is my fantasy." And kiss me he did. My neck, my breasts, my stomach. Then he parted me and kissed me on my heated flesh. As I welcomed my first climax, he eased into me and drove me over another endless wave.

Chapter 17

"So the widow believes her husband was framed for the store owner's murder?"

Gabe didn't glance away from the Marlins baseball game he was watching on the TV in the living room. "We've already covered this."

Unable to sit still, I wandered around my living room. "We're missing something. I need to go over your interview again."

Shrugging, Gabe said, "Señora Lopez says they were recent immigrants. Why would her husband risk the only job he could find?"

I paused in my pacing to stand in front of him. Big mistake. Still shirtless, he lay sprawled on the sofa, his bare feet crossed and propped on the top of the coffee table. He epitomized a man enjoying his Sunday afternoon.

He looked good there, I realized with a double-edged

sword of longing and panic. Having him underfoot and in my bed over the weekend had run the relational gamut from aggravating to exhilarating.

A commercial came on, and he looked up, frowning. "You look weird, like when one of my sisters can't make up her mind what to wear. What's wrong?"

Oh, I knew what I wanted to wear. Him. Naked. Now and tomorrow and the next day. But I had no time for this personal angst. None at all. The trial began tomorrow. Most of the time I was comfortable with the demands of my career, at times chewing up weekends and holidays.

I swallowed and shook my head. "Nothing's wrong. I was just thinking."

Gabe's lips curved in that long, slow smile and reached out for me. "Thinking's a dangerous thing for a woman to be doing on a Sunday afternoon. Come here."

I neatly sidestepped his hand. "Why did Mrs. Lopez think her husband was framed? After all, if he was new to the country, seeing the grocery store's till filled with money could've been an incentive for anyone desperate."

Gabe dropped his hand. "New to the country, didn't speak English, no friends. He cleaned the store after hours. Perfect man to set up."

"Or to commit the crime."

"That's what the jury found."

"Due to Winewski's evidentiary rulings throughout the case." I picked up my pad of notes.

"Damn." Gabe sounded disgusted. I figured the Braves had gotten another hit. "I totally forgot to tell you one comment she made."

"What?"

"Someone approached her husband in jail and offered him money, big money, to say he was guilty."

I picked up a pillow and heaved it at him, hitting his chest. He only grunted. "Damn it, Gabe! Why didn't you mention this before?"

He tossed the pillow aside. "Don't blame me. It's your fault that I've been a sex slave for the past few days." He patted the cushion. "Speaking of which, there's plenty of room here for you."

"Oh, no you don't." I kept the coffee table between us and folded my arms. "You're not going to sidetrack me."

"Your loss," he said, flashing a lewd grin.

I rolled my eyes. "Your ego is unbelievable."

"No, Beautiful, you are."

Keep focused, Kate. You can't jump his bones. Yet.

"Did Lopez take the money?"

"He refused."

"Did his widow know who tried to pay him off?"

"No, only that he was Cuban."

"Your Castillo connection?"

"Yeah."

Gabe's expression hardened. I knew the morning after my run-in with Dumb and Dumber he had called Lieutenant Bowie while he thought I was still in the bedroom dressing. Since then Gabe kept his cell phone by his side; it even went into the bathroom with him. However, I had drawn a line about him bringing it to bed.

Bending over a stack of folders, I grabbed one filled with microfilm copies of newspaper articles. I scanned one clipping. "This is what bothers me. The killer beat the owner to death."

"That makes it a crime of rage or warning."

"Exactly." I pulled out the police report Gabe had managed to dig up on the old crime. "The investigators found the bat in his garbage can. Pretty damning."

I thought about the neighborhood I had seen when we had gone to visit Isabella Montoya. "Gabe, that bat had to be planted." Pacing, I ticked the facts off on my fingers. "One, Lopez had no car. He walked to work. Two, we're talking about July, when the murder happened around seven-thirty. It's still light. Lopez walked home carrying a bloody bat and no one saw him?"

I was close. I knew I had to solve this murder to find the answer to Grace Roberts's death. The two were linked and if I pulled out the thread of truth on the old case, the new one should unravel.

The doorbell rang. I frowned. Interruptions I didn't need right now. "Gabe, could you answer that while I work out a timeline?" I hurried toward the office but glanced out the window. Oh no. A sleek silver Mercedes sat in the driveway behind Gabe's battered truck.

I spun around. "Gabe, wait—"

Too late. As he scratched his stomach Gabe opened the door.

"Well, really." Hilary's voice dripped ice.

"Mr. and Mrs. Wilkes." Gabe straightened and ran his hand through his hair. Hilary swept past him, followed by Colin.

I sighed and dropped the folder onto the nearest table. Of all the rotten timing for them to visit. I plastered on a smile. "What a pleasant surprise."

Colin looked sheepish as he planted a kiss on my cheek. "I'm sorry, Katherine. We should've called."

"Don't be ridiculous, Uncle Colin," I murmured as I studied Hilary standing near the kitchen counter, studying the stacked dishes bearing the remains of breakfast. "I'm glad you stopped by."

Gabe, who had disappeared into the bedroom, re-emerged with a black T-shirt on. I gestured toward him as he sauntered over to my side. "You remember Gabriel Chavez."

"Yes, course." Colin shook hands with him.

"Would you mind telling me what this is all about?" Hilary's question came out as a command.

I opened and closed my mouth in disbelief. What did she need, a gigantic billboard with the word *Lovers* on it?

Gabe came to the rescue. "With all the threats to Kate's life, I'm staying with her until the trial is over."

Hilary's lips pressed together, but, with a slight nod, she accepted the white lie meant to tidy a dirty situation. "All the threats? Has something else happened?"

"Thursday night she was almost abducted."

The bald statement startled even me. I hadn't really thought about the implications of the incident in that vein.

Colin whitened. "Someone tried to take her?"

"No," I rushed to reassure him. I knew that one of the greatest fears of the wealthy was kidnapping for ransom. I shot Gabe a quelling look, but he didn't appear repentant. "I'm sure it was because I had found Shirley Cameron."

Hilary slowly sank into the wingback chair. "Jonathan's secretary? What on earth did you want with her?"

"I think the question is what did those men want with her," I said dryly.

"Katherine."

I took a deep breath. "I've been investigating Grandfather's disappearance."

"My God. Have you lost your mind? That happened years ago. Didn't I tell you not to waste your time?"

I planted my hands on my hips. We needed to have this out. Here. Now. "I don't get it, Aunt Hilary. Why don't you want to know the truth about your brother's disappearance? Where he's buried?"

She flinched. Colin rushed over and put his arm around her shoulders. "Katherine! There's no need to be so disrespectful to her."

"Sorry, Uncle Colin. But I'm tired of avoiding the topic of Jonathan Rochelle. He was my grandfather, your friend, her brother. Doesn't anyone care what the truth is?"

Hilary looked at me. "Don't you think we tried to find out what happened? We hired an investigator at great cost. He found evidence of recent deposits into Jonathan's campaign account. Large deposits. The investigation was hurting, not helping, to clear my brother's name. We let it drop."

I had only heard the rumors that my grandfather was on the take but never knew the evidence concerned bank deposits. Given the extent of the Rochelle fortune, this didn't ring right to me. If my grandfather had any connection to the Mob, it would be for reasons other than financial.

Gabe's phone rang. "Excuse me." He grabbed it and walked out of the room.

I crossed to my aunt and bent down. I did something I'd rarely done my entire life. I took her hand. Incredibly, she didn't pull away. Although I could feel in her grip the strength of years of keeping in shape, I could also feel the frailty of age setting in.

A sense of urgency settled in me. Hilary and Colin were getting old. I owed them at least some peace of mind.

"Trust me. Believe in me. I will find out what happened thirty-five years ago and clear Granddad's name once and for all."

I expected at least relief in Hilary's eyes. I didn't expect resignation. However, she squeezed my hands. "I know you will, Katherine. If anyone can solve Jonathan's case, it would be you."

Stunned by the praise, I sat back on my heels. Hilary's compliment wasn't a kissy-huggy moment, at least not with her, but it was momentous, none the less.

In the end, my throat tight with suppressed emotions, I simply said, "Thank you, Aunt Hilary."

"That's why we dropped by, Katherine," said Colin from behind us. "We wanted to wish you best of luck with the trial."

Releasing Hilary's hands, I rose. Colin was a different matter when it came to expressing emotion. I flung my arms around his neck. "Thanks, Uncle Colin."

He patted my back. "You're a good attorney, Katherine. You care, and that's what makes you different. You're the kind of attorney that I dreamed of being but never accomplished."

Surprised, I drew back. "Uncle Colin, never say that. You've been my role model my entire life. I went to law school because of you, of the way you served the people as attorney general."

Colin's eyes misted. "Thank you, my dear." He kissed my cheek. "Sometimes those years seem like a different lifetime."

I gave him a fierce hug. "I'll just have to keep reminding you."

"No, sweetheart. I want you to blaze your own trail."

Over Colin's shoulder, I saw Gabe walk in with a satisfied look on his face. I stepped toward him. "Good news?"

"Bowie got Dumb and Dumber, and they're talking."

Tension that I hadn't been aware of drained away. I didn't know how many of the attempts against me had been due to those two men, but not having to look over my shoulder every second was going to be nice.

I also knew how important this was to Gabe. I crossed over to him. When he opened his arms, I stepped into them and pressed my cheek against his chest.

"Is this the break against the Castillos that you've been looking for?"

His arms tightened around me. "Yes. Marcos Castillo isn't going to walk away from this one."

"Castillo!"

I twisted slightly. Astounded, I saw the usually mild Colin rigid with his fists clenched. "Castillo is involved in this?" He gestured toward me. "He's responsible for the attempts on Katherine's life?"

"Yes."

Colin's throat worked, but before he could speak, Hilary rose and placed her hand on Colin's arm. "Come, dear. We should be going."

"But, Hilary, Katherine's in danger."

"Was in danger." She gave Gabe a long glance. "I think the very capable Mr. Chavez here will make sure no further harm comes to her, isn't that correct, sir?"

"Yes, ma'am."

I rolled my eyes. "I'm quite capable of taking care of myself."

A ghost of a smile touched Hilary's lips. "To be sure. After all, you are a Rochelle."

She turned to Colin. "We must be off. Everything will be all right. With the trial, all this disruption will end."

Strangely deflated, Colin simply nodded. He came to me and kissed my forehead. "Love you, sweetheart."

Touched, I blinked back tears. "Love you, too."

He followed Hilary out the door. Moments later I heard the Mercedes pull out of the driveway.

Gabe drew me closer. "I take it that highly charged

emotional scene was a breakthrough moment in the Rochelle household?"

Drawing comfort from his solid strength, I sighed. "Yes. Touchy feelings aren't expressed."

"So a guy shouldn't expect you to break out in declarations of love very often."

I stilled, took a deep breath. "No, but that doesn't mean the guy shouldn't break out in a love poem or two."

"How about flowers?"

I grinned against his shirt. "That would work as well."

"Mind if I ask a question?"

This was it. He was going to say something about our relationship. "Not at all." I raised my head as I wanted to see his face. Instead of having the expression of a man in love, Gabe wore his cop face.

"Why was your uncle so upset at the mention of the Castillo family? What's his connection to them?"

"Connection? None that I know of." Stunned, I took a step back. Gabe was right. For years now Colin's emotions had been submerged in his afternoon bourbons. His outburst a few minutes ago was so uncharacteristic.

The Castillos had tried to bribe Lopez and had succeeded with Winewski. But how many others had they tried to turn? Did it take more than one to throw a trial?

I crossed my arms. In the search for the truth about my grandfather, could I hurt the man who had served as my father?

Gabe stared at me. "There's something else Mrs. Lopez mentioned that you should know about."

"The State will prove beyond a reasonable doubt that the deceased Grace Roberts was in love with the defendant Lloyd Silber." Jared Manning paused in his opening statement, turned around at the podium to point at my client where he sat. Like a well-oiled machine, the jury members likewise pivoted in their chairs to stare.

"When he refused to divorce his wife, the victim threatened to disclose their affair. Late one night, he snuck back into the courthouse—" the prosecutor curled his thumb as if he was firing a gun "—and in cold blood he killed her with one shot to the head.

"Grace Roberts, a lovely young woman taken all too early from this life, has only one chance at justice. The State will prove beyond a reasonable doubt that Lloyd Silber took that life. Thank you."

Jared took his chair and adjusted his jacket sleeves.

"Ms. Rochelle. Opening for the defense?" Judge Rodriguez asked.

"Yes, Your Honor." I took a deep breath and rose. Twelve pairs of eyes watched me as I approached the podium.

Jury selection hadn't gone well. Since it was the beginning of the week, the jury pool was fresh, but this batch from the venire list of driver's licenses clearly had been plucked from a nearby retirement community. While this might have been a dream pool for a personal-injury action, for a murder trial, not so good.

I had tried to use my challenges to create a panel of mainly women, figuring that they would be sympathetic to my client and unsympathetic to the victim, but one too many people had believed in the death penalty. During the voir dire when both attorneys got to question the prospective panel, one man had said, "Fry the murdering scum's balls off." I hadn't even bothered to point out that Florida's death penalty was by injection. Since the man had smugly insisted he could be fair and impartial, I'd had to use a precious peremptory challenge.

While the court allowed unlimited number of challenges for cause, due to a juror's obvious bias to serve, we only received ten peremptory challenges to eliminate those we simply sensed would be a rotten egg on the panel.

Consequently, eight men and five women—one an alternate—most over the age of fifty, comprised our jury. Great.

My hand inched toward my pocket for my antacid roll. Instead I gripped the sides of the podium.

"May it please the Court, ladies and gentlemen of the jury. I have the privilege and honor of representing Lloyd Silber. You have listened to the State paint quite a pretty picture of Grace Roberts. But like a digital photograph can be manipulated for a desired image, the truth has been altered in this case."

Slow down, I warn myself. You're talking too fast. I kept my breathing steady.

"The evidence will show that Grace Roberts was an ambitious woman, and her ambition led to her death. She was an opportunist, a user and a social climber. Whether it was men…"

Good thing the rule had been invoked and no witnesses would be permitted inside until they had testified. I wouldn't have relished seeing the fiancé Charles Taylor Chase's face at this moment.

I took another breath and continued, "…jobs or blackmail, Grace used whatever she could to obtain money, power and position. She lied, cheated and stole."

I gazed at each juror. "My client Lloyd Silber was only one of those victims." I had to tread carefully here. By acknowledging he was a victim, I was also ascribing a motive. But I had to humanize him since I had no intention of letting him testify.

The judge didn't permit attorneys to approach the jury

without permission, but I could walk to my client. I placed my hand on his shoulder. "Lloyd Silber's a devoted married man, a longtime resident of this county, reputable, and an organizational genius. If there was a community project, Lloyd was the person to direct it to a successful conclusion. Because of his reputation, Lloyd was hired to put the courthouse restoration back on track.

"However, taking on this daunting task also brought him into a collision course with the enterprising Grace Roberts." I squeezed Lloyd's shoulder before returning to the podium.

"Over the next few days you will hear a lot about motive, means and opportunity. The evidence will not only show that many others had a motive purportedly greater than my client's, but also they had the equal means and opportunity to kill Grace Roberts.

"If others equally could have killed the victim, then my client is not guilty beyond a reasonable doubt." I smiled. "On behalf of my client and myself, I thank you for your time and attention over the next few days." I returned to the defense table, which was closest to the jury box, and sat down.

"All right, Mr. Manning, you may call your first witness."

Jared Manning proceeded with a scripted but logical sequence of witnesses. First up, the lead police investigator who described the crime scene and with a diagram showed the jury where the body had been found. Not much I could do here and I limited my cross-examination to help clarify the location of various items in the room.

Next up was the medical examiner to establish the time and manner of death. "Any cross, Ms. Rochelle?" the judge asked.

"Yes, Your Honor." I rose. "Dr. Wang, would you agree

with me that your testimony regarding the victim's time of death was not exact?"

The coroner gave me the condescending smile that all experts bestow on attorneys. "I don't."

"In fact, you gave a range, did you not?"

"Yes, ma'am."

"Unlike the mystery genre books or movies, here there was neither a broken watch nor a clock frozen in time to give you a precise time."

This time the examiner's smile was natural. He chuckled. "I would agree. I had no *X* marks the time of death. Based on the morbidity of the body, it appeared the victim was killed between eight and ten at night. The responding officers found nothing unusual with the room's temperature that may have impacted on the decomposition."

Perfect. A two-hour range would allow me to poke holes into others' alibis. "Thank you, Dr. Wang. I have no further questions."

I lined up my pens as I studied my notes, expecting a ballistic expert to be called next.

"Your Honor, I call Cindy Overbeck."

I frowned slightly as the bailiff led Lloyd's secretary to the witness stand. After she was sworn in, she perched nervously on the edge of the chair, facing away from the jury. Jared stood to the jury side of podium side, one arm propped carelessly on top. He flashed a smile. "Good afternoon, Ms. Overbeck."

Cindy turned slightly to face him. "Hello, Mr. Manning."

Nice unobtrusive move, I thought, to bring the witness to face the jury members. I'll have to remember that technique.

Jared led Cindy through her job and how she knew both the victim and the defendant. I had pre-marked her phone pad to be identified as an exhibit so I prepared to lead her through a few short questions.

"Now Ms. Overbeck, when did you last see Grace Roberts alive?"

"The night she was murdered."

What? According to my interview, Cindy had last seen Grace that morning. Wearing an attorney's version of a poker face, I studied her as she licked her lips. Why was she so nervous?

"Tell us what happened."

"Well, I had pottery class that night, but I forgot my dictation notes. Mr. Silber—" Cindy barely whispered his name "—had dictated a letter to me last thing. He said I could type it up the next morning. However, I knew it involved an important contributor, so I planned to do it on my home computer after class. When I entered the outer office, I heard Grace in Lloyd's office yelling at him."

I wrote a question mark on a pad and pushed it to Lloyd. He shook his head slightly and wrote the words "no, not true" underneath.

"Did you hear what she was saying?"

"Not really. Something about how he would pay. She was mad. I could tell from the tone of her voice. I didn't want her to see me, so I grabbed my notepad and left."

"What time was this?"

"I'd say about seven-thirty."

"Thank you. I have no further questions."

Gathering my thoughts, I slowly walked to the same spot where Jared had stood. I wanted the jury to see her expression.

"Ms. Overbeck, do you remember speaking with me on a few occasions?"

"Yes, Ms. Rochelle."

"Why didn't you ever mention that you were in the office that night?"

She licked her lips. "I didn't want to get Lloyd...Mr. Silber in trouble."

"You like Mr. Silber, don't you?"

"Yes."

"You care about him."

"Yes, of course. He's my boss."

"You also care for him as a man, don't you?"

Her hand crept to her throat. "That wouldn't be proper."

"Because he's married?"

"Yes."

"It may not be proper, but that doesn't stop you from feeling, does it?"

She looked down at her hands. I continued, "While the staff has cubicles with partitions, Mr. Silber has an actual office?"

She nodded. "Yes, of course he does. He's the director."

"When you returned that night, wasn't the door closed?" The cross-examiner's wisdom is to never ask a question you didn't know an answer to, but given this twist in Cindy's testimony, I had to take a risk. However, I asked the question in the negative, inviting her to agree with me. My tactic worked.

"Yes, it was closed."

"And you heard only Grace, correct?"

"That's correct."

Okay, I had her in a pattern of agreeing with me. "You never heard the other person's voice, did you?"

"No, I wanted to get out before—"

"Grace saw you?"

"Yes."

"That's because she was always mean to you."

"Yes," Cindy said in a voice barely audible. Some jury members leaned closer to hear her. Perfect.

"She made fun of you, degraded you in front of others."

"Yes." A tear slowly slipped down her cheek.

"Mr. Silber stood up for you, didn't he?"

"Yes."

"You didn't like Grace Roberts, did you?"

"No."

"Sometimes you could almost hate her, couldn't you?" She nodded. "Yes."

"You don't drive, do you?"

"No."

"That's why you go to the pottery place on Clematis, because it's within short walking distance of work."

"Yes."

"Then someone in the class gives you a lift home?"

"Yes."

"You've been doing this long enough that at times you finish ahead of others and have to wait?"

She shrugged. "At times."

"Can you explain why, on the night of the murder, when Trish Lyons tried to find you to take you home at eight-forty-five, you were nowhere to be found within the store?"

Cindy's face turned ghost-white.

"No answer, Ms. Overbeck?"

"I don't know."

I turned and walked away. "No further questions."

Chapter 18

That evening as I stepped inside my house, I breathed a sigh of relief. What I needed to ease the tension was a good swim.

Right. What I really wanted was Gabe to massage my neck, but after dropping me off at the court this morning, he had mysteriously headed off. Lieutenant Bowie had called him first thing so I assumed the Castillo family had been the hot topic.

No matter. After a swim I needed to focus on my preparation. The prosecutor had nearly thrown me for a loop by breaking the State's traditional sequence of witnesses and calling Cindy Overbeck to the stand. He wouldn't catch me by surprise again. I was going to assume a worst-case scenario and be ready.

I dropped my bag by the sofa, but it landed on its side, spilling the contents. I knelt, but as I began to replace my cell phone, I noticed that I had never turned it on after court. I pressed the switch and when the screen lit up, I checked for any messages. I listened to voice mail encouragement from both Carling and Nicole. I should call them and bring them up to speed on the trial.

Then my pulse kicked when I noticed I had a text message. To date Gabe was the only person I knew who sent text messages. That usually meant he wasn't free to speak to me on the phone.

I opened the message. "Meet me. Grandfather's office tonight. Urgent. I found the connection. Gabe."

What? I punched in his number. When I only got his voice mail, I said, "Gabe. I'm out of court. Call me."

Tapping the phone against the palm of my hand, I rose. What was going on? Had Gabe succeeded in connecting the Lopez case to the Castillo family today? I looked at the grandfather clock in the foyer. Seven o'clock. It would be dark by the time I reached the old courthouse, but they had tightened security since Grace's death.

I strode toward my bedroom to change clothes but ducked first into my office. I went to the safe, opened it and took out the Beretta I kept there. Hilary had drilled into me to be prepared for any exigency. A little safety insurance this time wouldn't hurt. After all, every time I'd been on the premises over the past few months, someone had tried to kill me.

Less than an hour later the security guard let me in. Other than a construction crew working late, no one else was there, he assured me. At least I had my answer how Gabe had gotten inside. He had gone back to working undercover with my ex's crew.

I climbed up the dimly lit stairs to the last floor and then walked down the silent, empty hall. Where was the work crew? As a precaution, I moved my gun from the tote to the pocket of the jacket I wore. I'm not sure what I had expected, but I had dressed for stealth and speed like a cat burglar—head-to-toe in black, including my athletic shoes.

Or a female version of Gabe, I wryly acknowledged.

The only light spilled from the office that had been my grandfather's. Quietly, I stole to the door, pausing, listening for any noise that would indicate someone was there. When I heard nothing, I stepped inside. The room was empty. The only sign of life was the desk lamp switched on. A few papers on the desk fluttered as if a breeze stirred them.

The silence had an expectant quality, as if the room had been waiting for me. The scene was so surreal that the hairs on my neck stood on end. Yet I sensed no threat.

Get a grip. Aggravated, I yanked out my phone and punched in a text message to Gabe. "I'm here. Where are you?"

No telling how long he'd be since I still couldn't hear the crew. They must be on the other side of the courthouse. I wandered over to the desk and aimlessly shifted through the papers. Apparently, no one had taken over Grace's tasks of readying the office for the museum. A labeled expando caught my eye: Original Contents From Judge Rochelle's desk.

I frowned. I didn't recall this being here the night Gabe and I had been shot at. I smoothed out a crumpled sticky note affixed to the front. "Found wedged behind Grace's desk. Cindy Overbeck." Hmm, the enterprising Cindy certainly hadn't wasted any time checking out Grace's work area. Maybe I'd better recall her to the stand to find out what else she may have found.

I sat down, removed a stack of documents and flipped through them. Letters and notes in my grandfather's handwriting. I would ask the acting director Derek Jones if I could borrow them to review at my leisure. They represented one more connection to the man Jonathan Rochelle had been.

I came across a rubber-banded bundle of photographs and pursed my lips. Careless. Since the rubber could damage the paper, they should be in a protective envelope. Handling the photos by their edges, I removed the band and looked through them. I froze at the sight of the eight-by-ten family portrait. My grandfather stood smiling with pride, his hand around my grandmother. Tucked into his other side was a young girl, equally beaming.

My mother.

I waited for the usual flood of bitterness whenever I saw her, but none came. How could I hate this girl, her face so full of innocence and happiness?

Perhaps once this trial was over, once I vindicated my grandparents, I could confront my feelings about my mother and at last move on.

It's time.

I jumped. I hadn't spoken, but the words echoed in my mind, almost as if someone else had whispered them. Well, it may be time, but not this precise moment.

Defiantly, I placed the photograph to the side and looked at the next one, clipped to a sheet of handwritten notes. Faded and blurred, I had to squint at the group shot of four men, all dressed up for a charity function, judging by the crowd in the background. Despite the thirty-five-year difference, I immediately recognized three of the men. I glanced at the sheet of notes, began to set it aside and halted, stunned by the implications before me.

What had Shirley Cameron said? That Jonathan always wrote out his decisions.

My hands shook as I held the edges of my grandfather's last decision in the matter of *State versus Lopez*. When I'd finished reading, I had my answer.

Bribes normally consisted of money, but not always. A bribe could also be the promise of power.

How many did it take to fix a trial? Answer: three.

A low sound came from the hallway. Was someone moaning? Quickly, I stuffed the photo and decision in my bag, stood and walked to the door.

The sound came again, to my right.

Hugging close to the wall, I crept down the hall. Once I left the circle of light from my grandfather's office, the corridor became pitch-black. Blessing lessons learned from Gabe, I pulled out a pencil-thin flashlight and turned it on.

As I continued, I spied a denser dark spot in the wall across from me. Shining the light on it revealed a gaping hole and a protruding boot. A boot with a foot in it.

My heart in my throat, I ran across the hall. "Gabe!" I gave out a low cry as I knelt in the opening. He lay in a sprawl as if someone had dragged him inside and dumped his body in what once must have been a utility closet. I flashed the light in his face, causing his eyelids to flutter, but he didn't open his eyes. A long, dark wound slashed across his forehead.

My God. He had been shot. I felt for his pulse with relief sweeping through me when I found it weak but steady.

Help. I needed to get help. I fumbled for my phone, juggling the flashlight, when an errant beam caught a dull gleam of white. I swallowed—hard—and raised the light.

Propped against the back of the small room were two skeletons, side by side, shoulder to shoulder. The faded tatters of clothes evidenced their sex: a man and a woman.

At long last, I had found my grandparents' grave.

I pressed the back of my hand against my mouth to suppress the scream welling deep inside of me. By my grandmother an object glittered on the floor. Gathering the frayed edges of my control around me, I reached forward to pick it up. The movement saved my life.

Wood and plaster splinters showered me as a bullet slammed into the wall above my head. I dropped the flashlight, dragged my gun out of my pocket, twisted and fired. Off balance and blind as a bat, I didn't stand a prayer of hitting anything or anyone, but I wanted my attacker to know I wasn't helpless.

As my gunfire echoed in the hallway, I rose to a crouch and then ran down the hall, blessing the fact I wore black. I hated to leave Gabe, but if I stayed in its narrow confines, the closet would have become our tomb as it had been for my grandparents. As the new target, I could at least draw the attacker's attention from Gabe.

A muffled oath and then the squeak of a sole against the marble floor told me the chase was on. My options were limited. Most rooms would be death traps on this level. If I could reach the stairs, I could go up to the roof or go down.

When I stubbed my toe, I fell forward, cracking my knee and losing my gun as I hit the floor. Despite the blinding pain, I could almost feel the killer's excitement intensify as he honed in on my location. I rolled to my feet and, for a few precious seconds, ran my hands over the floor, trying to find my gun. My left grazed something hard but it was a piece of wood rather than the gun. Probably construction debris, but it would have to do.

The killer was behind me. I curled my fingers around the wood and rose. Limping, I made my way to the stairwell. Deliberately, I scuffed my foot on the floor as I removed the clip from my hair. I waited for two heartbeats and then tossed the clip down the stairs.

At the clatter I pressed myself into the slight alcove of a door. I didn't even dare to try its handle. Holding my breath, I prayed the killer couldn't hear my hammering heart.

Oh no. My blond hair. Once I had ridden along with the county's drug SWAT team as an observer during a night-time drug raid. The captain had made me wear a dark knit cap, stating my hair made me a perfect shooting target.

Not daring to move again, I craned my head back.

The sound of my attacker's shoes stopped. His breathing sounded close, too close. A powerful flashlight panned down the hallway past my hiding place. I gripped the wood tighter. Then the beam disappeared and the killer ran down the stairs.

In the glow of the light I saw his face, and another piece of the puzzle fell into place.

After waiting for a few more seconds, I made my way back down the hall. When I passed the closet, I yearned to check on Gabe but knew I couldn't afford the time. Even now our attacker might have discovered I had duped him. I couldn't underestimate him.

I slipped into my grandfather's office, grabbed a few sheets of paper from the desk and hurried to the inner door that led to his courtroom. I turned the handle and opened it. The creak of hinges sounded like a gunshot.

Damn.

I slipped through and closed the door behind me. Although the room was as dark as a tomb, I knew I was on the upper balcony. As part of the restoration this two-level courtroom had been brought back to its former grandeur. On the upper level columns flanked the door and several rows of chairs crowded the narrow space. I knew at the base a construction rail ran the length of the balcony.

Running down the steps, I scattered the paper across one of the risers. Then I returned to the top and ducked behind the column on the left, my opponent's vulnerable side as he was right-handed. I pressed as close to the wall as much as I could and, with my free hand, tucked my hair under the collar of my jacket. After this was all over, I was going to give serious consideration to dying my hair dark.

The squeal of the rusty door hinges wailed out. I raised the board I still carried. The flashlight's beam split the dark and a figure appeared at the top of the stairs. He panned the light over the rows of chairs and then honed in on the paper.

"Come on out, Katherine," called out my ex-husband.

Juan went down one step. In the eerie glow from his flashlight I could see the gleam of the revolver he carried. "Game's over. I took care of the guard and locked the lower-level doors so there's no escape."

He took another step. "It's only you we want. I'll let that precious boyfriend of yours go."

Right, that's why Gabe was already in the closet. I was only going to get one chance. As I tightened my grip, the air stirred behind me. Was someone else in here? I peered but saw no movement. No matter. My window of opportunity was upon me. I had to take it. I stepped from behind the column.

Juan bent to pick one of the sheets of paper. "Does he make you hot, Ice Princess? Are you a woman yet?"

More woman than Juan could ever handle.

I dashed down the steps. Juan must have sensed me for he straightened up. Instead of his head, my swing caught him in the chest. Still, he staggered back to the edge of the balcony. Again, I swung the board but this time he threw up his arms and blocked the blow.

"Bitch! I'll make you pay for this. I'll put a bullet in that lovely face of yours. I almost got you the last time you came to your grandfather's chambers. This time I won't miss."

I struck at him again.

This time I caught him on the shoulder. He howled and crashed against the railing.

Juan cried out again but this time with terror. He flailed about wildly. A sharp crack reverberated throughout the chambers followed by Juan's screams as he fell through the broken rail. His cry came to an abrupt halt with a sickening thud.

I slowly made my way to the railing and looked down. Juan's body lay sprawled like a broken doll's in the center aisle of the courtroom.

I took a deep breath. When this was all over and done with, I would have a lot to tell the police and Gabe, but there was one thing I would take to my grave. In those last moments before Juan fell, I felt my grandfather's strength around me.

Wrapping my fingers around my necklace, I whispered, "Thank you, Granddad."

I raced up the steps, through the office and back down the hallway. My flashlight and bag still lay where I had dropped them in the closet.

Gabe had moved! He had shifted positions to lying on his back. I dropped to my knees and crawled in beside him.

"Gabe, can you hear me?" He winced but didn't respond. I pressed my two fingers against his throat. His pulse didn't seem quite as thready.

Pulling out my phone, I dialed 911 and called in the emergency. Even though the police station was just a few blocks down Banyan, it would still take a while for the first crew to arrive. In the meantime I had to wait helplessly.

Damn the first-aid training. I needed to hold him. I scooted as close to him as I could. Carefully, I raised his head and propped it in my lap. His eyelids fluttered open. "What took you so long, babe?" His voice was hoarse and rough, but it was the sweetest sound I'd ever heard.

Avoiding his wound, I stroked the hair from his forehead. "Oh, you know how traffic is always a bear at this time of the night."

"Took a bullet when I went to investigate the hole in the hallway. Kept fading in and out. But Juan bragged about using my phone to lure you here." Gabe lifted his hand and I gripped it. "Did you get Juan?"

A memory of Juan's face when he had been young and vibrant flashed in my mind. The man had been my first love and now he was dead because of me.

No! Not because of me. He was dead because he had taken the wrong path years ago. He had thrown our life together away because of greed.

I pushed away any regret, raised Gabe's hand and kissed it. "I got him."

"Good girl." Gabe closed his eyes. "I knew you could."

And Gabe's belief in me and the events over the past few months had made all the difference in the world. I no longer was the innocent girl Juan had seduced or the insecure woman Harold had betrayed.

The Kate Rochelle who sat in this musty closet, holding the man she loved, was a woman I could respect and be at peace with.

A glint of gold nearby on the floor caught my eye. I had almost forgotten about the piece of jewelry that had saved my head from being blown apart. Without jostling Gabe, I reached out, picked it up and with a jolt recognized the medallion's significance.

I looked at my grandparents' remains huddled together in death as they had been in life and whispered, "I know the truth now. Justice will be served."

A sense of calm stole over the closet as I waited for the police to arrive.

Chapter 19

The next afternoon, on a great swell of anticipation, I entered the courtroom. Last night when I had called Judge Rodriguez, without hesitation she had granted me a recess until two o'clock today. Working late, I had prepared witness subpoenas to be served for today's proceeding.

First thing this morning I had been on the phone with Carling to get a process server when Gabe, with a white bandage across his forehead, had shown up on my doorstep. Despite my concern about his condition, he had been all too delighted to serve this particular set of subpoenas. As important as the service was, I had been happy to leave them in his capable hands.

At my approach down the court aisle, Jared Manning rose. "Katherine, are you all right?"

Juan's death in the old courthouse had been news item number one on all the early-morning news programs. I smiled smoothly, revealing nothing of my inner tension. "I'm fine."

"I told the judge you could have a continuance if you needed one."

Touched, I shook my head. "I don't need one, but thank you." I handed him a list of the witnesses I expected to call. They had all appeared on the pretrial, but neither side had anticipated calling them. Last night had changed that.

Jared let out a long, low whistle. "Hell, I'd hate to be at your family's dinner table tonight."

I couldn't have agreed with him more as I saw the couple enter the chambers. So Gabe had been successful in his endeavors this morning. Hilary held herself stiffly and icily ignored me as she found a seat. Colin shot me a look filled with confusion, hurt and…fear?…before he followed her.

I sighed, wishing for one moment, that I was anywhere but here. Straightening my shoulders, I sat down. When Lloyd was escorted to our table, I spoke to him briefly, but my focus remained on what was about to occur.

I had to break down someone I loved in order to get justice for my client.

My roll of antacid tablets was in my pocket, but now was not the time for a crutch. I had to meet this head-on.

"All rise," called out the bailiff as Judge Rodriguez entered the room. She took her chair and looked at me.

"Call your first witness, Ms. Rochelle."

"Yes, Your Honor." I rose. "The Defense calls Colin Wilkes."

I watched my uncle take the witness box and be sworn in. He held his head high as he affirmed his testimony would be the truth. I prayed that it would, as I was counting on it.

Quickly I took him through the preliminary background

questions, ignoring the murmur that swept through the jury and gallery when he disclosed that he was my great-uncle.

"Mr. Wilkes, were you the defense counsel in the matter of *State versus Lopez?*"

"Objection, Your Honor." Jared stood up. "Relevance."

"Judge, I'll be connecting it."

"Ms. Rochelle, I'll grant you some leeway, but if you don't furnish this court with the relevance within short order, I'll strike the testimony."

"Understood, Your Honor." I looked at my uncle. "Do you need me to repeat the question, Mr. Wilkes?"

Colin flushed. "Of course not, Katherine. I may be old, but I still have my memory intact. The answer is yes. I defended Manuel Lopez when I was a public defender. Over thirty-five years ago, I might add."

I smiled. "Your memory is indeed excellent. Is it not true Mr. Lopez was found guilty of murdering a Cuban grocery store owner?"

"To my regret, yes. He got a life sentence and died of a heart attack in prison." Still a politician, Colin twisted toward the jury. "You never forget a case you lose."

"Mr. Wilkes, the judge on that case was Kurt Winewski and the state prosecutor was Paul Schofield, correct?"

"That's right." Colin faced me again.

"After the trial, Mr. Lopez retained a new attorney, did he not?"

"Yes."

"Isn't it true this attorney made allegations that you were incompetent?"

"Yes. The accusation was ludicrous. He said I never interviewed witnesses who would've supported my client's innocence." Colin spread his hands. "The public defenders' budget was so limited back then. No money for investigators."

"His charges went beyond that, though, didn't they? His motion stated that the trial was fixed."

"Preposterous. There was no reason—"

"Wasn't there, Mr. Wilkes? Didn't Mr. Lopez tell you that he had been approached in jail by a representative of the Castillo family?"

Colin's face paled. "No."

"No? He never once told you that he had been offered money, big money, to plead guilty? Be careful, sir. Mrs. Lopez has given a sworn statement that she was with her husband when he told you about the bribe. She's willing to testify to it in court."

A bead of sweat formed on his brow. "He may have. It's been years. I didn't take much note of it if he did."

"Really? Someone on behalf of a reputed crime family tries to bribe your client to take a fall for a murder and you ignored the information?"

"I thought Manuel was just desperate."

"But the chief presiding judge at that time, Jonathan Rochelle, conducted an inquiry, did he not?"

"Yes."

"And while he was investigating the case, he disappeared, didn't he?"

"You know he did."

Yes, how well I did. What no one else knew was that my grandparents' bodies had been found. Lieutenant Sam Bowie had agreed to keep that quiet until tonight.

"Did you know Diego Castillo?"

"Only by reputation."

"Really?" I walked to the clerk, who handed me the faded photograph I had previously marked for identification.

"I show you a photograph that has been marked as Defense Exhibit Twelve. Do you recognize the men?"

Colin studied the shot for a long moment and then looked at me with a bleak expression. "Yes. It's a photo taken of Paul, Kurt and me at some bar function." His lips twisted into a rueful smile. "I had forgotten this existed."

"And the fourth man?"

"Is Diego Castillo. Yes, I knew him."

"Turning your attention to the present, you knew the victim Grace Roberts was working on the collection of Judge Rochelle's memorabilia."

He returned the photo to me. "Apparently, she was more successful in her endeavors than I knew."

"Did she try to blackmail you?"

"Over a picture of me with Diego? How preposterous. Of course not."

"No, Mr. Wilkes. Over accepting a bribe for throwing the Lopez case."

Colin half rose from his chair. "How dare you! I've never taken a bribe in my life!"

The judge intervened. "Mr. Wilkes, please sit down."

Colin subsided. "I may have done a lot of things I regret, *Counselor,* but I've never stooped that low. Yes, Diego approached me during the trial, but I turned him down flat."

"What about Paul Schofield?"

Colin's smile was bitter. "You know Paul. No one presses his buttons, he pushes theirs."

I paused in my questioning. My uncle had just handed me, on a silver platter, the reason for what happened all those years ago.

But I needed to push Colin a bit more.

"Did you suspect that Kurt Winewski had been paid off?"

Colin hesitated, and then nodded. "With his evidentiary rulings being so outrageous, I suspected something was wrong."

"Those rulings included excluding any evidence that no money had been taken from the cash register, which was allegedly your client's motive?"

"Yes."

"Also excluding any reference that no blood was ever found on Mr. Lopez's clothes?"

"Yes." Colin shook his head. "Had Lopez not fired me, to this day, I truly believe I could've gotten his conviction overturned on appeal. As it was, any friendship I had with Kurt was over after the trial."

He leaned forward. "But you're wrong about Paul or me. We never would've taken money."

"There is more than one way to bribe a person, Mr. Wilkes," I said quietly. "The promise of power and position, for instance."

Colin opened and closed his mouth.

"No further questions."

Jared half rose. "No cross."

"Call you next witness, Ms. Rochelle."

"I call Hilary Wilkes to the stand."

Hilary and Colin passed each other without even a look. My great-aunt was positively regal as she was sworn in. She looked the part of a queen, well dressed in a sky-blue designer knit suit and her stylist-coiffed hair.

Composed, she looked at me with a lifted brow, the glint of challenge in her eyes.

Game on.

Once more the battery of preliminary questions to establish who she was. Out of the corner of my eye I saw the reporter Jim Grabkowski in a seat of the front bench.

"Mrs. Wilkes. Jonathan Rochelle was your brother, correct?"

"That's correct."

"Would it be fair to characterize that relationship as being strained?"

"As is the case always with family, we had our moments."

"Did those moments include jealousy and resentment?"

"Perhaps. Since he's been gone for over thirty-five years, I try to remember only the good times."

"Objection, Your Honor," Manning said. "Relevance?"

"Ms. Rochelle?"

"Your Honor, I'll make the connection shortly. I just need a bit of leeway."

"Make it quickly or I'll strike it from the record."

"Thank you, Judge." Turning back to Hilary, I continued my quest for the truth.

"You were aware Jonathan was investigating your husband for taking a bribe?"

"Yes, it was total nonsense."

"Did you think it was true?"

"What? Of course not."

"Paul Schofield was a friend of the family's back then, wasn't he?"

"Yes."

"A close friend?"

"Absolutely." A smug look crossed her face. "That's why Paul was named your godfather."

"When you learned your brother was investigating Colin, did you go to Paul for help?"

She shrugged. "I may have consulted him."

"Did Paul tell you that he thought Colin had been bribed?"

"No."

"No? Didn't Paul say Colin had been incompetent, so incompetent in his handling of the trial that the only possible explanation was he had been bribed by Diego

Castillo? Didn't Paul tell you that the Rochelle name was about to be ruined in scandal?"

"No!" A man shouted from behind me.

I turned to see Colin gripping the top of the seat before him. "Hilary, tell me that you didn't believe Paul! I never took a bribe. I swear."

"Order in the court!" The judge banged his gavel. "Mr. Wilkes, any further outbursts like that and I'll have you arrested and removed from these chambers."

Colin sank down and covered his face.

When I turned back, I caught Hilary staring at me with a look of absolute hatred.

"You bitch!" Venom accentuated each word. "You are so like Jonathan. So full of self-righteousness."

"I have to finish this."

"Of course you do. I knew from the moment my husband's love child was dumped on my doorstep this day would come."

My whole world overturned on me. I gripped the podium as a lifeline from the deep void that had opened in me.

She tilted her head. "Oh yes. Your worthless tramp of a mother wasn't content with seducing every man in the world. She had to also seduce my husband. I couldn't have children but yet had to bear the contrition of raising you."

"Punishment for murdering her parents." I reached into my pocket and pulled out the medallion. Glittering in the light was the figure of a swimmer.

"Do you recognize this?"

Hilary only gave a half glance at the award that had been given to her years ago for winning a prestigious event in California, the win that had placed her on the Olympic team.

"I wondered what had happened to it. Did Grace find it?"

"No, I did…when I found my grandparents' bodies concealed in a utility closet in the old courthouse last night."

Hilary's shoulders sagged.

Pandemonium rang out as people began talking and cameras were clicking. Judge Rodriguez banged the gavel once more. "Order. Order this minute."

When quiet fell again, I said, "Mr. Wilkes made a comment that no one pushed Paul Schofield's buttons, he did the pushing. Thirty-five years ago, he pushed yours, didn't he?"

"Yes." In the span of a minute, Hilary had aged as if her vitality had collapsed, leaving an older woman's shell. Only her pride continued to burn fiercely in her eyes. She would battle me to the bitter end.

"You went to the courthouse and confronted your brother."

"Yes. I begged him not to ruin Colin. But he refused to discuss the matter with me. He said the truth would come out."

"You brought a gun with you."

"Yes. I actually planned to use it on myself, but when I pulled it out, Jonathan lunged for it. We fought. The gun went off. Jonathan was dead."

"What happened to his wife, Marguerite?"

Hilary's laugh was bitter, but she continued focusing on me as if we were the only ones present. "Like the good, devoted wife she was, she had stopped in to drop him off dinner. She walked in on me standing over his body. She screamed and ran. I tried to catch her, to explain it was an accident, but she wouldn't listen."

"What happened?"

"Construction was going on. The place was a mess. Marguerite tripped and fell down the stairs, breaking her neck."

She looked down at her hands. "I was strong back then. I carried her up to Jonathan's office and then called Paul. Diego Castillo himself showed up with a few of his henchmen. We put the bodies in the back closet as it had no vents, no outlets so that no one would smell anything. Then the men plastered over the door, nice and deep so that it became a tomb.

"Next Diego let it be known that there was a gas leak so the entire building was closed. When the courthouse reopened, the construction was finished."

Hilary shrugged, her eyes once again defiant. "With money paid to the right people, the police never tore apart the courthouse. With time and the renovations, the closet became forgotten."

"Then all these years later, with the courthouse restoration project, the past came back to haunt you."

"Yes. First Diego's son Marcos became worried about the bodies being discovered. He arranged for all the construction delays until he could get his own people in control of the site."

"Juan Delgado's company," I prodded.

Hilary gave an aloof nod. "Your worthless ex-husband finally proved to be useful. But with all the preparations for the museum on the upper floors, he had trouble accessing the closet without being seen."

Her mouth twisted. "Marcos and Juan, having not an ounce of imagination between them, planned to trot out the gas leak routine again."

"But in the end you were the one to do the replay."

"Grace Roberts, the opportunistic bitch—" Hilary's eyes were slits of blue fire "—became curious about Jonathan's disappearance. She found his docket sheet and put enough information together that she called the house, wanting to speak with Colin."

"She thought Colin had been bribed."

"Yes. Foolish girl. I took the call and made arrangements to meet with her that night."

Hilary's expression grew distant. "It was déjà vu. Like all those years had melted away. They hadn't ever changed the lock on a side door. I got in the same way and made my way upstairs without the guard ever seeing me."

Then the old Hilary with her shield of arrogance looked me directly in the eye. "You want to know the truth? Killing was easier this time, a lot easier."

The judge leaned forward. "Bailiff, arrest this woman." She pointed her gavel at the prosecutor. "Mr. Manning, do you have a motion for me?"

Jared rose. "Yes, Your Honor. The State dismisses the charges against Mr. Silber. We will be filing murder charges against Hilary Rochelle Wilkes, as well as looking into the roles of Paul Schofield and the Castillo family."

Colin pushed his way through the crowd to reach Hilary's side as she was being led away. There was a look of shock on her face—at what she'd said or because she'd been caught—but she never looked at either Colin or me. We watched her disappear.

"Uncle Colin—" I stopped short. He wasn't my uncle. He was my father.

He lifted a hand toward me before dropping it. "Katherine. We'll talk later. I need to get Hilary a good attorney."

"Thank you for trying to help me. That was you on the phone that one night, warning me, wasn't it?"

"Yes. After all, you're my daughter. I'm so sorry. I've screwed up so much in my life." He drew in a deep shuddering breath.

"I'd always been suspicious of what happened thirty-five years ago, but didn't want to believe either my wife or friend was involved. Too caught up in the handling of the Lopez case. I started drinking. However, I couldn't bear the same thing happening to you that happened to Jonathan."

Slowly, Colin turned and walked down the aisle. Halfway to the door, he paused.

"I'm proud of you, Katherine. You're the attorney I never was or could ever dream of being. I'm proud to call you my daughter at long last." He walked outside.

Then reporters and others swept down upon me, and I was too busy answering questions to think. A teary-faced Lloyd and his wife thanked me and left. Soon the room emptied and I began to pack up my pads and folders.

I should have been feeling elation, but right now numbness absorbed me. At last I had found justice for my grandparents but at what personal cost? My great-aunt was a murderess and would be spending the rest of her life in prison.

My uncle was the biggest lie of all. My entire life I had looked up to him, even modeled my career decisions on him, and yet he had been my father. In seeking the truth, I had managed to disrupt the very foundation of my life. Where could I go? What was I to do?"

"Ms. Rochelle?"

I turned at the soft, hesitant voice. An overweight, middle-aged black woman stood behind me. She wore a simple blue dress and gripped the handle of a black purse. I didn't recognize her.

"Mr. Chavez said you would listen to me."

I looked past her shoulder and saw Gabe, dressed in a tan suit with a black open-neck shirt, leaning against the doorjamb, his arms crossed.

"Oh? What do you need?"

The woman twisted her hands on her purse. "My name's Mabel Smith. My daughter's just been arrested for murder."

I sighed. The last thing I needed was listening to another's troubles. "I'm sorry, Mrs. Smith, but—"

"My baby's killed her husband. He was a mean son of a bitch. He hurt her all the time. This afternoon he came home drunk, having been fired again. He took it out on her, beating her within an inch of her life. She grabbed a knife and stabbed him."

Tears roll down the mother's cheeks. "She killed him but it was self-defense. Now the police have her in lockup and she needs a doctor and a lawyer. I heard what the people said in the hallway about you. That you're good. My baby needs the best."

The girl was in lockup after being beaten? That wasn't right. I could make a quick call to the judge on duty. Then we would need witnesses to the beatings. Maybe medical records.

I looked up and saw Gabe grinning at me. "What are you doing just hanging around, Chavez? We have a client to represent."

I put my arm around the now-sobbing mother's shoulder. "Don't you worry, Mrs. Smith. We'll get your daughter to the doctor. And I would love to represent her."

As we walked up the aisle to where Gabe waited, I realized the dark void inside me had dissipated. As long as our society lasted, there would always be justice to be pursued and served.

And I was that woman who could do it.

Spotting a trash receptacle, I pulled out my roll of antacid tablets and pitched it with a perfect arc into the can. Score another victory for me.

"Ready?" asked Gabe.

"I'm ready." He swung open the door and on we went to our next case.

* * * * *

*There's more Silhouette Bombshell
coming your way! Every month we've
got four fresh, unique and satisfying
reads that will keep you riveted....
Turn the page for an exclusive excerpt
from one of next month's release*

*THE PROFILER
by Lori A. May*

*On sale August 2005
At your favorite retail outlet.*

When the cabbie drops me off at the scene, Cain is standing outside the building with Detective Severo, who's talking to a middle-aged woman. I wasn't expecting to see him here, only now that I do I'm curious as to why.

"Nice Thanksgiving?" he asks as I step up to the curb outside the mission.

I shrug my shoulders, not interested in small talk. "Fine," I say. "Burnt the turkey." Regret for confessing my culinary taboo immediately follows. Severo doesn't need to learn one of my flaws so easily.

"How ironic," he says then lifts his cardboard take-out box of stale-looking nachos, offering me a sample.

Shaking my head no, I step closer to Cain to see what's going on.

"Angie, thanks for getting over here quick. This is the housekeeper for the mission." I shake the woman's hand

and note her fearful eyes, desperate for answers to which I myself know not the question. "She was checking on one of the resident spiritual advisors when she found him…. Hell, I'll let you have a look for yourself."

As I offer a smile to the lady, trying to provide comfort for something I don't yet understand, I notice the many guests of the mission. People are lined up outside the building, food in their hands, protective of what is likely the best meal they've had all week—or longer.

The building itself has an unassuming decor, only now it looks like a disco with the strobe lights of emergency vehicles dancing across its plain concrete exterior in the darkening night.

We climb the narrow staircase to the upper level and I take in the stink of kerosene mixed with something potent.

Burnt human flesh.

Inside the advisor's room, barely lit in this evening light, I see the corpse propped upright in an unstable wooden rocking chair.

One thing doesn't make sense. The room has no fire damage.

"Matthias Killarney. Fifty-two. Caucasian. Dead."

The monotone of Cain's voice signals the beginning of a long shift and I step closer to the body, interested to understand. A few investigators are rounding up the forensic evidence and I'm careful not to step into their boundaries.

"This is Severo's deal," Cain says to me as I lean closer to the man's body, covering my nose and mouth with some gauze. "The detective and I were enjoying our own holiday feast of wings and nachos down at Dooly's Pub when he got called on this one. He was kind enough to invite us over to check it out. You know, so you can get your feet good and stuck in the mud."

"How considerate," I mumble, wondering how much Cain had to convince the detective to extend that invitation, but I keep my focus on the crime scene.

The man is sitting in a firm position, placed in the wooden chair as though he were a puppet. Rigor mortis has taken its full extent, letting the victim's posture become static and as flexible as a brick. This condition can last anywhere between twelve and forty-eight hours, and may also provide an estimated time of death for the crime scene unit and medical examiner.

To the obvious eye, the room appears calm and untouched by any intruder, but trace will undoubtedly disprove that naivety.

I step back from the body and pull the cloth from my face. Despite the stench, I need to breathe freely. "What do we know?"

Detective Severo flips through his notepad and runs through the time of discovery and a few comments from resident workers. "But most importantly, albeit obviously, this guy was set up here on display. We don't know where the actual crime took place yet, just that he was brought back to his home and propped up for someone to find. Excuse me a moment," he says, and I watch as he meets up with some of his teammates for a discussion.

Cain leads me through to the outside, letting Severo's team do their job. "The medical examiner will provide clues as to the fire. Whether this guy died in blazes or what."

"Why would someone go through all that trouble?" I lean on a weathered tree and watch as the detective makes his way to meet us outside. I look to the both of them, realizing in some ways they are complete opposites. I look to the both of them, realizing in some ways they are complete opposites, yet by some arguments they are one and the same.

Cain's hunched body, beaten with age and the streets, is deceiving. His appearance may be worn, but this profiler is like wine, only getting better with age. His exterior is unforgiving of the solid, analytical man inside. His reputation alone…well, it's enough to make a fresh agent like me drool with envy.

Though Severo is much younger, Cain obviously has respect for him so there must be worlds of experience beyond his facade.

Cain lights up a cigarette and peers at me with narrow eyes. "You'd be surprised, kid. And that's for you to figure out, my little profiler-in-training."

"But burning this man, and then bringing him back here—especially seeing how this is a busy place this time of year—it's like he wanted to make a point. Why not just leave him at the original scene. He'd be found there, too." As I speak aloud, I find myself running the events through my mind, trying to make sense of the chain.

"The housekeeper says the last time anyone saw Killarney was yesterday afternoon. Wednesday," Severo interjects. "But anything could have happened overnight, when only resident staff are around and likely asleep. But, yeah, seems risky."

Before much silence has passed between us, Cain turns toward his car and motions for me to join him. "Come on, Angie. We'll let the detective do his job here. And Severo— you know where to find us. If you don't mind, once your CSU team cleans the place I'd like to give Angie here a chance to mull over the findings."

I slide into Cain's passenger seat and look back at Severo, who peers at me suspiciously before walking back into the mission.

"You know Detective Severo well?"

As we drive along the dimly lit street, spotted with decorations in preparation for the holiday season, I try to look occupied with my seatbelt so Cain doesn't get any funny ideas as to my inquiry.

"Severo? We've had our moments."

He pulls up to a street corner deli cart, hops out to retrieve two extra-large coffees then shuffles back into his seat before starting back on the road. I hold the take-out cups as Cain slides his seatbelt over his chest.

"Ah, he's a pain in the ass, sometimes. His bark is worse than his growl, though, that's for sure." I hand Cain a steamy cup to balance while driving. "Thing is, kid, working in this city is like fighting for your corner of the playground, ya know? Everyone has their turf and no one likes sharing the dirt. You better get used to that, and quick, too. Best advice I can give you is don't piss anyone off unless you have good reason."

"Nice," I say, vowing to remember that bit of insider knowledge. Quantico was definitely competitive, but Cain's making NYC sound like a battlefield.

"Don't get me wrong, Angie. The guy knows his stuff and he's a pro on the job, no argument there. He's a good guy to let loose and slink a few beers with, too." He leans his head in my direction and briefly lifts his brows as if to emphasize, then returns his focus to the road. "But his noggin. He got messed up by a dame and I think it's got him all in a bunch, you know?"

I nod my head and sip at my coffee. Almost a week in his presence and the guy can't remember that I take cream, so the black liquid is a little harsh to the palate. As I swish the beverage in my mouth, letting its strong taste cool before swallowing, I try to imagine Severo in a relationship. Just doesn't seem to suit him.

Maybe his hard-to-read exterior is just a front. Guess I won't be playing poker with him anytime soon.

"Yeah, he got dumped, all right," Cain says, barely containing a tainted laugh. "She did a job on him, boy. Just a few days before the wedding, too."

The information jolts me, and I look to Cain for more.

"He's got a chip on his shoulder about the whole thing. But, he's a dedicated sap, whether with women or on the job, so whatever makes him tick is apparently working. Unlucky in love, but damn good detective. Schmuck."

I tail Cain's echoed laughter through the white-walled halls of the New York FBI Field Office, ready to start in on our night of business. Cain has much to familiarize me with yet in the office I'll be calling home for at least four years to come. It's good to get the formalities over and done with so I know what to expect of my work environment…and of my coworkers

Though, I still can't shake the concept. Carson Severo hurt by love? Anything's possible. I guess it explains his suspicious glances toward me. Maybe he thinks I'm one of the bad guys.

Then again, I've never been all that skilled at being good.

Silhouette®

BOMBSHELL™

brings you the talented new voice of author
LORI A. MAY

It takes talent, determination and an eye for forensic detail to make it in the elite world of FBI criminal profilers.

Angie David has what it takes. But with her mentor looking over her shoulder, a homicide detective dogging her every move and a serial killer intent on luring her to the dark side, she'll need a little something extra to make her case....

The Profiler

August 2005

Available at your favorite retail outlet.

If you enjoyed what you just read,
then we've got an offer you can't resist!

Take 2 bestselling love stories FREE!

Plus get a FREE surprise gift!

BOMBSHELL™

COMING NEXT MONTH

#53 DEVIL'S BARGAIN by Rachel Caine
Red Letter Days

Desperate to clear her partner of a murder conviction, former police detective Jazz Chandler made a deal to start her own P.I. agency. The agreement included a loose-cannon new partner and one all-too-sexy lawyer—and making any case that arrived via red envelope top priority. The seemingly innocuous cases soon threw her into a shadowy world of clandestine societies and hidden agendas where Jazz would have to choose between two evils to save them all.

#54 RARE BREED by Connie Hall

Young, idealistic Wynne Sperling put her life on the line every day working as a park ranger in Africa. Protecting the endangered animals she loved was certainly better than pushing paper in Washington. But when Wynne's attempts to thwart a deadly poaching ring got her into hot water, would her trusty slingshot and help from a mysterious smart-mouthed Texan be enough to prevent *her* from becoming extinct?

#55 SHE'S ON THE MONEY by Stephanie Feagan

She should have known better than to take on a client called Banty. But Whitney "Pink" Pearl couldn't say no to billable hours—and now the fearless CPA was knee-deep in trouble and sinking fast. Seems the oil-well scam she was uncovering led to secrets someone would kill to keep. And with death threats, tangled paper trails and two amorous suitors to juggle, it would take some bold moves to keep Pink out of the red.

#56 THE PROFILER by Lori A. May

A serial killer was on the loose in New York City, and FBI agent Angie Davis was on the scene. But this case was straining even Angie's highly developed profiling abilities…not to mention trying her patience. It was bad enough that she had to work with maverick NYPD detective Carson Severo, but as the body count rose, an unsettling pattern emerged—the victims all shared a connection to Angie. Was she next on the depraved killer's hit list?

SBCNM0705